To:

ESCAPE FROM PRAGUE

January 2017

By
Colin Knight

Copyright © 2017 by Colin Knight.

All rights reserved. No part of this publication may be reproduced, distributed or transmitted in any form or by any means, including photocopying, recording, or other electronic or mechanical methods, without the prior written permission of the publisher, except in the case of brief quotations embodied in critical reviews and certain other noncommercial uses permitted by copyright law. For permission requests, write an email to the author, titled "ESCAPE FROM PRAGUE RIGHTS" to the address below.

a.colinknight@gmail.com
www.colinknightbooks.com

Publisher's Note: This is a work of fiction. Names, characters, places, and incidents are a product of the author's imagination. Locales and public names are sometimes used for atmospheric purposes. Any resemblance to actual people, living or dead, or to businesses, companies, events, institutions, or locales is completely coincidental.

ESCAPE FROM PRAGUE / COLIN KNIGHT

1st paperback edition 2017.

ISBN: 978-0-9940219-5-3

Also by Colin Knight

Some People Deserve To Die

Public Service

Bad Analysis

For my wife, children, family and friends: Thanks.

Prostitution will always lead into a moral quagmire in democratic societies with capitalist economies; it invades the terrain of intimate sexual relations yet beckons for regulation. A society's response to prostitution goes to the core of how it chooses between the rights of some persons and the protection of others.

    BARBARA MEIL HOBSON, Uneasy Virtue

We say that slavery has vanished from European civilization, but this is not true. Slavery still exists, but now it applies only to women and its name is prostitution.

    VICTOR HUGO, Les Misérables

One

Anna needed money. Fast. Only in Wenceslas Square, despite the risk, could Anna earn the money she needed. The square, in the heart of Prague, once famous for the 1989 mass marches of the Czech Republic's Velvet Revolution, had become the uncontested home of Prague's pimps and prostitutes.

Five or six clients, three thousand five hundred Koruna each, would be enough. The plan, made in haste and desperation, required Anna to get about fifteen thousand Koruna, go to the airport, and call her sister Krystyna. Krystyna would tell Anna where to go.

More a boulevard than a square, Wenceslas stretched almost a kilometre in a northwest-southeast direction. Southeast ended at the Czech neoclassical National Museum, while the northeast end bumped up against the border between New Town and Old Town Prague.

Anna wiped fluid from her inner thighs and chin for the fifth time in two hours. Scuff marks on the knee of her jeans and abrasions on the palms of her hands reflected the preferences of her clients. Better that way. She didn't have to see and fear the disgust and anger that hovered beneath the fleeting ecstasy of each loveless liaison.

Casting for clients in the upper half of Wenceslas Square, between the grand stone statue of the "good Czech king" and the railway lines behind the National Museum, Anna avoided the greedy eyes of municipal and state police officers. Both sought payoffs from prostitutes, drug dealers, or beggars in return for "permission" to ply their trade. Desperate for money, Anna had paid neither police force, and she had little time before they demanded their payments or worse.

Corrupt police were one problem. Russian, Ukrainian, and Romanian women and their pimps and gangs who controlled the square were another much more dangerous problem. If caught without the protection and presence of her pimp, Edvard, Anna would be severely beaten. But luck favoured Anna. Crowded with men wanting sex, the darkened doorway of a disused newspaper kiosk had prevented people from noticing Anna's furtive solicitations.

Afraid Edvard would find her before she had enough money, Anna peeked through the worn boards that covered the broken window of the kiosk. Since Krystyna had disappeared two months earlier, Edvard had kept Anna close. Cruel and sadistic, Edvard swore a painful death for Anna if she tried to follow her sister.

Escaping from Edvard's control to earn money for her departure had sickened Anna. In need of something to incapacitate Edvard, Anna had traded herself to a drug dealer and his three brothers in return for a mixture of Temazepam and other street drugs to put in Edvard's drink. Temazepam, promised the dealer, "would knock a horse out for days," but dealers could not be trusted. Anna counted the hours rather than days before Edvard woke and came for her.

Anna pushed a wad of Korunas into a zipped pouch stitched inside the knee-length boots she never took off, even for a client, and stepped from the kiosk doorway. Frightened, Anna glanced with direct stares and pouted lips for what she hoped would be her last trick in Prague and, if Krystyna had been successful, the last trick of her life.

~

The drug dealer had lied. Edvard woke much sooner than expected. A broken drawer and Anna's missing identification filled Edvard with a rage that muffled the drug induced noise in his head and the ache behind his eyes. Certain Anna needed money, Edvard raced to the square.

In less than ten minutes, Edvard found Anna and watched as she led a fat American into the kiosk. Two more men entered and exited the kiosk while Edvard observed Anna with growing contempt and malice. Only the prospect of Anna earning more money before he beat her kept him at bay. The more she earned, the more she would hurt.

Luck liked Anna one last time. Client number six, a fit, muscular man, who performed sex as though on a treadmill, had a sense of chivalry. Edvard, patience exhausted, thrust past number six as he left the kiosk, grabbed Anna, pushed her to the ground, and kicked her in the back and stomach. Before Edvard could make a third kick, a vicious punch lifted Edvard from the ground, broke several teeth, and disoriented him long enough for Anna to scramble from the ground and disappear into the crowd.

Doubled over, clutching her stomach, Anna patted the inside pocket of her fake jean jacket for the one thing more important than the money she needed. Through the fabric, Anna felt the hard shell of the cell phone her sister had given her the night she had left Prague forever. The phone was her only link to her sister.

Two weeks earlier, Anna had lost that link. The phone had fallen out of her pocket and bounced under Edvard's bed when Edvard, drunk and high, had raped Anna. Only when Edvard had fallen unconscious with the Temazepam from the drug dealer had Anna found the courage to retrieve the phone and smash the locks on the drawer where Edvard kept her identification. Now, with money, identification, and the phone, Anna stopped a taxi and climbed inside.

~

Václav Havel Airport Prague is eighteen kilometres from Wenceslas Square and about forty minutes via taxi. Anna didn't know where she was going or how far she could get on the money she had earned in the square. She did know multiple airlines served all EU countries many times each day, and according to tourists, flights from France, Germany, England, and others were not expensive. But what was expensive?

As the taxi dodged traffic on the Horákové/Městský Okruh/Pražský okruh, Anna grasped the cell phone and prayed the battery had not died while it had lain under Edvard's bed for two weeks. A soft chime sounded as the phone powered on. Anna checked the battery and signal strength. Four bars for signal, but only two per cent for the battery. Frantic, Anna pressed the speed dial number she had entered into the phone. Anna held her breath as fifteen numbers pulsed on the screen while the international telecommunications system searched, synchronized, and connected. Two, four, six rings, then voicemail. Disbelief forged a grimace on Anna's face, a tear leaked, and her hand trembled as she pressed redial.

On the half-ring, the system connected. Breathless, Anna sobbed into the phone, "Krystyna, Krystyna! Oh God, are you there, Krystyna?"

"Yes, yes, Anna. I'm here. I . . ."

"Edvard is coming for me. He will kill me."

"Where are you?"

"I'm in a taxi going to the airport."

"What has happened, Anna? Are you all right?"

"There is no time to explain."

"Are you hurt, Anna? You must . . ."

"No time. Yes, yes . . ."

"What? You're hurt. What . . ."

"I mean no. I'm OK, but the phone. The battery is dying. Where do I go, Krystyna? Where are you?"

"England, Anna."

"England?"

"Yes, a farmhouse near Manchester."

"Where? What is the place, the address, Krystyna? Hurry?"

"I, I don't know, Anna."

The skin of Anna's face pulled taut as her mouth widened and scrunched her cheeks to squeeze tears from her eyes. "What? But how will I find you? Krystyna, Krystyna . . ."

"It's OK, Anna. Calm down. I don't know exactly where the farmhouse is. The men would not tell me, and I have found nothing with an address."

"What, what am I supposed to do? Oh God, Edvard will take me, and how will I find you?"

In front and beside the taxi, cars and trucks slowed, four-way hazard lights blinked, and the hiss of air breaks sounded.

"Listen, Anna. Stop and listen to me now. I have some details. You must write them down."

"I, I don't have a pen or paper. Oh God, Krystyna, the power light on the phone is blinking. Tell me now. Where do I go?"

"The house is somewhere near a bus shelter on Higher Road between Altringham and Didsbury. From Manchester, take bus number . . ."

Anna, tears welling, concentrated on what Krystyna had said. Something about a bus on a high road near some kind of ring or berry. It made no sense. Drawing on the strength from her hard life, Anna focused on what did make sense: getting to Manchester and calling Krystyna again. First, she had to get out of Prague. Stowing the phone in her pocket, Anna noticed the taxi had stopped on the highway. She caught the driver's eyes in the rear-view mirror.

"An accident," explained the driver. "Probably fifty minutes delay. Other way, via Pražský okruh, is clear, but I have passed the turn-off. We shall have to wait."

While they waited, Anna watched the metre turn, and the driver watched Anna. When the metre reached eleven hundred Koruna, the driver, sensing Anna's apprehension, turned and said, "I have seen you in the square. I can turn off the metre."

Anna did the math. She had only thirteen thousand six hundred Koruna. Some of the men in the square had not paid as much as she had wanted, and she had no time to barter or pick other clients. With almost halfway still to go and an uncertain delay, the taxi fare could reach two thousand, two thousand five hundred Koruna. She might not have enough for a plane ticket. Resigned, Anna nodded and said, "Turn it off now, and it stays off."

With the terms agreed, Anna moved from back to front while the driver cleared papers and garbage from the passenger seat. As Anna leaned over and inclined her torso and head to meet the bulge in the driver's pants, the taxi inched forward.

~

Fighting pain and struggling to speak, Edvard screamed and gesticulated for Boris, his bodyguard and enforcer, to get Anna. Fortunately, for Anna, Boris misunderstood Edvard. Instead of chasing Anna, Boris caught and beat Anna's chivalrous protector. When Boris returned, he wiped the blood from his knuckles and waited for Edvard's praise. Instead, Edvard, a dirty rag, handed to him by his driver Petr, pressed against his mouth to stem the flow of blood, spat muffled curses.

"You idiot. Anna, get Anna. Both of you, now!"

With Boris and Petr dispatched, Edvard received some rudimentary first aid from one of the mobile emergency responders that patrolled the square on bicycle. Violence wasn't uncommon in the square, and only a few tourists stopped to gawk until two police officers, both recipients of Edvard's financial and other types of favours, moved them on. A few minutes later, Boris returned with news. "She jumped in a taxi on Stepanka Street."

Faint crimson blots dotted the bandage wrapped under Edvard's chin and over his head. He grimaced as he pushed words past broken teeth, "What taxi company?"

"Not sure, Praha or Halotaxi."

"Which way did it go?"

"Taxi did a U-turn and headed south."

"She goes to the highway and the airport then?"

Boris, long familiar with Edvard's manner, didn't respond. Petr, eyes fixed on the ground and used to Edvard's need for control, waited for orders.

"The car, get the fucking car now."

The black Mercedes, a staple of mid-level criminals, lurched and left rubber on the worn cobbles of the dingy side street that linked the square to Stepanka. Edvard, seated in the back, leaned forward and spoke to Boris. "Get more men to the airport. And get someone to call the taxi companies."

Boris dialled numbers and issued orders and threats. As the car sped up the on-ramp, Edvard threw a question at Boris and Petr. "Who do we have at the airport?"

Petr turned to Boris, but Boris was still on the phone. Forced to answer, Petr said what Edvard already knew.

"No one. The Plavsic control the airport. In fact, we should maybe call and tell them we are going, or they might . . ."

"Shut up Petr. I know."

Boris turned side on, leaned between the two front seats, and reported to Edvard. "Victor and Vlad are on their way with three men each. They are about ten minutes behind us."

Edvard prodded his chin for damage. A red blotch expanded on the bandage where Edvard's finger had pressed, and an unintelligible obscenity followed. The car slowed. Edvard stared past Petr.

"Looks like an accident," said Petr.

Ahead, the on-off red of brake lights indicated slow progress.

"Get off the highway, Petr. Find another way."

"Can't. We passed the exit a half-mile back."

A fist slammed the back of Petr's seat.

"It's OK, boss," said Petr in response to Edvard's fist. "She only left ten minutes before us. All the taxis take this route-it's the shortest. She will be caught in the same traffic."

~

Business concluded, Anna straightened herself in the passenger seat and avoided the still-leering eyes of the driver. Fifteen minutes after they passed the accident, the taxi slowed, took the off-ramp, and exited the highway.

Ahead, through the windshield, Anna gaped at the glass and metal of Václav Havel International Airport. With over eleven million passengers in 2014, Václav Havel is the busiest airport in the newer EU member states, and Anna, who had never before visited an airport, hesitated when the driver asked, "Where to?"

"I don't know. Let me out anywhere."

"Where do you want to fly?"

Before Anna could stop herself, she blurted, "England."

"England? A holiday?"

"No, I mean yes. England is the first stop, then on to America."

With a smirk, the driver said, "America. That is a long way to go without bags."

"Just let me out."

"Not here. You want Terminal One. That is where international flights depart. I will drop you there."

Anna caught the man's stare. A smile, hopeful and sincere had replaced the smirk.

"Thank you."

The taxi slowed curbside in front of a large rotating circular door. Anna pulled the handle on the car door and stepped out as the car lurched to a stop. To her back, the driver called out, "Good luck."

~

Inside, Anna paused. People, familiar with the airport and international travel, moved with purpose around her. Electronic boards, TV monitors, and advertisements behind huge glass boxes flickered, changed, and moved. Voices, real and mechanical, competed with a steady hum of activity and motion. Smells of food, perfume, and humanity clogged Anna's nostrils. Overwhelmed, Anna moved to stand beside a wall out of the stream of people. After a few moments, Anna noticed the information displays and followed the directions to the ticket counter.

Across the cavernous entrance, Anna watched people approach counters and hand over credit cards or cash in exchange for boarding passes. Inexperienced, Anna searched the signs above the counters for a place to buy a ticket to England. Instead, the signs listed counters designated for airlines or multiple airlines. At last, one sign made sense: British Airways. Logic suggested that British Airways would fly to England and, therefore, Manchester. At the British Airways ticket counter, logic was indirect.

"Oh yes," said the clerk, "we do fly to England, but our flights only go to London or Gatwick. From there, you will need a connection to Manchester. When would you like to leave?"

"Right away. How much is a ticket? And when does the flight leave?"

The clerk checked prices and availability, with a broad smile, and said: "A flight leaves for Gatwick in seventy-five minutes. If you have no checked baggage, you could make that flight. There is a wait of two hours for the connection to Manchester. Shall I book you on the flight?"

Anna, relieved a flight would leave so soon, said, "Yes, yes, how much does it cost?"

"Eighteen thousand and ninety-four Koruna for both flights."

Frustration replaced Anna's relief. Anna mentally counted her money a second time. She was still about five thousand Koruna short. Behind Anna, a well-dressed, business-suited man snorted with impatience. Anna leaned her hands on the counter. Her voice cracked as she pleaded, "I have thirteen thousand Koruna. Is there a cheaper flight, perhaps one that leaves a little later?"

With one eye on the businessman behind Anna, the clerk closed a hand over Anna's and spoke softly: "I'm sorry. That's our best price to Manchester. We only offer business-class flights to Gatwick. It is 8,000 Koruna cheaper if you just go to Gatwick. You know England is quite compact. Gatwick is not that far from Manchester."

Uncertainty creased Anna's face. She had no idea where or what Gatwick was and no clue how she would get from there to Manchester. Behind Anna, the man coughed loudly. Empathy crossed the clerk's face, and she leaned forward and whispered, "You should try Jet2 farther down. They have much cheaper flights than British Airways. But don't tell anyone I told you, OK?"

Anna mumbled a low, "Thank you" and hurried to the Jet2 ticket counter. The British Airways clerk had been right. Direct economy-class flights to Manchester were between two thousand and four thousand Koruna depending on when she wanted to leave.

"When do you wish to depart?" asked the Jet2 ticket clerk.

"Right now if possible," said Anna, her confidence restored.

"Our first available flight leaves at midnight, and it is also our cheapest flight. It is only one thousand eight hundred and forty-six Koruna. Shall I book you a seat?"

Ecstatic the flight was so cheap, and she would have money left over when she reached Manchester, Anna nodded and bent down to retrieve money from her boots. As she bent down, voices, coarse and urgent, called out: "Edvard, Edvard, the bitch is not here."

"Are you sure?"

"Yes."

"OK, we will check the other terminals."

Anna remained stooped. Through legs, bags, and carts, Edvard, a bandage wrapped under his chin and up over his head, nodded to an out-of-sight person before turning toward the signs for Terminal Two.

"Excuse me. Are you all right?" said the Jet2 counter clerk as he stood and leaned over the counter.

Anna, with Edvard no longer in sight, stood upright and faced the ticket clerk.

"Oh, yes. Sorry, I dropped something. Is there an earlier flight?"

"No, I'm sorry, midnight is our next flight."

Anna checked her watch — it was 5:30 p.m. That left more than six hours to wait and six hours for Edvard to find her. Even in an airport, Edvard would not hesitate to take her. With a note of impatience, the clerk asked, "Do you want to take the midnight flight?"

Anna thought, *what had the British Airways clerk said? Eight thousand less to fly to Gatwick only and that Manchester was nearby.* That would be ten thousand Koruna, which would leave her with practically nothing when she arrived in England. But the flight left in less than an hour. Should she wait six hours to save a few thousand Koruna and risk Edvard finding her? Resolved, Anna headed for the British Airways desk to book a flight to Gatwick.

Two

Half a crow mile, a boy's school, a small private fishing lake, and several acres of common land stand between the Railway Tavern Pub and the railway line from which the pub derived its name. On a clear day back in the early 1800s, when the pub served its first beer, patrons would have witnessed the belch of white steam and black smoke from coal-fired engines as they pulled their wagons in and out of Manchester's inner city.

Diesel engines now spew exhaust in the air, but since 1955, the looming presence of the Wellacre Academy School blocked any sight of the railway line or diesel engine exhaust.

Wayne Jones, "Taffy" to his friends or "Welsh Fucker" to his enemies, had graduated from the then-named Wellacre Secondary Modern School for Boys in 1977. However, he had yet to graduate from the Railway Tavern Pub.

Adept at handling beer glasses, Taffy placed four pints of John Smith's on the worn copper-topped round table that filled the small alcove made by the bay window.

"Well, lads," said Taffy raising his glass, "here's to us. It looks like we've gone and done it, eh?"

Beer had been instrumental in Taffy's life since his first sip at age seven. Beer had curtailed a promising soccer career, guided his seed to father an unplanned child, and shaped his body and mind into the archetypal pasty-faced and beer-gutted Englishman.

Granddad Jones, on his mom's side, had slipped his impressionable grandson a half-glass of John Smith's bitter outside the Railway Tavern on a hot Sunday afternoon. Taffy still remembered the light-headed buzz and the knowing smile of his granddad as he held out the glass for a refill. Taffy had been chasing that first buzz ever since. Three eager hands lifted a glass, and each man siphoned off a generous amount of the cool brown liquid.

Phil, six feet two and stick skinny no matter how much he drank or ate, drew the back of his hand across his mouth to remove the foam from his top lip and said, "Damn right we have. We should have done it years ago. You must be happy eh, Ham?"

Graham Williams, or "Ham" to his friends, nodded in agreement as blood rushed to his face in embarrassment. Of the four men, Ham was the least vocal or demonstrative about his sexual activities and the arrangements the men had made. And for good reason.

Taffy, already only one more gulp away from needing a second pint, nodded to Steve as said, "So, Tyrion, are you finally getting enough now?"

Steve Ennis, five feet five with an updraft, five feet seven with his lifts, hated the nicknames that had plagued him since junior school. "Inch high," "Lifty," "Runt," and "Squirt" had featured in his early days.

Since the '70s, "De Plane" and "Tattoo"—after the character in the 1970s comedy show, *Fantasy Island*—had been staples for many years.

More recently, Steve Ennis had to suffer the nickname, "Tyrion," after the *Game of Thrones* character who soothed his inadequacies with wine and self-indulgence. Irritated by the name, but experienced enough to accept it until another one came along, Tyrion snapped back, "I always get enough, Taffy. Quantity is not the problem. Quality is what I like, and yes, I am getting enough of both. And stop calling me Tyrion."

"Quantity and quality haven't improved your sense of humour, though," said Phil.

"What would you know about humour, Phil? You only laugh when you're stoned, and then everything is funny."

Smiling at the rightness of Tyrion's assertion, Phil pushed his chair back, nodded, and said, "Speaking of which, I think I'll just have a quick toke. Anyone else?"

"Hang on a minute, Phil," said Taffy. "Let's get the business done before you light up. Otherwise, we'll be here all night explaining things to you."

Phil, the affable smile of a regular marijuana user spread on his face, sat down. Tyrion, accepted as the group leader due to a combined need to compensate for his shortness and apathy on the part of others, handed a single typed sheet of paper each to Taffy, Phil, and Ham. As each studied the paper, Tyrion spoke:

"Right, here are the details so far. The house, electricity, property taxes, water, and all the usual stuff is as expected. Food, clothing, satellite TV are a bit more than we thought. It seems our lady friend watches a lot of movies."

"I wonder if she stars in any of them, eh?" said Taffy with a smirk as he rolled the bottom of his empty glass back and forth on the table.

"I doubt it," said Tyrion. "She watches Disney movies and old shit. Anyway, I guess we can't begrudge her that."

Ham, tapping a pencil on the paper, asked, "What about the phone, Tyrion?"

"The landline is disconnected, but she wanted a cell phone. I got one of those cheap flip phone jobs with no Internet or anything. I pick up prepaid cards and deduct the cost from her weekly payment, so the calls are on her."

Still tapping his pencil, Ham, who earned the least of the four, coughed and insisted that he could not pay any more than he already did.

"It's all right, Ham. We're good for now. Six hundred a month seems to be plenty. Not a bad deal for sex on tap, eh?" "Well, I have to agree," replied Ham. "Having a woman on tap is a lot easier and more convenient than the way we did it before."

"You mean having to coordinate our trips with Man United's Champions League games in Europe?"

"Yes, not to mention we'd be screwed this year because they didn't make the Champions League."

"And we don't have to buy game tickets or travel on buses and flights with fixed times. It was always a rush."

"So," beamed Tyrion, "you three finally agree that my idea to set us up with a nice bit of fluff here in town wasn't all that crazy?"

"Yeah, don't like to admit it," said Phil, "but you were right on this one, Tyrion."

"What's even better," smirked Tyrion, "is that our wives think we're more responsible for not wasting money on a soccer trip to Europe. Jesus, if they only knew."

Phil, lips curled in a tight smirk, said to no one in particular, "Yes, it's all pretty damn good, but she does ask a lot of questions sometimes."

"That," said Taffy, as he rose to go to the bar, "is probably because she is trying to distract you from tying her up and spanking the shit out of her. There were marks on her wrists and ankles yesterday when I got there."

"Hey," said Phil, hands splayed in contrition, "we agreed that we get to have her any way we want when it's our turn. I'm not hurting her. Anyway, she likes it. And she still asks a lot of questions."

"Yeah, she does go on a bit, but it's easy to shut her up eh?" said Tyrion, and he laughed as he poked his tongue into his cheek.

Three

Prague, a centre for the European sex trade, had exposed Krystyna to many perverse and cruel desires of men. Escape from Prague and her move to England had fuelled in Krystyna a hope that the extremes of depravity were behind her. However, while Graham Williams, the fourth man to whom Krystyna was contracted for six months, was not the worst she had suffered, his desires were unpleasant and painful. Their first Monday meeting, two months earlier, had been unusual because Ham, as his friends called him, had only wanted to talk.

"I am a mortgage specialist, and I am good at my job. I used to work for the government in immigration, but I didn't like that very much. I'm married. I am forty-five, and my wife is fifty-five. We have a son. He is nineteen and at university. My wife works in a flower shop, drinks a lot, and gossips all the time. She was married once before, and she picked me up when I was twenty-five. Our son Nick was born when I was twenty-six."

Ham's bedroom, like Ham, was impersonal. A double bed, mounted on a box spring, on a plain black steel frame with no headboard, and no flanking side tables, pressed head-first against one interior brick wall. To the left, a hard wooden kitchen, or informal dining chair, provided a bed-height perch for a single bulb lamp and an unused ashtray. A low three-drawer dresser with faded cotton doilies and cheap figurines of farm animals squatted under the window, which faced the rear of the farmhouse and several small outbuildings. Opposite the bed, a dark, oversized, wooden wardrobe, which smelled musty and creaked when opened, dominated the room. A room, Krystyna had thought, for an unwelcome guest. Uncomfortable on the hard chair, Krystyna had watched and listened as Ham, prostrate on the bed, talked.

"Rose, that's her name, doesn't like sex. She hasn't for years. We don't really like each other that much anymore, but we need each other."

Ham had talked for almost two hours, recounting his childhood, school, how he pretended to like punk, grunge, and pop music when he had preferred classical music which he listened to now. He told stories of how, even though he was no good, he played football with Taffy, Tyrion, and Phil, and that he knew they only let him play because he did all the organizing. Ham said that he didn't care because he liked being around the guys.

"I was, still am I guess, a little soft and pudgy, even though I bike every day. I work from home, and Rose takes the car. I could never run very fast. Anyway, I don't play anymore."

Men had talked before—about what they would do to Krystyna, what they had done to others, what their wives wouldn't do, about their jobs, their lives, pressures, and unfulfilled dreams. Almost all had talked to explain and justify why they needed Krystyna's services. Ham had talked and unloaded his "justification," then left. Krystyna had heard stories of men who paid women to listen and never demanded any sex. Krystyna had been skeptical that such men existed, but after Ham's long rambling, she was hopeful that he would be an easy client. She had been wrong: very wrong.

~

Reality struck the following Monday morning shortly after 10 a.m. when Ham returned, and the saddle bag from his bicycle thumped down on the bedroom floor.

From the bag, Ham boldly withdrew an assortment of rubberized sex toys. Large, thick, smooth, and ribbed, Ham arranged the equipment on the bed. As straps and buckles, to attach the toys to the body, followed, Krystyna guessed what would be required of her. Krystyna had endured such toys before and hadn't been surprised when Ham had also wanted to be on the receiving end.

Bringing Ham to climax wasn't the issue. Ham came quickly. The problem and the pain came when Ham adjusted the straps so that he could use two toys simultaneously on Krystyna. Despite his soft, pasty exterior, Ham pursued his desire as though engaged in a war of attrition to wear the other out.

Today, for the first time, Ham's sixth Monday morning visit ended early. Ham had explained that he had to get the car from his wife so he could collect his son, Nick, from the bus station. Nick, who rarely visited during the university term, was coming home because he had something to tell them. Krystyna, eager for Ham's departure, had grimaced when Ham parted with a sincere promise to "make it up next week."

When Ham's bicycle disappeared from the driveway, Krystyna eased herself downstairs and placed a short note in the volume of the *Encyclopedia Britannica* reserved for notes on Ham: *Ham, 10 to 12, Monday, left early to collect his son, Nick, who comes home from university to tell parents some news.*

Four

Blemished plaster and exposed brick, dulled by early evening light, filled the view from the window above the dirty well-used basin. Vibrations, emitted by the laundry machines on either side of the sink as they worked through the wash and dry cycles, rattled the basin. Krystyna pressed her pelvis against the dryer and let the warmth and rhythm of the machine ease the discomfort and soreness left over from the morning session with Ham. Lulled and tired, the shadow-filled wall drew Krystyna in and provoked suppressed memories of another wall.

The wall, built in 1999 on Maticni Street, Usti nad Labem in the Czech Republic, symbolized the systemic discrimination that plagued the Roma minority in the Czech Republic for centuries. Designed by bureaucrats to appease self-righteous, respectable, and employed homeowners who demanded separation from the "jobless, dishonest, and smelly" Roma families who lived in nearby city-owned flats, the wall haunted Krystyna's childhood memories.

Stigmatized and poorly educated due to a government policy that sent all Roma children to schools designed for the mentally delayed, Krystyna's parents, like ninety-five per cent of Roma adults, had been unemployed for years. Life, or existence, depended on the illegal use of land her parents and other Roma used to raise pigs and chickens and grow staples to supplement the state handouts that only maintained their poverty. Although only six years old when the wall appeared, Krystyna could still taste the bitterness, and she shuddered when the dryer stopped.

Tomorrow would mark seven weeks since Krystyna had arrived at Manchester Airport, England. Only one of the men, Steven Ennis, had met her at the airport, and he had driven Krystyna directly to the farmhouse where she now stood washing soiled sheets. Ennis, or Tyrion as his friends called him, had demanded sex the moment they arrived at the farmhouse. He hadn't even allowed her to use the bathroom first, which she really had to do after the flight from Prague.

Today, Monday, had been Ham's turn. Tomorrow, Tuesday, was Taffy's day. On Wednesday, Tyrion, Thursday, Phil, but no one had a schedule for Friday—however, any one of them could and often did show up. It all depended on whether or not they could fool their wives into believing they would be somewhere else.

Saturday had so far seen no visitors, and on Sundays, usually between ten and four, one or two of them would arrive for a "quickie" as they fit their visit in between or around the errands their wives had tasked them to do.

After replacing the dry sheets with wet ones, Krystyna took the clean bedding to the living room and held one of the silk pillowcases to her cheek.

Silk had caressed her skin before. When she arrived in Prague in early 2012, her first client had been a businessman staying at the five-star InterContinental hotel. The man, middle-aged, clean, and polite, had only wanted straight sex. He was done in less than ten minutes and Krystyna had earned five thousand Koruna or about two hundred US dollars. Flush with optimism and money despite the work, Krystyna believed she could control her situation and earn enough money to provide for herself and her sister, Anna, whom she had left behind in Usti nad Labem. Krystyna's naivety ended when Edvard, an experienced, and as it later turned out, brutal Prague pimp got his hooks into her. But Anna hadn't stayed in Usti nad Labem. She followed Krystyna to Prague and into Edvard's clutches.

Anna had always followed Krystyna: for love and protection. Their parents loved them, but the demands of Roma life, the discrimination, the poverty, and the depression, strained parental relations and limited the frequency and depth of affections their parents could provide. Anna, younger, sensitive, and fearful, needed more love and reassurance than most, and Krystyna, who could draw strength from being wanted, gave Anna the love she needed.

Protection had been another factor that drew and kept Anna and Krystyna close. Krystyna, taller and stronger than most girls her age, also had nerve and bravado, which she used many times to protect herself and Anna from unwanted interest from boys and men. Krystyna had begged Anna not to come to Prague until she had gotten a job and had a safe place for them to live. Of course, Anna, afraid without her sister, had arrived in Prague shortly after Edvard had trapped Krystyna, and now he had Anna too. Krystyna would never forgive herself. Not until they were both free of Edvard.

Thoughts of Edvard and Anna sent Krystyna's hand to her jean pocket. She withdrew a cell phone and willed it to ring. Almost three weeks had passed since Anna last called begging Krystyna to send her money to escape Prague and Edvard. She had tried to send money, but time, access, and the absence of a physical entity like a bank account number, a mailbox, or even another person's address, had prevented Krystyna from getting money to Anna.

In desperation, Krystyna had mailed three hundred pounds in an envelope in care of Hugo, a bellhop at the Prague Hilton hotel, who occasionally arranged clients for her and Anna without Edvard's knowledge. Hugo had never demanded sex in addition to the money she paid him for the secret hotel clients and she thought he might be trusted to pass the "letter" to Anna without opening it. Two weeks had passed since Hugo would have received the letter and money for Anna, and Krystyna accepted the probability that she had been wrong about Hugo.

Krystyna turned the phone in her hand. She wanted to call Anna, but the risk that the phone would attract Edvard's attention was too great. If Edvard discovered Anna had a second phone he would beat the truth out of Anna. And Edvard must not learn the truth.

The silk bedding was Tyrion's. He had arrived unexpectedly on Sunday morning and stayed just long enough to dirty the sheets with his seed and sweat before running off to collect his sixteen-year-old daughter, Beth, from her choir practice. At first, Tyrion had reminded Krystyna of her first trick in Prague: straight sex, in and out with efficiency, and nothing kinky. All he needed was an assurance that he was the best and that she had "really enjoyed it." Stroking egos required more skill and finesse than stroking anything else. However, that soon changed when Tyrion installed his medieval equipment.

With the sheets folded and placed in a laundry basket, Krystyna moved toward the large bookcase that dominated one wall of the living room. From the top shelf, she withdrew volume one of a 1965 edition of the *Encyclopedia Britannica* and opened to page seven. A single plain white paper, half filled with small neat ink-written notations, rested between pages seven and eight. Underneath the existing notes, Krystyna wrote: *Tyrion, Sunday, 10:15 to 10:55, while daughter, Beth, at choir practice.*

Five

Toot, toot. Two sharp honks, a short skid, a door thump, and a crunch as leather-soled shoes, which supported well over two hundred pounds, shuffled from car to front door across dry gravel. Wayne Jones had arrived. Krystyna eyed the overweight, drab-dressed man from the bathroom window. He was early, by almost half an hour. She had just returned and needed to shower away the sweat and overcome the disappointment of another unfulfilled wait at the bus stop. Wayne, or Taffy, had his own door key. They all did.

Krystyna stepped under the water and lathered herself with vanilla-scented body wash and shampoo. The products were cheap generic brands that dried Krystyna's hair and skin, but Taffy had provided them and insisted she use them when he visited. He said it reminded him of his first love, which Krystyna inferred had not been his current wife. When the shower ran, the pipes knocked, and Taffy would know where she was. As expected, Taffy entered the bathroom and lowered his pants before she had rubbed herself dry. Less than a minute later, when he was done, she brushed her teeth, washed her face, and joined him in his bedroom.

Each man had his own bedroom, desires, demands, secrets, and weaknesses. Taffy's room was plain and unadorned. A double bed, mattress, box spring, and flimsy plastic-covered headboard stood off-centre against the wall that abutted Phil's room. Crisp, starched, and ironed white sheets, half-covered by a fleece-like brown blanket, covered the bed, and two under-filled pillows lay against the wall. A white four-drawer dresser, scratched with two broken handles, loitered alone against the other wall. Matching side tables flanked the bed. A cloth covered reading chair, with a worn footstool, soaked up the light from the window, which had faded the fabric on one side. Carpet, greenish and plush, complimented the textured off-white wallpaper adorned with green plants and vines.

Taffy, thin beige curtains already closed, draped his pants, shirt, and jacket over the chair and leaned against it to remove his socks and underwear. Naked and flaccid, Taffy held out his arms and spoke as he beckoned Krystyna to him.

"I'm supposed to be over in Lymn showing some young executive from London a five-bedroom house with a pool, double-car garage, and a bloody tennis court. Christ, the kid can't be more than twenty-five, but he's looking at houses that cost almost a million pounds! Where the hell do these kids get that sort of money?"

"I don't know, but a lot of young people seem to make money from computers or investing."

"More likely he's a crook."

"Oh, I hope not. What if he doesn't pay your commission?"

"What? I hadn't thought of that. Well, I'll tell you he had damn well better pay me if he buys it. Do you know how much I'll make on a million pounds? You're a devious little bitch, are you?"

A dry towel, cinched above Krystyna's breasts but open at the thigh, drew Taffy's eyes as she adopted a soft pout to respond to Taffy's insult.

"I'm no bitch. It's just that in my country you always assume everyone is a crook, and no one will pay. It's easier that way."

"Well, this is England, and people don't do that. Besides, I got some contacts that will take care of any ponce boy from London who don't pay his bills."

With one leg placed on the bed to allow Taffy a view of her inner thigh, Krystyna spoke as she unknotted the top of the towel.

"Well, Prague is very violent, and I'm glad I don't live there."

"Me too," said Taffy as he hardened in response to signals from his brain.

"What's worse is that everyone smokes in Prague. I hate it."

Taffy had made his intolerance of smokers and smoking plain to Krystyna on his first visit when Taffy had disclosed that his wife, Angie, smoked. Since then, Krystyna had employed a mention of smoking to loosen Taffy's tongue to get him to talk about his life without having to ask direct questions. Today was no exception.

"Damn right too. I can't stand smoking. You know Angie started smoking a couple of years ago. Christ, I don't know why. She is skinny as a rake so there is no need to use fags for weight loss."

"It must be hard for you, you know, being with a smoker when you do this sort of thing."

The towel had dropped, and Krystyna had grasped and squeezed Taffy's stiffness. Between moans, Taffy continued.

"Yeah well, chance would be a fine thing. She seems to have lost interest since she began smoking. Worst part is that I think my daughter, Millie, has started smoking as well."

Sinking to her knees, Krystyna sympathized with Taffy.

"Oh, I hope not. That would be awful."

"Damn right. I'll bloody kill Angie if Millie starts smoking because her mom does it."

~

For Taffy, talking served two purposes. First, the human need to feel important and needed by having someone listen, and in Krystyna's case, to convey interest and reverence for everything he said. Second, talking, especially about work and family, distracted Taffy from the pulsing in his groin and the problem he wanted no one, except his most intimate partners, to know about.

Angie, whom Taffy had knocked up when she was just eighteen, had for many years managed his problem and ensured their sexual relationship had been mutually satisfying. More recently, and as he had told Krystyna, Angie didn't care anymore and the sex, when they even bothered, was over in no time at all.

Obscured under Taffy's protruding beer belly, Krystyna stimulated Taffy's manhood and carefully checked her watch to ensure she "bested" Angie's time. Four minutes. Another thirty seconds and she would bring Taffy to the edge of a climax before doubling over on the bed to allow his brief and messy visitation. Premature ejaculation was often a godsend to prostitutes who worked streets and alleyways, and most would prefer quick and messy to the long drawn-out rutting and aggressive frustration of alcohol-laden men.

Closeted in a private house with a man desperate for duration was rough on knees and throats, and Krystyna had been relieved when Taffy had revealed that Angie's "best effort," as he described it, had been three and a half minutes. So long as she bested Angie, it seemed that Taffy was satisfied. The first one, like the one in the bathroom, didn't count. Taffy had explained that part of her duties and their "routine" would be to provide a quick blowjob to take the edge off before the second, longer performance. There wouldn't be a third. Satiated, Taffy lay prostrate on the bed and awaited his massage. While Krystyna kneaded and rubbed, Taffy talked.

"So Krystyna, it's been six weeks now. How do you like the setup?"

"Very much, Taffy. Regular customers, and good ones like you, are much better than, you know, being on the streets in Prague."

"The farm, this house, it's pretty damn good too, eh? Everything you could want, I bet."

"Oh, yes, I have everything I need."

"Last week, you were telling me about your family and how you grew up in a nice house until your parents died. What happened then?"

"Oh, it was horrible. My uncle, Peter, he took me in and we moved to . . ."

Krystyna continued with a well-rehearsed and fictitious life story that she had told in differing details to each of the men. Taffy and the others must know nothing that might enable them to track her one day.

After fifteen minutes, Taffy showered and dressed while Krystyna poured him a beer. Only Taffy drank alcohol after a visit. The others preferred hot, sweet tea. After beer, Taffy, like Tyrion, sought assurance of his performance and confirmation that she was suitably satisfied. With appropriate assurances, Krystyna hovered by the front door to ensure that Taffy had left.

With Taffy gone, Krystyna went to the living room and located volume three of the *Encyclopedia Britannica*. From chapter seven, she withdrew a sheet of paper and added a notation to the already three-quarters full page.

Tuesday, while supposed to be showing a house with a pool in Lymn. Said he would kill Angie if his daughter, Millie, started to smoke.

Six

On British Airways flight BA 1234 from Prague to Gatwick, Anna's hand shook as she pressed her second double vodka on ice in a clean glass to her mouth. Vodka, straight from the bottle, had been the drink of choice for Anna and her peers since their early teens. In Prague, as a street-level prostitute, Anna discovered that vodka was much more than just a way for teens to get drunk. Vodka served Anna as a mouthwash, an agent to clean and sanitize, a way to calm nerves, dull pain, and to forget.

The first in-flight drink hadn't touched Anna's lips, but with little money, Anna had to make this one last. The sight and sensations of the runway acceleration, take-off, and the steep climb pushed sweat from every pore and tensed every muscle. Two hours later, the sweat and tension returned as the plane banked and slowed to begin its descent to Gatwick Airport.

Off the plane and through to the arrivals area, Anna had one priority. Call Krystyna. First, she needed money. Her two thousand seven hundred Koruna exchanged for seventy-three British pounds and ten Pence. With her cell phone dead and with no charger, Anna found a pay phone. Then she needed change.

Then she called Krystyna's number, but it didn't work. An automated message said that the international code for England was not required. "Please check your number and dial again." When Anna figured it out, all she got was a beep to leave a message. Anna left a message.

"I made it, Krystyna. I'm in Gatwick Airport. I will call again soon. Please answer, Krystyna, please."

Disoriented, alone, and unsure about what to do or where to go, Anna followed the baggage-laden crowd as they headed toward exits with signs for car rentals, taxis, coaches, buses, limousine services, and trains. Anna's budget would not extend to cars, limousines, and taxis, and besides, they would need a credit card, driver's licence, and/or a destination, none of which she had.

That left buses and trains. Buses were usually the cheapest form of travel, and Anna headed for the bus terminal. Before the bus terminal, a sign directed travellers to the "non-stop Gatwick Express" train to London for a one-way only price of 17.80 pounds. Anna liked trains. Krystyna and Anna, like many children, had used trains to escape the real or imagined brutalities and disappointments of their young lives. Not far from their home on Maticni Street in Usti nad Labem, trains, more than thirty each day, had roared east and west on the SZDC railway across the Czech Republic. The sisters, shoeless and hungry, had built and shared many dreams and hopes on the backs of those speeding trains.

Lost in memories, the tide of people swept Anna to the ticket office, onto the platform, and into a carriage for the thirty-minute express train ride to Victoria

Station in the heart of London. The train dawdled most of the time and only "expressed" on a few short stretches of track between built-up areas. The seats looked comfortable, but Anna didn't get to sit down, and instead stood sandwiched against the carriage wall with tens of hot, impatient, and irritated passengers. Over the shoulder of a small dark-skinned man who swayed rhythmically with the train, houses, factories, trees, and landscape blurred as Anna struggled for personal space.

After a long reduction in speed and an endless screech of wheels and brakes, the train entered Victoria Station. Passengers, sensing an end to their journeys, exited the train as though sucked by a giant vacuum.

Bustled by the throng of people, Anna halted in front of a large wall-mounted map that orientated Victoria Station in central London close to Westminster, Pimlico, and Belgravia. The names, like those of more suburbs such as Mayfair and Paddington, meant nothing to Anna. Only one place name brought recognition: Soho.

Men, often drunk and laying blame on Anna for their lack of release, had made many crass comments and comparisons between the whores in Prague and those in Soho. Using her index finger as a ruler, Anna estimated that Soho Square, for lack of any other destination, was about three kilometres from Victoria Station. With less than fifty pounds in her pocket, Anna began to walk. As she walked, Anna stopped at three public telephones to call Krystyna, but her sister did not answer.

~

After forty-five minutes and several wrong turns, Anna arrived at the end of Firth Street at the south-west corner of Soho Square. Tired of the traffic and exhaust fumes, Anna crossed the road, passed through the black iron gates that marked the entrance to Soho Square Gardens, and followed the well-maintained path to one of several wooden park benches. Fighting fatigue, hunger, and dehydration, Anna slumped on the bench. Pigeons, seeking food, milled around Anna's feet. People, intent or indifferent, passed without a glance. Through the trees, a neon sign blinked an attention-getting message: "Nude Espresso-OPEN." Intrigued, and in need of the caffeine that espresso implied, Anna left the gardens and entered the Nude Espresso, a micro roastery that offered fresh coffee, cakes, and pastries.

Inside, behind the counter and above an enormous black hissing espresso machine, a chalkboard with flowing letters intertwined with flowers and multicoloured smiley faces, listed a selection of coffee and pastries. With a large black coffee, water, and three plain croissants, Anna collapsed on a seat at a bench placed against the window overlooking the road and Soho Gardens. Rain, light and erratic, tapped the window and scattered across the glass. Two croissants, the water, and most of the hot black coffee had disappeared with neither thought nor taste before Anna, catching her reflection in the window, wiped crumbs and moisture from her lips and chin. Anna didn't look well.

Her face, drawn and thin on her best days, had sunken in, and her cheekbones protruded unnaturally below dark-rimmed eyes. Lips, dry and cracked, had stung when the cold water or hot coffee had touched them. Using the distorted reflection, Anna loosened an elastic from her hair and pulled loose the tangles with calloused fingers.

Silent and still, a misshapen figure hovered in the reflection behind Anna. Jolted, Anna turned. A woman, with neat short hair, large eyes, and pale white skin dressed in black pants and shirt with a black-and-white apron tied between breasts and knees, smiled and spoke.

"Hello, my name is Veronika. Are you all right?"

The woman, who spoke English with an Eastern European accent similar to Anna's, had been behind the counter making coffee when Anna ordered her food from the man who operated the cash register. Assured that the woman was not an agent of Edvard's who had somehow followed her to Soho, Anna replied, "Yes, yes, I'm all right. Just a little tired."

Veronika collected Anna's empty cup and croissant paper and said quietly, "If you need help, I will be done in an hour. I walk home through the gardens. I can meet you on the other side away from the café."

Veronika returned to work, and Anna, streetwise from hard years in Prague's Wenceslas Square, remained quiet, finished her coffee, and left the café. An hour later, with no other options, Anna and Veronika sat together in Soho Gardens.

"I don't have much time."

"What do you mean? What do you want?"

"I don't want anything. I don't even want to know your name. So don't tell me. Listen, I am from Belarus.

You are also from somewhere like that, from an Eastern country.

Listen, I don't want you to end up like me. You must get away from Soho before one of them finds you."

"What? How do you know someone is looking for me?"

"I don't, but I mean the men, they will take you and . . ."

"You mean pimps, don't you?"

"Yes, yes, they look all the time for girls who show up with no money, nowhere to go, and they offer you everything and then they trap you. Do you have somewhere to go?"

"Yes, I'm going to Manchester."

"I mean right now."

"No."

"Do you have money?"

Suspicious, Anna replied.

"A little."

"Don't worry, I don't want it. If you need a place to sleep, go to the SoHostel. It's not far from here on Dean Street. Go that way and turn left. It's cheap and clean, but don't stay long. Then you must get away."

Furtive and nervous, her hands trembling, Veronika checked her watch.

"I must go, I am late, and he will be suspicious."

Veronika stood abruptly and walked away. Anna called after her: "What? Who will wait? How can I thank you?"

Over her shoulder, Veronika called back: "Don't get caught."

Seven

Anna's call from the taxi tormented Krystyna. The call had ended abruptly, and Krystyna, who had suffered Edvard's brutality many times, had felt Anna's fear through the phone. Anna had not answered Krystyna's repeated calls. Had Anna escaped? Was she lying dead in a ditch beside the highway, or worse, had Edvard taken her back to Prague? Even if she had escaped, would Anna remember or understand the details of how to find her in Manchester?

Almost two months had passed since Krystyna had left Prague. Anna had called several times crying and afraid. Edvard followed her everywhere, would not let her have money, and had taken her identification. Edvard had also beaten Anna to find out where Krystyna had gone. Krystyna and Anna had agreed that the only way Anna could keep from telling Edvard where Krystyna had gone was if she really didn't know. Imagining Anna's suffering tortured Krystyna but it had been the only way. Anna's instructions were to get at least fifteen thousand Koruna, head for the airport, and call Krystyna. They both knew the plan had many flaws, but it was all they had.

Cursing herself for not having done more, Krystyna gazed through the living room window along the dirt track that led away from the farmhouse. At the end of the dirt track, almost a mile from the house, Krystyna had found a narrow hedge-lined road with little traffic. Krystyna had wanted an exact address to give Anna when she called, but she had been unable to discover the address. No mail arrived at the house, and questions to the men only prompted generalities and sarcasm such as "near Manchester" and "in England." Once, when she asked Tyrion directly, he became suspicious and asked why she needed to know. Since then, fearful of creating suspicion, Krystyna had tried other ways to discover her location.

A walk to the end of the dirt road had revealed two worn stone pillars with the words "Vale House" etched into the stone. No signage marked the road, and brief walks in either direction revealed only unmarked lanes and entrances to other distant farms. Her cell phone, a cheap pay-as-you-go phone which the men had purchased for her and deducted the cost from her payments, did not have Internet and GPS capabilities. In frustration, Krystyna had set off across the country to find an answer. One of her walks, up, over, and down a near-distant hill, had taken Krystyna to a three-road intersection with an ancient bus shelter and one unhelpful road sign: Higher Road. Underneath the sign, attached to the metal pole by twisted wire, another sign, handwritten on a small rectangular piece of wood, announced Badgers Hill with an arrow pointing back the way Krystyna had come.

~

Subsequent visits had established the bus schedule and some idea of the location of the bus stop. The bus, number thirty-eight, a single-decker that exuded dark diesel exhaust, stopped at the shelter twice a day at 9 a.m. and 5 p.m. In the morning, the sign on the front above the driver read "Didsbury," and in the evening, it had changed to "Altringham."

Constrained by visits of the men who kept her, Krystyna could not commit to meet Anna at a pre-arranged time or even a day. Instead, Krystyna would make the one-and-a-half-hour round trip to the bus stop when she could. In preparation for Anna's arrival, Krystyna had made a small 8 x 4 rectangular piece of paper with a horizontal blue triangle pushing a third of the way from the left into the paper. White and red filled the top and bottom. Krystyna made the Czech flag with half-used crayons she had found in the house.

Krystyna would arrive shortly before the bus, tape the flag to the glass of the shelter, and retreat into the trees to wait. Krystyna's plan was that if Anna was on the bus, she would see the flag and get off. If there was no flag, Anna would stay on the bus and try again the next day.

Krystyna kept the flag inside volume eight of the *Encyclopedia Britannica*. Anna had called from the taxi less than five hours ago, and if she had avoided Edvard, if she had enough money, if she had managed to get a direct flight to Manchester, then she might be able to find the number thirty-eight bus. Wanting to believe that Anna would be on the morning bus, Krystyna removed the flag from the encyclopedia. In the morning, she would go to the bus stop. If Phil, mean and hurtful, arrived before his usual 10:30 a.m. Thursday time slot, she might suffer. But Krystyna had suffered before, and one more visit from Phil would only strengthen her resolve.

Eight

The SoHostel, informed the poster in the window of the entrance, featured hardwood floors, bathroom facilities, bed linen, towels at a surcharge, as well as laundry facilities, a shared TV lounge, an onsite bar, and breakfast. Anna read the poster to the bottom: a room cost seventy-three pounds, which she didn't have. A bed in a dorm cost thirty-two pounds, which she did have and would leave her with seventeen pounds. Anna, in need of sleep, safety, and a shower, entered and paid for a dorm room. In the morning, right at the 10 a.m. check-out time, Anna, refreshed and full from the unlimited bagels and cream cheese breakfast, stepped out of the SoHostel into a bright, cool morning.

Anna had planned to ask the SoHostel reception for information on how to get to Manchester, but a sign said reception would open at noon and indicated a telephone number for emergencies only. Hesitant about which way to go, Anna searched up and down the busy street for inspiration. Instead, among the flow of people and vehicles, Anna noticed a man staring in her direction from across the street. The man wore a black, waist-length leather jacket, jeans, and boots. He was smoking a cigarette, and his furtive gestures into a cell phone jolted Anna. She had seen many men dressed that way in Prague. Had Veronika betrayed her?

~

Afraid, Anna walked the buzzing streets of Soho. Even early morning did not discourage the degenerates that worked London's Soho area. Pimps, prostitutes, drug dealers, and scammers; cheap homemade signs advertised "models" selling themselves for sex: Twenty pounds for a blowjob and thirty for another orifice. Most could hardly speak English and shouted coarse rehearsed lines provided by their handlers. All were after one thing: money. Anna sensed danger from some, but most were harmless souls seeking a few pounds to survive.

The man in the leather jacket, only thirty or so steps behind Anna, did not attempt to hide. Confident, the man waved and gestured for Anna to come to him. Unnerved, Anna quickened her pace and stayed on busy main roads where she hoped plenty of people would provide safety from whatever the man intended to do.

Leicester Square swallowed Anna as the man closed in. On her left, from a four-story glass-fronted building called M&M's World, the scent of chocolate penetrated Anna's senses. Crowds of people, entering and leaving the worldwide candy retail store, clogged the entrance. Anna entered the confusion and rudely pushed her way into the crowd. Anna had run from people before, and instead of entering the store, she huddled against a wall and used the crowd for cover. Moments later, when she saw the back of the man who followed her enter the store, Anna crabbed along the wall and into the street.

Out of the store and running, Anna saw a sign for St. James Park. The park had been on Anna's route from Victoria Station to Soho. Guided by familiarity, she made for the park. Out of breath, on the south side of the park on Great George Street, Anna rested. Traffic roared past, spewing exhaust and dust. A red double-decker bus stopped directly in front of Anna. On the side of the bus, a blue and white advertisement for National Express Coach Service announced "Bus service from Victoria Station to all major cities: London - Birmingham 7 Pounds / Manchester 10 Pounds / Leeds 13 Pounds."

Anna couldn't believe it. She had seventeen pounds. All she needed was to get to Victoria Station. Anna turned her head left and right to find street names. She was at the junction of Great George Street and Birdcage Walk, but which way to go? A hand gripped her arm, and harsh Russian-accented words spat from fat lips and stained teeth.

"You are lost, ya? Come with me, and I will help you."

Anna tried to shake loose, but the grip tightened. The man pulled Anna in close, and stale breath pushed into Anna's nostrils.

"Do not struggle. I can smell a whore a mile away. You will come work for me."

~

Strength, hope, desperation, resentment, and hate flowed through Anna. She clawed the man's face, kicked and wriggled herself free, and ran directly into the intersection. A bus skidded, a car honked. Anna reached the other side and fled along Old Queen Street and down steep steps into London's underground. Confused and frightened, Anna studied the multicoloured underground map. She found Victoria Station on the map but was unsure where she was or which line to take.

"Bloody hard to know which way is up eh, love?"

An elderly woman, sprite and vibrant in a bright red coat and matching hat, gestured at the wall map and said, "Where do you want to go? I've been using the tube for fifty years. Don't need no map."

"Victoria Station. I want a bus."

A smile accentuated the creases on the woman's face.

"Eh, you could walk there in half an hour. Save yourself the money. But you seem in a hurry, eh. You want the Circle Line for Victoria. It's only one stop. You can't miss it."

With a grin, the old lady turned and stepped confidently into the moving mass of people. Anna followed the old woman's instructions and ten minutes later emerged from the Victoria Line tube station and walked the three hundred metres to the Victoria Coach station. Inside, a helpful ticket representative sold Anna a one-way ticket to Manchester for ten pounds. The bus departed in fifteen minutes at 1:30, and made one stop in Birmingham for thirty minutes before arriving in Manchester at 6:50 p.m.

Anna, relieved, clutched the ticket and made for a bank of public telephones. This time, Krystyna answered. Mid-way through Anna's story, two men and a woman entered the bus station. One man, the one who had grabbed Anna earlier, rubbed the scratches on his face and surveyed the station waiting area. The second, tall, wide, and expressionless, stared straight ahead. Between the two men, eyes and lips swollen, Veronika cowered. Krystyna, unaware of Anna's peril, continued to ask questions.

"Anna, what happened when you got to Gatwick?"

"Never mind that, Krystyna. I have to get away now. We can talk later."

"I'll call you, Anna."

"You can't. The phone is still dead. I haven't been able to charge it. Just tell me where to go, Krystyna."

Anna listened as Krystyna explained the details of the bus shelter and the flag.

Across the waiting area, Veronika's eyes, laden with regret and fear, met Anna's, and an involuntary cry parted her swollen lips. The two men followed Veronika's gaze. The PA system sounded.

"This is the final call for bus 574 Manchester via Birmingham."

The men were between Anna and the boarding gate, and they moved to flank Anna. Rising to the balls of her feet, Anna got ready to run for the bus.

Thirty steps from the gate, the tall man snickered and licked his upper lip before his face widened into a smile. Soft words of greeting flowed from his mouth, and his arms opened in welcome. Distracted, Anna had not noticed the speed of the second man who was almost upon her. Ready for flight, Anna drew a breath as the men closed in.

A shrill, pain-filled shriek cut through the station. Screams followed. People scattered from an area behind the men. In the space, blood spread across the tiled floor. Centred in the blood, Veronika, still screaming as red liquid gushed from her neck, stumbled and wobbled as a short knife fell from her hand. The men, wanting no connection to the scene, left the station quickly. Anna, tears filling her eyes, murmured a faint thank you to Veronika and stumbled to the bus. As the bus left the station, the sound of emergency sirens wailed their approach.

Nine

Anna's call from the bus station in London spurred and worried Krystyna. Confirmation of Anna's escape from Edvard and Prague brought joyful tears, but another cut-short telephone call tightened Krystyna's chest with anxiety. Anna had called shortly after one in the afternoon. Krystyna did not know how long it would take the bus from London to reach Manchester, and she doubted Anna would have time to find and catch the number thirty-eight bus to the bus stop on Higher Road. Unable to act, Krystyna steeled herself for the arrival of Phil and the unpleasantness that accompanied each visit.

It was an old trick—one many experienced prostitutes used. Helga, well past her best and reduced to enduring bondage for impotent middle-aged men angry at their wives and the world, had shown Krystyna another use for Vaseline besides the obvious. Krystyna, expecting Phil's arrival, smeared Vaseline around her wrists and ankles. Just enough to ensure that the rope, or cord, or whatever Phil brought with him, would slide and slip with minimum friction. Redness and soreness could not be avoided, but at least the Vaseline prevented burns and broken skin.

Phil's room had two distinctive features. A small square table with metal legs, a green plastic top, and a wooden stool with a screw-type adjustable seat. At first, Krystyna had assumed she would either be on the table, the stool, or both. She had been wrong on both counts. Phil had a different use for the table and the stool.

Phil used the table, smooth and worn, to make marijuana joints, and he sat on the stool while he cut and mixed the marijuana with tobacco. Krystyna's job was to crouch under the table and caress and fondle Phil between his legs.

When Phil began rolling joints, the stool would be quite low, and Krystyna had plenty of head room. Then, every few minutes, Phil would adjust the seat upward until the top of Krystyna's head pressed against the underside of the table, at which point Phil would begin to thrust.

The first time Krystyna had been unprepared, and her head hit the table hard. Since then, Krystyna had to ensure that Phil's climax happened as close as possible to Phil's final chair-height adjustment. Phil had gotten wise to Krystyna's strategy and would try to outwit her and get her head as close to the table as possible. It was part of the game Phil played; the other was bondage.

Phil didn't speak much until he was stoned. Then he never shut up. Two things dominated Phil's drug induced angst: lost conquests and guilt.

Today, Thursday, while he rolled, Phil talked about his past conquests. They were always the same.

"Gaynor, a slut from the estate where we lived, was my first. I was only fourteen, and her dad was a policeman. She gagged on me at lunch time in the trees down by the school fence. She would do anything for a toke, and it didn't take long to get into her knickers. Silly bitch got pregnant at sixteen.

"Marie. Now she was hot. Took me ages to get her skirt up, but once she started, she begged for it all the time. Don't know what happened to her.

"Then there was Alison. She was eighteen, and I was fifteen. Massive tits and long nails. I liked that."

Each name would stimulate Phil as he relived his real or imagined experiences with the unfortunate girls from his youth. Climax arrived soon after Phil talked about the two friends, Helen and Abby, whom Phil described as the only ones who really understood him.

"Helen and Abby were the best of all. They knew how to behave and what men wanted. They wanted me to tie them together while I did them one after the other. Man, they were the absolute best."

Brought to climax by Krystyna's rhythmic expertise and the sordid recollection of Helen and Abby, Phil slipped off the stool and lay on the bed to smoke a joint. While Phil floated in drug-heightened, post-release pleasure, Krystyna cleaned her teeth and massaged her jaw before stripping down to underwear and bra.

Glassy eyed, Phil rose from the bed and opened the black gym bag he always brought with him. Krystyna subconsciously rubbed her wrists as Phil uncoiled about twenty feet of thick, rough rope, the kind used to tie a good-sized yacht to a wharf. A knife, long and sharp, followed the rope, and Phil cut the rope into various lengths.

He tied Krystyna's wrists and ankles to different pieces of furniture; today, both ankles to the legs of the bed, one wrist to the door handle, and the other to a hook in the ceiling that Phil had installed weeks before. Taut between the ropes, Krystyna would wait while Phil smoked again and undressed. Naked, Phil would slap Krystyna's torso and legs with his manhood before inserting himself in Krystyna at random intervals. Talk of his wife and the inhale and exhale of marijuana punctuated the slaps and insertions.

"You're not like my wife, Gillian. She is a good person. She looks after me. Always trying to get me to quit the weed and eat better. I think I am like one of her cases. She's a social worker, you know. She is always trying to save someone. Even whores like you. Says she wants to grow old with me. Can you believe it? She loves me so much. No matter what I do. She even lets me tie her up, but it's not the same. She doesn't enjoy it like you do. She pretends, but I know. She does so much for me. I'm supposed to be at a support group for dope heads today. I shouldn't do this."

Shallow sobs interrupted Phil's self-serving guilt, his thrusting slowed, and firmness ebbed. On cue, wanting Phil to be done and aware of his needs, Krystyna cooed as required, but stayed clear of speaking directly against or about his wife.

"It's not your fault, Phil. Men's needs are complicated. Men need to be strong and in charge like you, Phil. Women need men like you. I'm lucky that I have you to take me."

Ego fed and fetish justified, Phil swelled, thrust, climaxed, and collapsed on the bed. Sometimes Phil slept immediately, and Krystyna would remain tied for up to an hour. Sometimes, like today, Phil would untie one wrist so Krystyna could free herself.

"Bring me a joint."

"Here you are, Phil. You are the best. Thank you for having me."

Krystyna, sore and cold, showered for a long time and applied moisturizer and soft bandages to her wrists and ankles. Phil had left when Krystyna, dressed and restored, returned to Phil's bedroom to ask if he wanted anything to drink or eat.

On the bed, a short length of rope lay across the pillows. As previously instructed, Krystyna picked up the rope and placed it in a dresser drawer along with the many samples that Phil left her so that "You can use these to think of me and remember our pleasure when you are alone." The delusions upon which men founded their self-worth amazed Krystyna.

Downstairs in the living room, volume two of the 1965 edition of the *Encyclopedia Britannica* contained Phil's notes. Krystyna began a new page with a short notation: *Phil, Thursday, 10:30 a.m., while wife thinks he is at a drug support group.*

Ten

Krystyna did not sleep. Jumbled images of Edvard and Tyrion abusing her and Anna brought cold sweats and startled awakening from semi-conscious naps. Now, Friday, Tyrion, who had missed his Wednesday session, called at 7:40 a.m. to say he would arrive at ten. Recklessly, Krystyna fled from the house to meet the 9 a.m. bus.

Mumbled prayers and promises spilled across Krystyna's lips as she ran through the early morning mist to paste the flag to the bus shelter. More prayers to Saint Sarah, the patron saint of the Romani, flowed when the bus turned the corner. But the bus had not stopped, and Anna had not appeared. Back at the farmhouse just before 10 a.m., Krystyna showered and prepared for Tyrion's visit. Tyrion arrived in a foul mood and berated Krystyna with an unneeded reminder of her role.

"Let's get one thing straight. You are a whore. Your job is to fuck me any way, anytime, and any place I want. Do you understand?"

Little men with inferiority complexes who needed to dominate women were not new to Krystyna. Steven Ennis, about five foot five inches, broad across the shoulders, well-dressed, and overly confident, fit the mould perfectly. Higher than average heels on his shoes, and lifts inside, elevated Ennis to a respectable five foot nine inches, but if anyone asked, he always said he was "just under six feet." In fact, his driver's licence, which relies on self-stated details, listed Ennis as six foot one inch.

Krystyna, herself five foot eight, made sure to stoop slightly when standing near him and sat or kneeled as often as possible. The insecurities of clients were not to be trifled with, especially one like Ennis for whom sex centred on command and control rather than physical intimacy or prolonged sensuality. Another self-esteem prop for Ennis was his Land Rover SUV: A "step-up-and-into vehicle" that enabled the driver to look down on people.

Ennis, or Tyrion as his friends called him, had decorated and organized his bedroom to reflect his sexual preferences. Unlike the other three men, who had queen-sized beds, Tyrion's room had a single bed with silk sheets, one pillow, and no blankets or comforter. The bed was not for post-sex comfort or skin-on-skin relaxation: Tyrion, when he was finished with Krystyna's services, actually slept in the bed, alone.

Three chairs, each with a matching footstool, crammed the room. Worn brown leather covered one chair, rough yellowish fabric a second chair, and the third was solid wood. Behind the door, a rickety wooden hat stand served as Tyrion's clothing hanger. Each visit required Krystyna to contort herself over, or in, the front of the chair while Tyrion perched on the stool and inserted himself into Krystyna.

Then, for round two, Krystyna would sit on each stool in turn and provide oral attention. However, Tyrion saved his prized piece of furniture for his last relief. A reproduction medieval stock, positioned so that Krystyna faced the window, enabled Tyrion complete dominance over Krystyna and allowed him, erect and sweating, to prance around inserting himself at will.

Tyrion was all about insertion in prostrate and submissive positions, and ejaculation was always exterior and with Krystyna below him.

Unlike Taffy, Tyrion could hold his climax for a very long time; even worse, from Krystyna's perspective, Tyrion often needed three and sometimes four climaxes before he was satisfied. While Taffy only needed about an hour, Tyrion could and did take two, three and sometimes four hours before he quit. Then he would nap in his single bed while Krystyna prepared tea and a snack.

Fortunately, Tyrion's penis matched his height. At under five inches, Krystyna, except when forced into her mouth, had difficulty sensing the exact location of Tyrion's manhood.

Today, of all days, Tyrion was on a marathon. It was almost 3 p.m. At least she was in the stock and he should be done soon. She might still make the 5 p.m. bus.

Despite his differences, Tyrion, like most men, talked. Mostly about himself, his work, his accomplishments, other people's shortcomings, and how and who he had bested at something or other.

In keeping with his need to command and control, Krystyna did not speak unless directly asked a question.

Today, between furniture, props, and climaxes, Tyrion had talked.

"On Wednesday, when I couldn't get here, I was making a killing. It is incredible how gullible people are. This couple, both in their thirties, had saved a hundred and fifty thousand pounds in a savings account. Can you believe it? What a waste of money. Anyway, they were ready to invest the money and wanted me to manage the investments for them. "Sure," I said. They were so focused on how much return they could make that they never even asked what my fees were. Well, I suckered them into signing a gold-plated agreement that gives me money every time I make a trade, every time they receive a dividend, and on top of that, I get three per cent of the gross value of their investments every year. Dave and Samantha were their names: more like dumb and dumber if you ask me.

"As you know, I play squash on Sundays. Well, last Sunday, my club, the Sale and Altringham Executive Racquet Club, played a tournament against a bunch of yuppies from the South Heaton Squash Club. Well, we, I mean the other players from my club, were playing rubbish, and we were tied when it came to the last game. I, of course, had to play the last game, and it was against Heaton's club champion. It just happens that I had heard about this player, and rumour had it that he absolutely hated being hit by the ball. Apparently, it would put him right off his game. Anyway, I managed to hit the ball at him twice in the first three points, once right on the back of his calf. He squealed like a girl and complained instead of just getting on with it. I whipped him three games to zero.

"My wife, Joanne, an accountant, thinks I'm at an investment seminar in the city. As long as I'm home by seven and remember to drop some brochures about investment on the counter when I get home, she will never know."

At 3:15 p.m., Tyrion finally announced he would take a short nap.

"Wake me at four with my tea and snack."

Tyrion's SUV scattered gravel as he pulled away from the house shortly before 5 pm. In the front room, in "Tyrion's" *Encyclopedia Britannica*, Krystyna wrote: *Tyrion, Sunday, 10:00 to 5:00, while wife thinks he is at an investment seminar in the city.*

Too late to meet the bus, Krystyna would go tomorrow, on Saturday.

Eleven

Moisture, dense and cold, obscured Badgers Hill. Erratic wind, gusting east to west, mixed and rolled the moisture up and over the hill. At 7:30 a.m., only nature's voices sounded in the valley as Krystyna pulled the farmhouse door closed behind her. No visitors were expected on Saturdays, but as her contract stipulated, she had to be available twenty-four seven. Krystyna left a note:

Gentlemen, I have a headache and have gone for a walk. I won't be long. Yours, Krystyna.

Draped over Krystyna's shoulder a bag, stuffed with bread, cheese, fruit, water, a blanket, and money, carried her hopes for herself and Anna.

Despite the cold morning, sweat soaked Krystyna's armpits, back, and brow as she peeled Scotch tape from the plastic dispenser to attach the homemade Czech flag to the dirty glass of the bus shelter. Flag attached, Krystyna withdrew to her observation place behind some bushes across the road from the shelter and checked her watch: 8:45 a.m. In fifteen minutes, Krystyna prayed Anna would arrive.

Two cars and an ancient tractor pulling an open trailer loaded with damp hay and potatoes crept through the dim light of the intersection. Nine a.m. came and went. No bus. Nine thirty, worried and willing the bus to arrive, Krystyna stepped from her hiding place and strained to see down the road. At nine forty-five, shivering from cold and disappointment, Krystyna reached up to retrieve the flag from the shelter.

Dim headlights, a squeal of breaks, and a bus slowed. Startled, Krystyna, leaving the flag in place, moved out of sight behind the shelter. Krystyna listened to a pneumatic hiss as the doors of the bus opened, and a concerned voice spoke to someone about to step off the bus.

"Eh luv, are you sure you want to get off here? There isn't much around for miles."

"Yes, yes, I am certain. Thank you. This is the right place," responded the slight figure silhouetted against the light of the bus interior.

The door closed, gears ground, and the bus pulled away. Anna waited a few moments, then moved inside the shelter. The flag, the one Krystyna said would be there, hung precariously by one piece of tape on the inside of the grimy glass panel. Nervous, Anna grasped the flag, held it to her chest, and leaned against the back wall of the shelter. Krystyna, uncertain but hopeful, stepped cautiously from behind the shelter.

"Anna!"

"Krystyna."

Anna, the ordeal and fear of her journey sapping the last of her strength, stepped, stumbled, and fell into Krystyna, pushing them both to the ground. On the cold, damp dirt, the sisters held each other, words unable to communicate their relief.

Krystyna stroked Anna's hair, kissed her forehead and hugged her close to ease Anna's heaving sobs. As Anna calmed, Krystyna opened her bag and spoke.

"I have water and food, Anna."

Anna shook her head.

"Tell me we are safe, Krystyna."

Cool and strong for Anna, Krystyna assured her younger sister.

"Yes, Anna, we are safe."

Tears flooded Anna's cheeks. Krystyna held a bottle to Anna's mouth, and water, past dry cracked lips, dribbled into Anna. Small pieces of bread and cheese followed until dry heaving sobs shook Anna, and tears flooded her cheeks. Krystyna tilted the bottle again, but Anna pushed it away.

"I don't need water. I just want to be with you. Do I come to the house with you?"

Krystyna, wrenched by Anna's frailness and fear, wanted to take Anna to the house where she could care for her. Reluctant, Krystyna said, "I'm sorry, Anna, but no, not yet. We must move out of sight. Come, there is a place in the bushes where you can eat more and we can talk."

Arm in arm, the sisters crossed the road, climbed the waist-high bank, and pushed through the bushes. In a small space between the base of a Wyche Elm tree and the roadside Blackthorn bushes, Krystyna spread a blanket she had brought with her. As Anna ate and drank, Krystyna listened to Anna's story of how she escaped Edvard in Prague, and of the men in London, and the woman Veronika who had saved her life.

"What happened when you got to Manchester?"

"I sat beside a woman on the bus from London to Manchester. She was from Manchester, and she told me how to get to the main city bus depot. When I got there, I asked at the information desk for number thirty-eight like you told me. Two bus routes had number thirty-eight, but when I asked for one that went on a Higher Road, the man knew which one I needed. I arrived too late for the 5 p.m. bus, so I walked around Manchester all night and slept in a doorway. On Friday, I was on the 9 a.m. bus and the 5 p.m. bus, but there was no flag and I kept going. The 5 p.m. bus route ended in a place called Altringham. I only had enough money left for two more bus rides but I didn't want to go with any men. I slept in a park and got the bus this morning. I don't know what I would have done if you hadn't been there today."

Krystyna held her sister's hand.

"I love you, Anna. I will always be there for you."

They hugged, drawing strength and resolve from each other, until Krystyna withdrew and said: "Now, Anna, you must listen. We have escaped Prague and Edvard, but we still have much to do before we are truly free. I cannot stay long. One of the men might come to the house, and I am supposed to be there whenever they come."

Anna pulled Krystyna back to her and whispered, "Do they hurt you, Krystyna?"

Unconsciously rubbing her wrists, Krystyna replied, "No more than any man has, Anna." Anna sobbed again, but Krystyna shushed her. "The time for tears is over, Anna. You have work to do."

Krystyna explained what Anna needed to do. When Krystyna finished, Anna gasped, "Oh god Krystyna could we really do it?"

"We must Anna."

"They will kill us."

"It's our only chance, Anna. I've prepared for weeks. I have lots of information already. All we need now is some proof, some evidence."

"But we are in England. We have gotten away from Edvard, and he will never find us. Let's just leave. We can take the next bus. We can, we can . . ."

A hot rage swelled in Krystyna. Colour filled her cheeks, and her lips stretched wide. Krystyna reached for Anna's shoulders and pulled her close, her own suffering bubbling to the surface.

"What, Anna? What can we do? Go back to spreading our legs and opening our mouths for more men until another Edvard comes along. No, Anna. These men are the last ones that will use me."

"But I don't want to die, Krystyna."

Krystyna met and held Anna's eyes. With more conviction than she felt, Krystyna said, "They won't find out, Anna. I promise."

Silence hung between them until a bird chirp, loud and sharp, ended the tension. Gathering herself, Krystyna returned to business.

"But first, before you get anything else Anna, you must buy a cell phone, and text me the number. I must be careful, and I will call you when no men are at the house. When you have what we need, we will meet here, and you will give me everything."

"Do we have money?" asked Anna, resigned to her sister's plan.

"Yes, the men pay me cash each week. I have saved for the past two months. There are four thousand pounds in the bag. That is enough for what we need and for you to find somewhere to stay for a few days. I have written a list for you. Get the equipment as soon as possible, Anna."

Anna, with a dirty face, tangled hair, and crumpled clothes, squeezed Krystyna's hand.

"Can you stay with me until the bus comes?"

"No, Anna, I cannot. I want to, I really do, but the men must have no suspicions. There is plenty of food, water, and cigarettes in the bag. Take the bus to Manchester and . . ."

"I'm afraid."

Anna's words dried Krystyna's throat. Anna had said those words before. Once, when Anna had been fourteen and Krystyna eighteen, Anna had pleaded not to be left alone with the younger brother of Alex, a Roma boy from a visiting community. Alex, also eighteen, who had chased Krystyna for weeks until she had agreed to a date with him, had a younger brother, Erich, and had suggested that Erich and Anna keep each other company while he and Krystyna walked out together.

Erich was very big and strong for his age and, like most boys and men of the close-knit Roma community, the mechanics of procreation held no mysteries for him. Alex and Erich had similar intentions, and while

Krystyna had fought Alex off, Anna had been less successful.

Anna had not confided in Krystyna about what had happened until Alex and Erich had left. Guilt had overwhelmed Krystyna, but Anna's forgiveness had pulled them together more than ever. Krystyna swallowed hard and reassured Anna.

"There is no need, Anna. You have made it this far. We have a plan, and it will work. In one week, perhaps two, we will be together and free of these men forever. You can do this, Anna."

A shared hug, long and tight, hid the doubt in Krystyna's face.

"Now I must go, Anna."

Twelve

Dictated by the norms of the Victorian times when the pub first opened its doors, the Railway Tavern had two rooms: one for men, one for women. Through the front door to the left, women would have entered a small snug. In the snug, a beautiful, curved wooden bar sat atop a locally-quarried, tiled floor, which separated the bar from a grand stone fireplace. The snug led to a spacious, carpeted lounge where patrons could sit on seats built into the pub's bay windows or on chairs and stools that surrounded copper-topped round and square tables. To the right of the entrance was the men's vault.

A traditional Northern vault where men drink, banter, play darts or cards, and in the winter, crowd around the Victorian fireplace. Even in the twenty-first century, with Victorian shackles discarded, few women chose to enter the vault, while men readily shared the snug with the women.

Tucked away in the pub's vault, Tyrion, buoyed by the four hours he, Taffy, Ham, and Phil had spent drinking in various other local pubs, held quite a court with his fellow adulterers.

"So, my friends, almost two months in, and things are going very well, I would say."

"Yeah, no complaints here," said Taffy.

"Mm, yeah, man, me too," said Phil. "She's a good un. Nice fuck, and knows how to do as she's told. I like that."

Tyrion, like a benevolent host asking his guests if the accommodations were suitable, gestured and spoke to Ham.

"And you, Ham," a slight teasing lilt in his voice, "what about you? Does our little whore meet your needs?"

Ham, ever fearful his particular needs would become common knowledge, nodded agreement as he sipped beer.

Pleased with the response and the implicit affirmation of his plan to establish a shared concubine, Tyrion held his almost empty pint glass and said, "Right then, lads, I think we have time for another, eh?"

Before Tyrion rose from his chair, Phil, still short of breath from the partial toke he had hurried on their way between pubs, half-coughed and half spoke a question to Tyrion.

"What if I want to have more visits?"

"What do you mean, Phil? You want an extra day?"

"Not exactly, I mean you know, just more."

"Look, Phil," said Tyrion, irritation entering his tone, "we all agreed, one day a week each and an occasional emergency if needed."

Ham, his beer glass empty, smiled at Phil and chipped in.

"I only need my one day. In fact, it's more like half a day for me. If you want my half day, Phil, you can have it."

Surprised by the offer and eager to accept, Phil gushed, "Wow, man, that's great. That's really fucking great. Thanks, Ham."

Ham's smile widened to a grin, and he clarified his offer.

"Hold on, Phil, I didn't say I was giving it to you. You have to pay for it, of course. Say half of my share for half of my time?"

"Fuck off, Ham," said Phil, his gushing acceptance cut short. "That's not right. The cost doesn't work out like that. Look if you're not using it, what's the problem?"

"Something for nothing, that's you all over, Phil. Well, fuck you. If you don't want to pay, you don't get. You . . ."

Taffy, concerned about other ears in the small room, butted in. "Jesus, keep it down, for Christ's sake. Now's not the time or place. We can talk about this somewhere else."

"Anyway," said Ham ignoring Taffy, "I've been thinking that I should probably be paying a bit less than you guys anyway. It's too much for what I get."

Phil, a little pissed at Ham for his false offer of more time, seized the chance to snipe. "Hey, it's not our fault that you can't get it up often enough. What's the matter, Ham, your 'old' lady making demands on you suddenly?"

"At least I don't need chemicals to get me going."

"Maybe a little weed would make you last longer, and you could get your money's worth, ya tight bastard."

Tyrion placed his empty glass on the table, leaned in and spoke with a leader's authority.

"Listen, both of you. We made an agreement for six months. After that, we can revisit it and change things if we want, but for now, what we agreed on stands. Phil, if you want more, then take a bit on Friday or Saturday, but don't get greedy and fuck her up for the rest of us. And I want your fucking jizz gone before I get in there. Understood?"

Perplexed by his empty glass, Taffy butted in. "Let's all calm down. I'll get us a pint before last call. Jesus, I can't believe we're arguing about this."

Tyrion's phone buzzed as Taffy stood to go to the bar. With the phone extended at arm's length, Tyrion read a text message and exhaled a terse "fuck me."

Phil smirked and asked, "What's up? Wife wants you home already?"

"No. Fuck. It's our girl. A pipe has burst in the kitchen. Water is everywhere. Wants us to get over there and do something."

"What? We can't leave now. What the fuck? Tell the bitch to turn the water off."

Another text buzzed its arrival. Tyrion read it and said, "OK, it's OK. She has turned off the main tap in the laundry room, but she says there is a lot of damage."

"More fucking money then," said Ham as he took a pint from Taffy and turned to watch the soccer highlights on the wall-mounted TV in the far corner of the room.

Thirteen

Anna's arrival on Saturday, safe and unhurt, had lifted the guilt Krystyna endured since leaving Anna in Prague. Moreover, with Anna in Manchester, Krystyna began to believe that her plan might really work. With no unexpected visitors, Saturday day and Saturday evening had dragged as Krystyna paced and waited for contact from Anna. On Sunday, after a restless night, Krystyna paced and clock-watched until, at 10 a.m., Anna sent a text from her new phone. Krystyna called Anna immediately. Anna answered on the half-ring.

"Anna, how are you?"

"I'm good, Krystyna. Thanks to you. I have a hotel room in the city near the bus station. It's quite cheap. I had a bath for an hour and then another one after that. I'm sorry, Krystyna, but I slept a long time. I was so tired. Then I had a meal in a restaurant. I haven't spent much. I . . ."

"It's OK, Anna. You did the right thing. You needed rest and food. Do you feel OK now?"

"Yes. I am about to go and buy the things on the list. I'm not sure where to go, but I will ask at the hotel desk. There must be a big store near here."

"That's good, Anna. Remember, everything must work on batteries. I can't have things plugged in. OK?"

"Yes, I got it. I'll call you later when I have the stuff."

"No, Anna. You must not call me. I will call you if I can."

"What do you mean, if you can?"

"There is a problem with the house. One of the men is coming sometime today. So don't worry if I don't call."

Panic entered Anna's voice. "What's wrong with the house? You are not leaving, are you?"

"No, of course not, a pipe broke in the kitchen. There is water damage, and I had to turn the water off. One of them is coming today to fix it."

A heavy breath and a sigh rushed from Anna as she whispered, "Is it bad, Krystyna? The men, are they cruel?"

"They are men Anna. They stick their dicks in and they take them out."

"Do they hit you?"

"No, thank god. One is a little rough sometimes, but it's nothing like Prague."

"They have wives?"

"Of course; they lie and cheat like all men who use us."

Relieved by Krystyna's assurances, a smile crept across Anna's face as she asked.

"Anything weird?"

"No Anna, it's under the table, tied up, over this or that, front and behind. Nothing we haven't seen before."

"A regular work week then."

"Yes, there is even one who comes so quickly, I would have to give him a discount if we were in Prague."

Anna laughed, but her smile quickly faded. A strong voice replaced Anna's lightness. "If they hurt you, Krystyna, I will kill them."

"Don't worry, Anna; what we have planned will be worse than death."

"OK. OK. Please call me if you can, Krystyna, just to tell me you are all right."

"I will, Anna, I will. I love you."

"I love you, too."

With the call ended, the quiet of the farmhouse unnerved Krystyna. The confidence Krystyna had shown Anna slipped away. Her stomach cramped as she contemplated the price she and Anna would pay if their plan failed.

Fourteen

Focused on boring a hole through a half-inch of wood while contorted and perched on a stool, Krystyna did not hear the tires crunch gravel. Not until four car doors thumped closed did Krystyna register that someone had arrived. Startled and frightened, Krystyna pushed the corkscrew and the chips of wood to the back of the shelf. A wool blanket followed to cover the mess before Krystyna closed the door of the wardrobe in Taffy's room. Footfalls on gravel and raised voices approached the front door. A key turned. Krystyna, flustered, met the men at the bottom of the stairs as they entered the farmhouse.

"Oh, hi," breathed Krystyna hurriedly, "I didn't know you were all going to come."

Phil, a petulant scowl plain on his face, moved inside and whined.

"Yeah, well, neither did we, but it seems that we are all needed to fix the leak."

"Don't be like that, Phil," said Taffy, as he followed Phil into the hallway.

"We are all supposed to have gone to the Man U game together in Tyrion's car. We have to stay together in case one of us is seen without the others, and it gets back to the ladies. So stop your whining."

Phil continued to whine as he slumped down on one of two wooden chairs that stood like watchman on either side of the front door.

"Ah, fuck it. I could have gone to the game and met up with you later at the pub. It doesn't take four of us to fix a leaky pipe."

Tyrion, uncharacteristically the last man through the door, rounded on Phil.

"Look, Phil, you're right, but look on the bright side. Last night, you said you wanted more time with our lovely whore. When she's shown us where the leak is, you can head upstairs for a little extra."

Happy with the prospect of some extra, Phil relaxed and smiled to acknowledge his agreement with Tyrion's suggestion.

Krystyna, surrounded by the four men in the small hallway, shuffled and her eyes darted as though seeking an escape.

Ham stared at Krystyna, nodded toward her, and asked, "What's up with you? You scared of something?"

Krystyna was scared. The closeness of the four men highlighted her vulnerability. Thoughts of Anna's warning that no one would know if anything happened to her knotted Krystyna's stomach. Coughing lightly to cover her nervousness, Krystyna held Ham's stare and said, "No, no. It's just that you haven't all been here at the same time since the first day months ago. I'm just surprised that you all came. That's all."

"Right," said Tyrion, his attention on the problem rather than Krystyna, "let's get on with it. Where's this damn leak?"

Krystyna led the men to the kitchen and pointed to the open cupboard doors under the sink.

"When I came in the kitchen last night, I saw water running out from the cupboard all over the floor."

Everyone looked down at the wooden floor. Tyrion and Phil slid their feet side to side on the wood.

"Well, it's wet all right," observed Phil, "but the water must have drained through the boards and into the cellar. It's a dirt cellar under the kitchen, so I doubt it's gonna be a problem."

Tyrion took charge and issued orders. "Yeah, you're probably right, Phil. Taffy, get your fat arse under the sink, and see what's up."

Used to doing Tyrion's bidding, Taffy duly knelt and crouched, with the seat of his jeans straining to contain his arse, under and into the sink cupboard. After a few moments, Taffy reported, "I see it. Nothing much, a joint has worked loose. Probably happens when the pipes knock. You know, when the water runs."

"Can you fix it?" asked Tyrion.

"Yep, just need my toolbox and some plumber's tape. I'll loosen the joint, slap some silicon tape on it, crimp it back, and it should be fine."

"How long will it take?" asked Phil.

"About an hour, maybe less."

Phil grinned and nodded to Krystyna, who pushed a smile on her face and moved to follow Phil out of the kitchen.

"Come on, time for some Phil time. Let's go."

Tyrion, as Phil made to leave, touched Phil's arm and gave out more orders.

"Only half an hour, Phil; I'll have a quick go, as well."

Turning to Ham and Taffy, who had extracted himself from the sink cupboard, Tyrion continued. "What about you guys?"

"Oh yeah," said Taffy, "might as well while we're here. Soon as I'm done with the pipe."

"Ham?"

"Er no, I'm good. I'll just wait in the living room and check out some books."

Phil, a lecherous grin on his face, patted Krystyna's behind and chuckled. "Looks like you gotta busy afternoon, honey. Let's go."

Obedient as required, Krystyna followed Phil to the stairs. She hadn't the time or notice to put Vaseline on her wrists and ankles, but Phil didn't have a bag with him, so maybe she would just be under the table.

As expected, Phil made for the stool and pointed Krystyna to the table. Under the table, as she unzipped his jeans, the sound of rustling cigarette papers signalled Phil had begun to roll a joint. To Krystyna's surprise, Phil relieved himself in a few minutes and got up from the stool. He tucked his t-shirt, zipped his jeans, and exasperated, despite his relief, blurted to Krystyna, "Aw, fuck. It's not the same with everyone else in the house. I'm done. I'm just gonna lie here and smoke a fat one. You can go."

Relieved in a different way, Krystyna was quick to leave Phil to his joint. She stopped by the bathroom to dry-brush her teeth, then went downstairs to find

Tyrion. The sooner she got it over with, the sooner they would leave. Pausing at the doorway to the living room, Krystyna saw Tyrion. He stood with his back to the room gazing out of the window while Ham studied the literary offerings on the bookcase. Tyrion, unaware of Krystyna's presence, spoke to Ham without turning. "Anything worth reading, Ham?"

Ham, his index finger slowly tracing left to right across the spines of the books on the second shelf of the bookcase, lamented softly, "Not really. It's mostly gardening, bird watching, and cooking. There are some books on local history stuff, but nothing much."

Finished with the second shelf, Ham looked to the top shelf and exclaimed, "Hey, there is a 1965 *Encyclopedia Britannica* set here. Might be worth a few quid if they are in good condition."

Krystyna's heart stopped. Ham reached for one of the Britannicas and began to wriggle it free. Desperate to stop Ham before he found her notes on the men, Krystyna faked a stumble and knocked a vase off a table. The crash startled Ham and Tyrion. They both turned.

"What the fuck?" shouted Tyrion.

Ham turned from the bookshelf and complained.

"You'll have to pay for that. Probably an antique."

"I'm sorry. I tripped on the rug. I'll clean it up."

"Where is Phil?" asked Tyrion.

"He's done. He is smoking upstairs."

A sly grin pushed skin on Tyrion's face.

"He's getting like Taffy."

Tyrion stood and moved toward Krystyna, who had knelt to pick up pieces of the broken vase.

Indifferent to the vase and eager for his own satisfaction, Tyrion barked at Krystyna, "Leave the mess. You can clean later. Take care of me first."

As Krystyna followed Tyrion from the living room, Tyrion mocked Ham, "Hope you find something 'stimulating' to read."

Wanting to divert Ham's attention away from the Britannicas, Krystyna stopped and pointed to the table.

"There are some books about famous composers under the coffee table. I know you like classical music, so they might be of interest."

Ham nodded, then moved to the table and picked up a book from the shelf under the tabletop. Out of Krystyna's sight, signs of a deep thought crossed Tyrion's face.

When Krystyna entered Tyrion's room, he seemed preoccupied. He put Krystyna in the stock, took his pleasure quickly, and left the room. Krystyna, apprehensive but unsure why, followed Tyrion downstairs warily. Taffy, tools in hand, stood by the front door and announced to Tyrion that he had fixed the pipe. He then nodded to Tyrion and went out to put his tools in the car. Phil, blurry eyed, swanned downstairs and Tyrion, Phil, and Ham, who had come into the hallway from the living room holding a book about Mozart, all went outside. Krystyna waited by the door and heard Tyrion say, without irony, "Don't be long, Taffy."

"I won't. Be there in a jiff."

Without ceremony or words, Taffy dropped his pants in the hallway. Keen to have the men gone,

Krystyna broke a record, and Taffy returned sheepishly to the car in less than a minute.

Tyrion pushed the gas pedal to rev the engine as Taffy hurried to climb in the SUV. Tyrion, spinning the wheels on the gravel, stared hard at Krystyna as she pushed the front door closed.

Fifteen

Maintaining the pretence of attending the Manchester United game, the men, as normal, arrived at the Railway Tavern at 5:30 p.m. Taffy, always eager to commence drinking, collected four pints of hand-pulled Sovereign keg beer from the bar and deposited them on the table. Wedged behind the table, up against the wall, Tyrion squirmed on the bench seat and sipped his beer. A frown accompanied the sip, and Taffy, worried about the beer, asked with concern, "What's wrong with the beer?"

"Nothing, it's fine."

"What's with the long face then? Didn't get enough this afternoon, eh?"

Pensive, sipping more beer, Tyrion watched as returning Manchester United fans bustled in the vault and ordered pints and pies. Phil, half his pint already gone, answered instead of Tyrion. "Well, I had a very nice blowjob and joint, thanks."

"Me too," added Taffy between slurps.

Tyrion ignored Phil and Taffy and turned to Ham.

"Ham," said Tyrion.

Ham, focused on the football highlights on the TV, didn't respond.

"Ham!"

"What?"

"At the farm today, when we were in the living room."

"Yeah, what about it? She is gonna pay for that vase."

"Not the vase. I don't care about the vase."

"What then?"

Phil and Taffy began to pay attention.

"Remember when you were looking for something to read?"

"Yeah, so what?"

"Krystyna told you there were some books about music or something on the coffee table that you might like."

"So, I like classical music. It's not a crime."

"I know. I'm not on about that. I don't care what you listen to, but how did she know you liked classical music?"

"I guess I must have mentioned it sometime. I don't know. Why, what's the problem?"

"Well, it got me thinking about what and how much she knows about us."

Phil, pint momentarily paused, chipped in, "What do you mean?"

"Have you lot seen the news reports about that dating service Ashley Madison?"

"Oh yeah," answered Taffy, "that's the website that lets you cheat on your wife, right?"

"Yeah," added Phil, "the one where those dumb bastards posted everything about themselves, and it got hacked, and all their cheating was posted for everyone to see. Some men actually killed themselves over it."

Ham, attention focused as a commercial interrupted the football highlights, motioned to Tyrion. "What's that got to do with us and our little setup? We don't have anything on a website. Only we know about her. No one else. What're you on about, Tyrion?"

"You're right, Ham. Only we know about her. But what if someone found out about her and decided to tell people or our wives about her? We would be right fucked."

"Who the hell is gonna find out?" demanded Taffy. "We're not telling anyone. We all have too much to lose. What's the problem? You are making something out of nothing."

"Am I, Taffy? What does she know about you?"

"Nothing; I go, I fuck her, and that's it."

"Do you talk to her?"

"Well, yes, I suppose so. She doesn't talk much. I mean, I talk and she listens."

"What about you, Tyrion?"

"Well, I have to confess that, yes, I do talk to her. I hadn't really given it much thought. It's like part of the routine."

Ham, one eye back on the TV, mumbled, "She's not nosy, though. She hardly ever asks questions anymore, right, Phil?"

"That's right. In fact, all she does is listen, which I like 'cause I get enough earache at home without another woman . . ."

"Shut up, Phil. I'm serious. Think about it for a minute. What have you, we, told her about ourselves?"

Efforts to remember and tally fought with satisfied smiles across each man's face as recollections of sex sessions competed with thoughts about conversations, comments, and off-handed remarks. In unison, comprehension squashed their self-satisfied smiles.

"There, see what I mean?" said Tyrion as he interpreted the men's expressions. "I'll go first. I, er well, I do sometimes tell her where I'm supposed to be when I am with her."

"Taffy?"

"Yeah, me too."

"Phil?"

"Last week, I told her I was supposed to be at a rehab meeting."

"Ham?"

"What? Rehab? You? I don't believe it."

"Fuck, Ham, that's not the issue, is it? What have you told her?"

"Nothing. I don't talk much. Well, I might say why I'm going somewhere or something about what's going on. What the fuck, you gotta talk about something. I always talked with the hookers. Don't you, Tyrion?"

"Yes, I did. The difference is, or was, that we were in another city or country, and we would never see them again. This is different."

Taffy, uncertainty in his voice, tried to rationalize the situation.

"What the hell, Tyrion? So she knows a few details about our lives and such. It's not as though she knows where we live or has anything that can trace us. Even the house is in a shell company name. What can she do with a few snippets of information? And why would she, for God's sake? We pay her well, she has a place to live, and when she is done, she will have enough money to set herself up here in England. Why would she fuck all that up just to get at us?"

"I'm not saying she would. I'm just saying she could. Eh, Phil?"

"Never mind could. What would she use? It would be the word of some whore against ours. We pay her in cash, the shell company pays all the bills, and we deposit cash into the shell company. There is no paper trail. I don't know about you lot, but I don't keep anything personal at the house."

"I don't either. There is nothing to tie me to the house or her."

"DNA," said Ham with almost calm indifference.

"DNA? What the hell do you think she is? You really think she's gonna collect our DNA and have some laboratory match it to us and then tell the world we've been banging the shit out of her for months? You watch too much telly, Ham."

"All right, if not DNA, Phil, what about licence plates?"

"Oh, give it a rest, Taffy. What's next, dick prints?"

"I ride a bike."

"Fuck off, Ham," shot Tyrion. "I'm not saying anything is wrong, but maybe we should give it some thought. Maybe we should be more discreet about our personal lives, eh?"

Taffy, his empty glass causing him more concern than the possible information-gathering efforts of their resident concubine, gestured at Tyrion and lamented, "Well, you know how to put a damper on things. I'm getting a pint. Anyone else?"

Sixteen

The unexpected arrival of all four men had unnerved Krystyna. Alone and isolated at the farm house, she realized how powerless she would be if the four men decided to do something to her. Relieved the men had left, Krystyna showered long and hot to cleanse herself of Phil, Tyrion, and Taffy. Soothed by the shower, purpose replaced apprehension and Krystyna called Anna.

"Hi, Anna, how are you?"

"I am good. I feel much better and have good news."

"Good news?"

"Yes. I have everything you need."

"Already? That's great, but how did you get the equipment so soon?"

"Oh, it was easy. A man at the hotel reception sent me to a place called Realcamera. It's a few blocks from the hotel. Well, anyway, I just asked for the stuff you listed. At first, it was difficult to explain what I wanted because I didn't know the technical words in English, but the salesman used a website and changed the language to Czech. After that, it was easy."

"Anna, I told you to go to different stores to avoid suspicion."

"Oh, it's OK, Krystyna. I told them that we owned a day care for little kids and that we wanted to monitor how the workers cared for the kids. You know, we wanted to be sure the kids were OK when sleeping and stuff like that. I said we wanted to hide the cameras so we could get a true idea of what was going on."

"They weren't suspicious?"

"No, they said lots of workplaces have hidden cameras now. The man at the store, Connor, knew a few other daycares that had installed cameras. He even offered to install them for me. I think he, you know."

"Yes, I get it. Well done, Anna. And they all work with batteries and are easy to use?"

"Oh, yes. They are very small. The lens is on the end of a thin wire, and it's only the size of a penny. Connor said all you have to do is set it in place, and turn on the motion sensor. When something or someone moves, the camera will record."

"How long will it record for?"

"Six hours running all the time, and up to twenty-four hours or more depending on how often it has to turn on and off."

"What about printing photos from the camera?"

"I didn't quite understand that when he explained, but he said it's easy if you just follow the instructions. He sold me a small printer and a cable to connect the camera to the printer."

"Paper and ink, Anna?"

"Yes, the printer comes with enough for about fifty prints, and I have a package of paper."

"That's good, Anna."

"I miss you, Krystyna. I want to be there with you. When do I bring the cameras?"

"Tomorrow, Anna, take the morning bus."

"Oh, good, I was worried it would be longer. I can't wait to see you again, Krystyna."

"I'm sorry, but you won't see me tomorrow, Anna. Ham, one of the men, comes tomorrow, and I can't be sure when or if I can meet the bus."

"Then how will I . . .?"

"It's OK, Anna. Do you remember the bushes we sat behind on Saturday across the road from the bus shelter?"

"Yes."

"Buy a good waterproof bag, something dark, and leave the equipment in the bushes. I will collect it when I can."

"All right, but what shall I do until the bus comes back at 5 p.m.? Can I come to the house?"

"No, Anna, you must stay hidden. You can't come to the house. I told you one of the men is coming tomorrow and then another on Tuesday, Wednesday, and Thursday. I'm not sure yet. I have to get the cameras in position and to have pictures of all of them before we can proceed. Maybe you can come this weekend or early next week."

"I'm sorry, Krystyna. I know it must be hard for you, and you are taking a great risk. I, I just want to help, to be with you in case anything happens."

"You are helping, Anna. Without you, we couldn't do this. Now, Anna, bring the equipment tomorrow on the morning bus, OK?"

"Yes. I love you, sister."

"I love you too, Anna."

Seventeen

Dawn light pushed around and through the faded curtains, and Krystyna checked her watch. Five-forty-five a.m. Sleep, what little she managed, had not refreshed Krystyna. The image of Tyrion's face as he drove away had spurned a growing uneasiness that Tyrion suspected something. She wanted the cameras as soon as possible. If she could get them today and put one in Ham's room, she could have all the men photographed by Thursday. If not, she would have to wait until the following Monday after Ham's visit or even longer if there was a problem.

Wakefulness put Tyrion's hard stare in perspective. While Krystyna was certain she had given nothing away about her intentions, instinct forced Krystyna's decision. She would meet the bus and Anna at nine and run all the way back if she had to. A brisk walk took about forty-five minutes from the bus shelter to the farmhouse. If the bus was on time, if Ham adhered to his usual schedule and arrived shortly after 10 a.m., she could do it. She had already cut the hole in the wardrobe in Ham's room with the corkscrew. All she had to do was place the camera in the wardrobe and tape the camera lens to the hole.

Sun, bright and warm, had evaporated the morning dew, and Krystyna made good time over and down Badgers Hill to the bushes opposite the bus shelter. It was only 8:45 a.m., but before Krystyna could sit to wait, the bus arrived. Anna, a rucksack on her back, stepped off the bus. Elated, Krystyna opened her mouth to call, but another person, a man, had followed Anna.

The bus departed, and the man spoke to Anna. Krystyna couldn't hear the words, but the man's hands moved up and down and pointed different ways. On the verge of intervening, Krystyna braced to rush forward and rescue Anna from whatever the man wanted. Poised to leap from the bushes, Krystyna checked her step as Anna and the man laughed aloud. After more hand movements and laughs, the man set off down the road without looking back.

Chuckling, Anna crossed the road and stepped up the low bank and into the bushes. Krystyna stepped from behind a tree and called softly, "Anna."

A hoarse scream flew from Anna's mouth, and she scrambled backward toward the road.

"Anna. It's Krystyna. It's all right."

On the road, braced for the worst, fear raised Anna's voice to a shout. "Shit, Krystyna. You scared me. I thought you couldn't come. What is wrong?"

Krystyna embraced Anna for many moments. When Anna stopped shaking, Krystyna said, "Nothing is wrong, Anna. I just had a change of plan. I want this over with."

"Do I come with you now?" asked Anna, hopefully.

"No, not today, Anna. Look, everything is all right, but I must hurry. The man will come close to ten, and I must be back by then. Give me the pack."

Anna wriggled out of the arm straps and gave the backpack to Krystyna. As Krystyna put the pack on, she said, "Who was the man at the bus stop, Anna? I was worried."

"Oh him," said Anna, a wide smile on her face. "He's a boy, really, a university student. He studies geology and told me he is hiking the area for a few days to collect samples."

"What was so funny?"

"I'm not really sure. He was telling me some jokes about a geologist pickup line."

"A what?"

"He said, 'want to go behind that outcrop and get a little boulder?' I didn't understand, but he had a funny accent, and he made me laugh. He kept telling other jokes I think, but I didn't understand."

Krystyna wriggled her shoulders to centre the backpack and cinched the straps.

"It's good to see you laugh, Anna."

"Don't you want me to show you how the camera works?"

"There's no time, Anna. I'll figure it out. Stay out of sight until the bus comes. Do you have food and water?"

"Yes and some magazines."

"OK, Anna. I will call you when it is time for you to come."

Anna grasped her sister and held on tight. With her head pressed against Krystyna's bosom, Anna pleaded,

"Can't you stay for a little? Just for a few moments. I'm, I'm . . ."

With a gentle touch, Krystyna eased Anna's arms from around her waist. "I'm sorry, Anna. I can't stay. Soon, Anna, we will be free. I promise."

Reluctant, Krystyna turned and left.

~

Her lungs burned and her head ached, but Krystyna made it back to the farm house by 9:40 a.m., thirty-three minutes after she had left Anna. Inside, Krystyna locked the door behind her and checked the driveway. No sign of Ham. It was too early. She ran upstairs to Ham's room and spread the backpack on the bed.

The camera, probably the one the salesperson had used to demonstrate to Anna, was half out of its box, with the lens still attached to the camera by a cable. Her hands shook as she turned the camera over and found the "on" switch clearly indicated on the left side. A small LED screen activated and a prompt offered "motion on" or "motion off." Krystyna tapped "on." The screen changed, and Krystyna saw an image of a pillow. She flipped the cable with the lens upward, and the image on the camera changed from the pillow to the wall above the bed.

Trembling, Krystyna placed the camera in the wardrobe and taped the tiny lens up against the hole she had made days earlier. On tip-toes, Krystyna checked the image on the camera: with a wide clear view of the bedroom, the camera's auto-record function waited for movement. Krystyna checked her watch—9:49 a.m.—

plenty of time. She ran to her own room, stuffed the bag under her bed, stripped off, and jumped in the shower.

Krystyna need not have hurried. Ham was late. He arrived at 10:50 a.m., by which time Krystyna's nerves had frayed.

"What's wrong?" asked Ham as he entered the front hallway. "You look funny. What have you been doing?"

"Oh no, I'm fine. I, er, I was a bit worried about you. You know, on your bike, and that you maybe had an accident. But you're here now. I'm all right."

"Mm, I didn't know you cared so much. Anyhow, I've had a bastard of a morning, and I need some distraction so let's get upstairs."

Ham followed the routine, except he hardly spoke. Afterward, when Ham had left, Krystyna checked the camera. The images would not win awards; she would not get an Oscar, but the actions, the participants, and in Ham's case, the extra equipment, were clear.

Eighteen

Anna screamed and pleaded for Krystyna's help as Tyrion clamped her wrists and head in the stockade, but Krystyna, splayed and bound with Phil's ropes between the brown and yellowish chairs, could do nothing. Phil, erect, stoned, and angry, presented his manhood to Anna's closed mouth while Ham, his obscene sex toy gleaming between his legs, positioned himself behind Anna. Tyrion stood ready behind Krystyna and Taffy, already leaking semen, pressed his penis against her cheek. Tyrion's voice boomed. "Ready, boys. On my count of three, we will make a real fucking movie. One, two, three!"

Krystyna woke and ran to the bathroom. Vomit surged from Krystyna's mouth and splattered the bathtub and tiles. Dry heaves and retching followed until acidic stomach fluid, neither up nor down, stuck at the back of her throat. Grasping her stomach, Krystyna stumbled to her bedroom, curled up on the bed and focused her eyes on the digital numbers on the radio alarm clock as they blinked 4:30 a.m. She did not want to sleep again. The dream, vivid and repetitive, would not stop.

Unable to fight sleep, Krystyna got up at 5:30 a.m. She had a lot to do before Taffy arrived for his Tuesday session. Also, Taffy's arrival time varied depending on what appointments he could use to disguise his visit. After cleaning the bathtub and putting the shower curtain in the washing machine, Krystyna retrieved the camera and the other equipment from under her bed.

In the kitchen, Krystyna connected the portable printer to the camera and printed five colour pictures of Ham's exertions with one print clearly showing Ham's enjoyment at being penetrated. Krystyna held the prints dispassionately and reached for a kitchen knife. She placed the tip of the kitchen knife against her eyes and scratched until she obliterated her entire face from the picture. When she was done, Krystyna took the camera to Taffy's room.

The wardrobe in Ham's room, tall and dark, had been a perfect place to position the camera to capture the entire room. In contrast, the highest point in Taffy's room was the top of the white four-drawer dresser that stood alone against the wall and parallel to the bed. The space between the dresser and the bed was cramped, and Taffy usually stood at the foot of the bed where there was more room. With the camera on the dresser, Krystyna would need to position Taffy between the dresser and the bed while she provided his oral satisfaction.

Krystyna studied the dresser. One of the drawer handles on the top drawer was broken off, but the screws that once held the U-shaped handle were still in place. Using the flat tip of a butter knife, Krystyna removed one of the screws. From inside the drawer, she enlarged the hole with the same corkscrew she had used on the wardrobe until the diameter matched the tiny lens head of the camera. Scotch tape secured the lens, and extra bedding covered the camera. With the drawer closed, Krystyna stepped back and examined the drawer. To Krystyna, the camera was obvious, but then she was looking directly at it. To encourage Taffy to stand in the space between dresser and bed, and directly in front of the camera, Krystyna poured a kettle of water on the carpet at the foot of the bed.

Finished with preparations, Krystyna went out of the bedroom, re-entered, and imagined Taffy's actions and habits. Clothes hung over a chair, impatient, taking in her body and grasping the back of her head, then mounting her on the bed. Assured Taffy would not be interested or notice a missing screw head from the top drawer, Krystyna closed the bedroom door. With a clean shower curtain, Krystyna lathered herself with Taffy's vanilla-scented body wash and shampoo.

Towel-dried, Krystyna cocked an ear at the sound of tires on gravel. By the time she had slipped on a robe and reached the foot of the stairs, Taffy had already unzipped his pants. As he fumbled with his underpants, he nodded and said, "You look tired."

"Yes, I am. I didn't sleep well."

"Hm, is something on your mind?"

"No, I ate some leftovers last night, and my stomach was upset."

"Well, I hope you're all right now 'cause I'm loaded and ready to go. Last night, my wife . . ."

Taffy stopped mid-sentence.

As Krystyna slid downward, she said, "What was that about your wife?"

Abrupt, Taffy said, "Nothing, just get on with it, will you?"

Relieved, Taffy released Krystyna's head and hitched his pants as he climbed the stairs. Krystyna followed. In the bedroom, Taffy closed the curtains, removed and draped his clothes on the chair as usual, and moved to stand at the end of the bed.

"What the fuck is this?" said Taffy as he lifted a foot from the carpet.

Krystyna, expecting the question, answered meekly, "Oh, I'm sorry. I was cleaning the room earlier, and I spilled some water. It hasn't dried yet."

Taffy stepped back and wiped the bottom of his feet on a dry section of carpet. Annoyed, he pointed at the wet carpet and announced: "I'm not standing in a fucking puddle."

Krystyna, naked and tweaking her nipples, moved between the bed and the dresser and knelt down in the narrow space.

"OK, how about over here?"

Indecisive for a moment, until Krystyna parted and licked her lips, Taffy complied. Routine followed, except Taffy spoke differently. He made no mention of his wife, daughter, or open houses. Instead, Taffy babbled about the weather, football, cricket, and beer. The change in conversation unnerved Krystyna but she didn't understand why. Mount, dismount, massage, and coffee followed. Then Taffy departed without a word.

Even though Taffy's bulk and movements had caused the bedroom floor to shake and slightly blur the video recording and the still images, there was no question who Taffy was and what he was doing. After obliterating her face from the printed photos, Krystyna took the camera to Tyrion's room.

~

Unlike the dresser in Taffy's room and the wardrobe in Ham's, the three chairs, footstool, single bed, and the medieval stock in Tyrion's offered no obvious location to place a camera. No drawers or wardrobe cluttered the room, and Tyrion hung his clothes on an old-fashioned hat stand behind the door.

Frustrated, Krystyna lay back on the single bed and closed her eyes. When she opened them, no solution had presented itself. A light fixture, above the bed and flat against the ceiling, would be perfect if Krystyna had the time, tools, and expertise to install and disguise the camera somehow. But she didn't. She needed something easy. Sitting up on the edge of the bed, Krystyna looked out of the window. Usually, Krystyna viewed the window from the stock with her head and hands firmly clasped in the rough wooden holes.

Countless times, Krystyna had gazed through the grimy window at the lush countryside to disassociate herself from Tyrion's thrusts and grunts behind her. Now, without the need to "be elsewhere," Krystyna noticed for the first time the unused planter box that hung outside the window. With an idea forming, Krystyna opened the window. The box, filled with dirt, loose leaves, and weeds, hung level with the base of the window frame.

Back on the bed, Krystyna stretched out the cable that attached the camera lens to the camera. Confident the cable would be long enough for her purposes, Krystyna left the bedroom to search for other materials she would need.

Half an hour later, her hands snug in some tattered gloves she had found in the laundry room, Krystyna carefully scooped soil and leaves out of the window box into a bucket. When she reached the wooden bottom, Krystyna enlarged the space to accommodate a medium-sized Tupperware container she had brought from the kitchen. The thin cable, that connected the lens to the camera, protruded from a small hole in the lid of the container.

Krystyna closed one side of the two-door window and pressed the lens end of the camera to a small area she had cleaned at the bottom corner on the exterior of the window pane. With clear Scotch tape, she attached the camera lens in place. Krystyna lifted the lid of the Tupperware box, flicked the "motion on" switch on the camera, closed the window, and left the room. Outside the bedroom, Krystyna waited for sixty seconds until the automatic motion detector on the camera switched off.

After the minute, Krystyna re-entered the bedroom and mimicked Tyrion's movements and her position in the stock. Then she got the camera and reviewed the recording. The images were not good. Some kind of reflection distorted the recording. The camera manual provided no help, and Krystyna was about to remove the camera and cable when she noticed that the lens had slipped the tiniest bit off the window. The lens needed more tape to hold it still, especially when she closed the window. Additional tape, a gentle close of the window, and another check solved the problem. With the camera in place, she replaced the soil and leaves and closed the other side of the window. It was 7:30 a.m. With the window open, a cold dampness had entered the room, and Krystyna hoped the room would warm up before Tyrion arrived.

By 8:45 a.m., Tyrion hadn't called. Of the four men, only Tyrion called to say when he would arrive, and so far, he had always called around 8 a.m. By 9 a.m., Krystyna was worried: she needed Tyrion there today. She didn't want to wait another week. At 9:40 a.m., unannounced, Tyrion's white SUV sped up the driveway and slid to a stop. Tyrion vaulted from his car, burst through the front door, and demanded, "Are you ready?"

Flustered, and a little frightened by Tyrion's sudden arrival and more than usual directness, Krystyna mumbled, "Yes, yes, I'm ready. But why didn't you call first? I could have . . ."

Tyrion shed his coat, dumped it on one of the chairs by the door, and demanded, "Why should I call? Do you have something to hide?"

Krystyna, a flush rising up her torso, through her neck, and onto her face, took Tyrion's coat and turned away from him to hang on a hook on the hallway wall. With her back to him, Krystyna said, "No, of course not. It's just that you always call and that gives me time to, you know, get in the mood."

Tyrion huffed and pointed to the stairs as he expressed his opinion on Krystyna's need to be prepared. "Mood: I don't care if *you* are in the mood or not. Now, let's get upstairs because *I'm* in the fucking mood."

~

In the mood was an understatement. Tyrion used Krystyna for three hours, stopping only for water, to dry his sweat, and to allow Krystyna use of the bathroom. As Tyrion exerted himself, Krystyna listened to a monologue of the past few days and his plans for the following week. The commentary was unusually specific, and Tyrion glanced at Krystyna with each reference to a date, person, or place. Finally done, Tyrion dismissed Krystyna to prepare his tea. At the door of the bedroom, as Krystyna pushed an arm into a robe, Tyrion said, "Ashley Madison. Have you heard of her?"

Naked and sore, Krystyna, hesitated. "Yes, it's been on the news. It's a dating website for married people."

Up on one elbow, Tyrion stared hard at Krystyna. "What do you think of it?"

Cinching her robe, Krystyna pasted a confused expression on her face and responded with a jest, "Oh, I haven't really thought about it. I'm not married. Anyway, I'm too busy and happy with you and the others. I don't need to cheat on anyone. Why, is it . . . something for you?"

Tyrion, a sly smile stretching his lips, said, "No, no, just wondered about it, you know. I can't believe people would give their personal details to an organization that sets up appointments to fuck someone else's wife. It's asking for trouble. Now, go get my tea ready. I'll be down soon."

Tyrion appeared in the kitchen before his tea had brewed and announced that he had to leave right away. Krystyna watched Tyrion's car depart from the back of the living room. Unnerved and anxious at the manner and tone of Tyrion's visit, as well as the changes in Ham and Taffy, Krystyna forced herself to wait a full hour before she removed the camera from the planter box outside Tyrion's bedroom window.

The video and printed pictures of Tyrion were better than expected, but Krystyna was worried. First Ham, then Taffy, and now Tyrion had acted strange, especially Tyrion. His account of what he had done and what he had planned had been too detailed, and she sensed Tyrion watching her reactions to the information. Then the question about Ashley Madison had shaken her. Krystyna had seen the news reports about stolen personal data used to blackmail people. Krystyna's hands trembled as she put Tyrion's pictures with the others. Did Tyrion suspect something?

~

That evening, following Tyrion's unusual behaviour, the dream returned. This time, Edvard entered the room, but instead of joining the assault and rape, he hummed and laughed as he unzipped a large canvas bag. From the bag, Edvard withdrew two white folded jumpsuits with straps and buckles attached to the cuffs of each arm. Two face masks, also with straps and buckles, followed the white suits. As Edvard lay the suits lengthwise on the floor, he spoke to Tyrion: *When you are done, put my girls in the suits and carry them outside to the truck. And make sure they can breathe. It's a long drive to Prague.*

It's a long drive to Prague, haunted Krystyna throughout the night. Unable to sleep, Krystyna used the time to prepare for Phil's visit.

~

Krystyna stood in the centre of Phil's room. A wicker laundry basket in the far corner of the room held her attention. After inspecting the basket, Krystyna nestled the camera in a bed of towels mid-way down inside the basket. The lens she wedged between the wickers. With the lid placed on top and more towels draped on the lid, the camera and lens were invisible. Krystyna had the room ready by 5 a.m. and unwilling to sleep, for fear of her dreams, brewed and drank tea until the sun rose over Badgers Hill.

Phil's arrival time on Thursdays varied. Sometimes he would come at 9 a.m., sometimes at 11 a.m., and once as late as 12:45 p.m. By 1 p.m., Krystyna began to worry. The odd behaviour of Ham, Tyrion, and Taffy, together with the stress of using the camera, had Krystyna on edge.

Phil had never missed a day before. Krystyna, torn between the logic that it was normal to miss an appointment sometimes and a growing paranoia that the men had discovered her actions, paced and fretted. The urge to run, to take what she had and get away before something happened, overwhelmed her.

The more she analyzed the past few days, the more she thought about the change in the men, especially Tyrion, the more frightened Krystyna became.

Apprehensive and vulnerable, Krystyna collected the files hidden in the *Encyclopedia Britannica*, the photographs hidden under her mattress, and started to pack a bag. In the bathroom, as she collected her few personal items, a text buzzed its arrival. Krystyna pulled her phone from her jean pocket. The text was from Phil. A terse message said, "My car is fucked. I will come Friday."

Krystyna paused. The message language, terse, rude, and dismissive, was normal. Also, Phil did drive an older car, and he had mentioned a few times a problem with his car's transmission.

Krystyna slumped down on the toilet. Her legs jumped and her hands shook. Her body folded forward, and she fell to the cold tile floor of the bathroom. It was dark when she woke. Stiff and cold, Krystyna pulled herself level with the bathtub and leaned to reach the taps. While the tub filled, Krystyna undressed. Naked, she lifted a leg over the side of the tub and rolled into the hot water. Somewhat revived by the bath, Krystyna returned, unpacked the bag, and re-hid the photographs and files. Krystyna's body, responding to her physical and emotional exhaustion, remained functional until she reached her bed and hid from the world under a blanket.

Ten hours later, at 7:15 a.m., Krystyna woke. Sweat, hot and sour, ran down her neck onto an already wet pillow. Frantic, Krystyna grasped at her neck to pull away Phil's pieces of rope which had entered her nightmare and joined with another to slither and coil around her neck and torso.

Phil arrived at 9 a.m. Antsy and vocal about his car, which had required several hundred pounds of repairs, Phil was eager to begin. Without preamble, Phil ejaculated, smoked, rambled, and tied, this time with white electrical wire, Krystyna as usual. Everything as normal, and as Phil often had, he up and left while Krystyna showered and soothed her wrists and ankles. When Krystyna returned to the bedroom to collect the camera, she expected to find a short length of the electrical wire on the pillows for her to "remember Phil," but the bed was empty. Krystyna went to the drawer. It too was empty. All of Phil's ropes were gone.

Nineteen

After Phil left with his ropes, Krystyna, the weight and danger of her situation straining her resolve and strength, called Anna.

"Anna, it is time. You must come today at five."

"Yes, yes, of course. I am ready. I will be on the 5 p.m. bus."

Krystyna's voice cracked. "Be sure, Anna. You must come, you must."

"Of course, I will come. What is it, Krystyna? You are scared. What has happened?"

"I'm not sure, Anna. It may be nothing, but the men, they acted differently this week. I think they may suspect something, or maybe they have some second thoughts about our arrangement."

"God, Krystyna, you can't stay there. They could do anything to you, and no one would know. You must leave now, Krystyna. Just leave. We will be all right. We can survive."

"No, Anna. I, we have worked too hard for this. This is our chance to escape this life. There will never be another one."

"But, but, it's no good if, if they kill you."

"Anna, I am OK. They have done nothing to me. It's just a sense I have that they are preparing for something. Anyway, Anna, I have all the photos and recordings we need. You come today and help me with the last preparations. Then we will leave together on the morning bus on Sunday."

"Oh, Krystyna, are you sure it's safe? Can we really do it?"

"Yes, my sister, we can do it, and then we will start a new life."

Bruise-coloured clouds pitched and rolled like an angry upside-down ocean. Rain, cold, hard, and relentless, beat on the kitchen window, its rhythm, erratic in tone and frequency, hypnotizing Krystyna into listlessness. Noon slipped away. Three thirty p.m. arrived. Lightning, like veins, spread across the sky, thunder echoed, and Krystyna shivered. Tea, that she didn't remember making, stood untouched in a cracked mug on the table. Pushing the weariness away, Krystyna went to the hallway and dressed for the weather and her walk to meet the bus and Anna.

Water had penetrated her clothes long before she reached the bushes opposite the bus stop. She turned up the sleeve of the raincoat and checked her watch. The bus was fifteen minutes late.

~

At 5:20 p.m., its dim headlights hardly visible through the driving rain and early evening twilight, the bus arrived. Anna exited the bus and popped a large golf umbrella. Krystyna stepped from the bushes, crossed the road, and initiated a long embrace to convey what words couldn't. Huddled together under the umbrella, they sloshed their way to the farmhouse. By 7 p.m., the sisters, showered and dry, sat at the kitchen table. Krystyna sipped coffee and watched tears slide down Anna's cheeks as the still photographs of the men abusing Krystyna shook in her latex gloved hands.

"It wasn't so bad, Anna."

"These men are pigs, Krystyna."

"All the men who use women are pigs, Anna. Just like in Prague."

"Yes, yes, but in Prague, the men were gone in half an hour, and we almost never saw the same men again. But here, you had to suffer them again and again. You knew what they would do. Oh my God, Krystyna, I'm so sorry."

"Knowing what they would do made it easier, Anna. I, I could manage them most of the time, and I just thought of you and us and how this would set us free and . . . ."

Anna wrapped her arms around Krystyna, stroked her hair, and collected tears on her fingertips as the pain of the past two months leaked from Krystyna. Choking off the leak before it turned to a flood, Krystyna unfolded Anna's arms and held her sister's face.

"Now we must be strong, Anna."

"What should I do?"

"Three things, Anna: First, bury the printer. I don't want them to try and trace where and when you purchased it."

"Surely, they wouldn't do that. They are just filthy men who like to do nasty things to women. They're not police or detectives or anything like that."

"Anna, we are going to destroy their lives. They will try everything and anything to find us. Now, after you have buried the printer, there is some old wood with nails by the shed in the backyard."

Puzzled, Anna asked, "What am I to do with old wood and nails?"

"A precaution, Anna. Take several pieces of the wood with the most nails sticking up to the front yard. Walk to the end of the driveway and place the wood between the two stone pillars where cars must pass."

"What if they come tonight? They will go crazy."

"They don't come at night. And today is Saturday. The men drink together, and then they have to go home to their wives and families. Besides, if they do come tonight, it would be better if their cars were disabled."

"OK, I will use some mud and the puddles to hide the wood. What is the third thing?"

"Fingerprints, Anna. We must remove my fingerprints from this place. Make sure you keep those latex gloves on everywhere you go, including outside and with the wood. Begin with the men's rooms, then my room, and then the bathroom. Then start on downstairs."

"What will you do?"

"I will prepare the files on each of the men. When I am done, I will help you with the kitchen and hallways. We will sleep in the living room tonight."

With Anna upstairs, Krystyna went to the living room, withdrew the first four volumes of the *Encyclopedia Britannica* from the top shelf and returned to the kitchen table. From each volume, Krystyna took several sheets of paper and an equal number of photographs of the papers and laid the papers and photographs next to the corresponding photographs of each man. On Friday, even in constant fear one of the men would arrive unexpectedly, Krystyna had photographed and printed copies of her handwritten pages. In addition to the notes she had taken on each man's ramblings, Krystyna listed home, work, driver's licence numbers, and other details she had collected from the men's wallets.

Arranged on the table, ten weeks of Krystyna's sordid and painful life as the resident whore for a bunch of repugnant men whose lives relied on lies, deception, and perversion lay before her. Krystyna allowed the memories to harden her as she placed a pen to a single sheet of plain white paper. With clear and precise words, Krystyna explained to Ham, Taffy, Phil and, most of all, Tyrion, the true cost of their degenerate desires.

Krystyna didn't sign the note; they would know who it was from. Krystyna sorted the photographs into four piles and topped each pile with a clear image of the man in a sexual position with a woman without a face. Staring at her own faceless body, Krystyna wished memories could be rubbed out so easily.

Twenty

With the obligatory Friday evening with their wives out of the way, the men relished their Saturday night routine: they met at the Fox & Hounds at 6:30 p.m., drank for an hour, drove to the Bird in Hand for another hour. After that, a taxi to the Church Inn until, at around 10 p.m., they took another taxi to their "local" pub, the Railway Tavern.

At each pub, they bantered with friends, added fuel to gossip, speculated on football and politics, and drank. Now, after edging their way into a window seat at the back of the Railway Tavern, the issue they had avoided for several hours broke free and confronted the men.

Taffy, well into his ninth pint of the evening, slurred his thoughts to Tyrion and the others. "I think you were right, Tyrion. I thought about everything I've said to our little whore. The more I thought about it, the more fucked I would be if she ever decided to tell anyone."

Tyrion, his own words thickened by drink, eyed Taffy and spoke with uncharacteristic softness. "What things, Taffy? What did you tell her?"

Beer, mostly froth, turned and clung to the sides of the glass as Taffy swirled the last of his drink. "Well, it's not so much that I deliberately told her things. It's more like I was just talking out loud, you know?"

Phil, munching potato chips and slurping beer to feed his marijuana-induced hunger, spoke through food-laden teeth. "Yeah," agreed Phil, "she never really asks questions. Well, not lately, anyway. I mean, I think at first she used to, but . . ."

Tyrion, softness gone, spilled a little beer as he jibed at Phil. "Jesus, Phil, I'm surprised you can even remember that you fucked her let alone what you told her, or if she ever asked you any questions."

Ambivalent to the rightness of Tyrion's remark, Phil laughed and said, "Don't get 'short' with me, Tyrion."

Ham, smirking at Phil's short reference, blurted, "I remember."

"What, Ham? What do you remember?" asked Tyrion.

"Where I grew up, my school, about my job, my wife, my son, about how I . . ."

"Jesus, Ham, what the fuck were you thinking?"

"I wasn't, I guess. I always tell the hookers stuff. I know they don't really listen and don't give a fuck anyway, but I just do it."

Tyrion, soberness creeping into his voice and manner, asked, "Did she ever ask you questions about your life or work?"

"Not really. She didn't have to. I just told her."

Pensive for a moment, Ham added, "Well, maybe not recently, but in the first few weeks she might have asked me something then."

Taffy, who had drained his pint three times, but not moved for a refill, added his own confession: "Yeah, Ham, now you mention it. At the beginning, she asked me a bunch of basic questions. But it was always kind of indirect. Like she would say something about marriage or kids or the type of jobs people do, and I would, well, just tell her about myself."

Phil, his eyes fixed on some distant point, mumbled to Tyrion, "I told her about all the girls and women I've had and about Gillian."

"Gillian. What the fuck did you say about your wife?"

"Well, you know."

"No, I don't."

"Oh, shit. Look, I bet you all told her things about your wives. Come on; don't look at me like that. Oh, all right, mostly I told her what Gillian wouldn't do. There, I've told you."

"You mean things Gillian wouldn't let you do to her?"

"Yeah, man, stuff like that. Gill's a bit lame when it comes to sex."

Tyrion, without humour, challenged the others. "Anyone else told our whore bitch what your wife will and will not do in bed?"

Taffy studied the bottom of his empty glass to avoid Tyrion without success.

"Taffy. Look, Taffy, we all fucking know you can't hold it in. It happens, but what did you say about it?"

Red flush swamped Taffy's pudgy cheeks as he stammered, "Well, I might have said a few things about Angie's skills, you know."

"Fuck," said Phil, "I'd like to hear about those too. Give you a nice hummer, does she?"

"Shut up, Phil," shot Tyrion.

Ham, his tongue loosened by beer, had a go. "What about you, Tyrion? You're not exactly renowned for your modesty."

Hesitant, Tyrion confessed, "I've been as big a blabbermouth as the rest of you."

"What?"

"Yes, all right, I have talked about my wife and job also. It just happens, but from what you all say, and from my own observations, I think Krystyna is a very clever bitch and possibly a dangerous one."

Before anyone could challenge him, Tyrion held up his hand.

"Listen, she's a good listener. In my case, I like it that way. My wife, as you know, never shuts up and, unlike our hooker, she is not responsive to my dick in her mouth."

Familiar with Tyrion's wife Joanne, snickers escaped from Phil and Taffy.

"It's time to stop fucking around, Phil, Taffy. The other thing I told her, probably a few times at least, was where I was supposed to be when I was at the farmhouse."

The snickers ended as each man reflected on past conversations with Krystyna. Tyrion judged their expressions and said softly, "I guess you've done the same a few times?"

Taffy, Phil, and Ham nodded in unison.

"So, not only does she know about our jobs, families, wives, sexual issues, but she also knows about whatever lies we have told our wives about our whereabouts when we've been at the farm."

Phil, concern clearing some of his marijuana fog, became serious.

"What the fuck does it matter? It's not like she is going to remember any of the details anyway. And look, we don't have any proof that she is going to do anything with what she knows. Man, as far as I can tell, things are going pretty well."

"Just 'cause you can't remember fuck-all, Phil, doesn't mean she can't," spat Taffy.

"She could just write it down."

"What's that, Ham?"

"Write it down. The details, whatever you told her."

"She isn't doing any writing while I'm fucking her, that's for sure," said Phil with confidence.

"Afterward, you dick, when we have left. I mean how hard would it be?"

Agitated, Tyrion slammed his glass on the table. "She could have a whole fucking file on us."

"Look, this is stupid," said Taffy. "We're getting all worked up over nothing. We don't have any proof. It's you, Tyrion. You're paranoid."

Silence hung between the men. Bodies squirmed and fingers tapped until Taffy spoke up. "What the fuck are we going to do, Tyrion?"

"We're gonna search the farmhouse."

"What? When?"

"Tomorrow, early morning, we'll all go, and we'll search her room and everywhere else in the house."

"She's gonna be suspicious."

"I don't give a fuck what she is."

"Let's go now. Catch her by surprise."

Tyrion, calmed by the prospect of action, asserted his leadership role. "Not something to be done while we're all piss drunk. Besides, who the fuck is gonna drive? No, we need clear heads for this. We go tomorrow morning, early."

"What if we find something?" asked Ham.

A dark grimace distorted Tyrion face. "Then I guess we had better take a shovel, just in case."

"Fuck me," whispered Phil.

Up off his seat, Tyrion slipped on his coat. With determination, he said, "I'm going home. I'll pick you all up at seven tomorrow."

Twenty-One

Krystyna watched the alarm clock she had brought down from her bedroom silently mark 2 a.m. Anna, head cradled in Krystyna's arms, had fallen asleep around midnight. Exhaustion, physical and mental, wracked both of them, but Krystyna could not sleep. The plan, her plan, made in haste months earlier, as she packed a bag to leave Prague and escape Edvard, had really happened.

When the man, Tyrion, had first suggested she join him at a bar for a drink and to meet his friends, Krystyna had declined. His manner during their sexual liaison, while not unusual, had been dismissive and authoritative, and Krystyna had not wanted to meet more like-minded men.

Later, when Tyrion approached her in Wenceslas Square and asked again if she would join him and his three friends to hear about a proposition, Krystyna had assumed the men wanted a five-some. Uninterested, and thankful Edvard wasn't around to force her interest, Krystyna had shaken her head and turned away. Only when Tyrion had offered 5000 Korunas just to listen, did Krystyna join the men in a coffee shop.

Initially, as the men explained what they wanted, Krystyna suspected Edvard had put the men up to it to test her loyalty. She had expected Edvard to appear any moment and reward the men with free access to her body before he beat her. Instead, the more the men talked, the more she realized they were serious. And the more the men talked, the more Krystyna saw her opportunity.

Krystyna's first thoughts had only been of escape, of hope for herself and for Anna. Later, after she had agreed and taken money for the flight to Manchester, England, did Krystyna begin to think darker thoughts. Thoughts of more than just escape from Edvard, but escape from all men like Edvard and the life she was destined to live. The meeting with the men occurred at 5 p.m., and they told her to take the 8 a.m. flight the following morning. The men would catch the evening flight, and one of them would meet her in arrivals at Manchester Airport the next day.

The speed of the discussion, the offer, and the terms happened so quickly that the possibility of what could happen to her alone in a foreign country with four men she had only met for half an hour only surfaced later that evening when she found Anna on the other side of the square. Huddled together in a side street, away from prying eyes, Krystyna told Anna about the men. Anna, ever afraid and uncertain, clutched at Krystyna.

"What do you mean you are leaving Prague? Where are you going?"

"I can't tell you, Anna. Not yet. For your own sake, you cannot know where I am going."

"You can't, you can't just go. Who are these men?"

"I don't know, but they seem ordinary enough."

"You're crazy, Krystyna. No. You're mad. They could murder you. Chop you into little pieces or, or keep you as a slave. They could do anything."

"I'm not crazy or mad, Anna. I'm sick of this life."

Taking Anna's hands, Krystyna pulled her sister close and held her eyes.

"Anna, it's a chance to escape. To start over. After six months, they will be done with me. I will be free of them, I will have money, and I will send for you. It's a chance for both of us, Anna."

Anna cried, clung to Krystyna, and pleaded, "Take me with you. I can't stay here alone. What will Edvard do when you disappear?"

Taller than Anna, Krystyna pressed Anna's head to her chest and stroked her hair. Anna's body trembled, and Krystyna swallowed hard as she described what they both knew would happen when Krystyna disappeared. "Edvard will beat you. He will beat you until you tell him where I have gone. Then he will come for me. I don't know how, but he will."

"He won't believe I don't know where you have gone, Krystyna."

"I know, I know, but it must be this way."

Anna pulled away from Krystyna. "Will I ever see you again?"

"Yes, I promise, Anna. Tell Edvard I said I will come back for you. But only after he has beaten you, or he won't be satisfied."

They wiped their tears and faced each other. Drawing on resolve and determination, that her father said Krystyna had inherited from her grandmother, Krystyna took her cell phone from her pocket.

"Here, Anna, take my cell phone. I won't need it, but I will call you on this phone as soon as I can and give you a number to reach me. I will only call early in the mornings when Edvard is sleeping off his night and only on Mondays and Wednesdays. That way you can keep the phone hidden and turned off most of the time so Edvard does not discover it."

Anna's tears had ripped Krystyna's heart. Now, as she stroked Anna's hair again, the thoughts and guilt about the beatings Edvard gave Anna ripped her heart over again.

~

"Wake up, Krystyna, wake up. It's 7:20 a.m."

Groggy and disoriented on the floor of the living room, Krystyna flailed and grasped for Anna. "What, what's wrong?"

Before Anna could reply, Krystyna noticed the time. "Oh my God, Anna, the alarm, I didn't hear it. What happened?"

Anna, frightened by Krystyna's outburst, stammered, "I think I must have set the buzzer too low. I set the alarm for 6:30 a.m. like you said, but I only woke now. I'm sorry, I'm sorry."

Relieved that the problem wasn't more serious, Krystyna stood and held Anna.

"We still have time right, Krystyna?" said Anna nervously.

"Yes, but no time for showers. Just get dressed. I'll get the backpack."

Anna, wanting to be helpful and make up for the alarm, said, "OK, but I'm going to boil some water for tea. We can take a cup with us."

"Yes, that would be good, but be quick, Anna. The bus comes at 9 a.m. and we need an hour to get there."

Balancing steaming tea in matching mugs, Krystyna and Anna left the house at 7:35 a.m. and made for the crest of Badgers Hill.

Twenty-Two

By 7:15 a.m. on a foggy, wet Sunday morning, Tyrion had collected Ham, Taffy, and Phil. As they sped south on Irlam Road, Tyrion's driving was not helping his friends' hangovers. Phil, in the back, stifled and swallowed bile. Through a rounded fist at his lips, Phil spoke to Tyrion's back. "Jesus, Tyrion, slow down, or I'm gonna throw up."

"Don't you fucking dare, Phil, or you'll lick it up."

Ham, sitting shotgun in the front passenger seat, said, "Come on, Steve, take it easy. She's not going anywhere. No use getting a speeding ticket or stopped for a breathalyzer. We reek of beer, and I bet you would blow over."

Placated by Ham's advice, Tyrion eased off the accelerator, but kept slightly above the speed limits.

Taffy, sitting next to Phil and more resilient to hangovers, leaned back to look in the rear of the car. When Taffy saw a dirty, well-used shovel on top of a clean blue tarp, he exclaimed, "Hey, what the hell, Tyrion? You actually brought a fucking shovel?"

Focused on the road, Tyrion made no response. Taffy leaned a little farther back. The tarp was folded over, the two sides held down by the shovel. There was a large lump under the tarp. Taffy reached back, pushed the shovel aside, and lifted the tarp. This time, Taffy shouted at Tyrion: "Lyme, Tyrion! What the hell are we doing? What's going on?"

"Just being prepared, Taffy, that's all," said Tyrion with unnerving calmness.

Phil, indigestion adding to his discomfort, grabbed the back of Tyrion's seat and pulled himself forward. "Jesus, what the fuck are you thinking? I don't like it, Tyrion. I don't want any part of this."

Tyrion slowed to stop at a traffic light. "Listen to me, Phil, all of you. I was awake all night thinking about it. If we find something, we will have to deal with it right away. And, Phil, whatever happens, whatever needs to be done, we are all in this together. Understand?"

Silence, punctuated by Phil's burps and farts, filled the car, but no one laughed.

~

Tyrion, as the car slowed due to the narrow, bush-lined roads, announced: "OK, we're almost there. She's probably still in bed. I'll do the talking."

"What are you going to tell her?" said Taffy.

"That she has to take a walk with Phil while we check the house."

"Check for what?"

"Rodents, mice, and rats."

"Mice and rats; I doubt she will believe that."

"Like I said last night, Taffy, I don't give a damn what she likes or doesn't, or what she believes or not.

She will go for a walk with Phil, and we will search the place."

Phil, reluctance clear in his voice, said, "How long do I have to walk with her, Tyrion?"

"As long as it takes, Phil. I'll text you when we're done."

The SUV swung off the road, between the two stone pillars, and splashed through the mud and water left from the previous night's rain. Ten metres on, they all felt and heard bangs and scrapes on the underside of the car followed by screeches and vibrations.

Phil, still fighting the urge to vomit, grasped the back of Tyrion's seat and said to everyone, "What the hell was that?"

"Don't know," said Taffy. "We ran over something."

Tyrion, who had braked and stopped, rounded on Taffy. "No shit, Sherlock. Get out and see what it is."

Taffy got out, circled the car, and stopped at Tyrion's rolled down window.

"What is it, Taffy?"

"Shit, Tyrion. There is a piece of wood stuck up in the wheel arch on the back passenger side, and the tire is flat. And the front driver's side looks like it's partly flat too. It's hard to tell in the water."

Tyrion, Phil, and Ham joined Taffy to inspect the damage. Ham stepped in mud and shouted obscenities as he jerked his left leg upward. A short piece of scrap wood emerged from the mud attached to Ham's shoe by a nail.

"Jesus Christ," continued Ham as he shook his foot to loosen the nail from the sole of his shoe, "what the fuck is that doing here?"

Tyrion, pensive and without sympathy for Ham, stared first at the wood, then the farmhouse, and back to the two stone pillars.

"Fuck," exclaimed Tyrion, "no way that wood got there on its own. Someone put it there on purpose."

"Why," said Taffy as he grasped the wood and pulled it off Ham's foot, "would anyone do that?"

"Why the fuck do you think, Taffy?"

"Are you all right, Ham?" asked Phil.

"Yes," said Ham, "my shoe took most of the nail. My foot seems OK."

"Phil," barked Tyrion, "get the shovel. Now!"

∼

Tyrion, red-faced angry, led the men on foot to the farmhouse. At the edge of the gravel, where the dirt driveway to the road ended, the men paused. Tyrion pointed at the farmhouse.

"No lights on. The bitch must still be asleep. Come on."

At the front door, Tyrion turned his key in the lock.

"Not locked."

"Must have forgotten," said Taffy.

"Maybe."

Hesitant, Tyrion entered.

Taffy followed Tyrion and paused in the hallway.

"Feels empty. It's weird."

"Ham," commanded Tyrion, "you and Phil check the living room. Taffy, search the kitchen and laundry room. I'll wait here."

Moments later, Phil's shrill voice echoed through the farmhouse.

"In here, in here," screamed Phil from the living room. "Jesus fucking Christ."

Taffy and Tyrion ran to the living room. Phil, pale, leaning against the bookcase, held a sheet of paper.

"What's all the shouting for? What's that paper?" asked Tyrion.

"It's the end. That's what it is. You were right Tyrion, you were right."

Tyrion snatched the paper from Phil and read it aloud.

You will each find a package in your room. My silence and your personal and professional lives will cost you one thousand pounds per month. There will be no negotiation. There will be no individual deals. If one of you fails to pay, you will all suffer. If you try to find me, I will send one package to one wife. I will contact Tyrion in a few days to arrange payment. You have used me for the last time. Now I will use you.

Ham collapsed onto the sofa and cried out: "No, no, no!"

Phil, stock still against the bookcase, croaked, "I'm fucked."

Tyrion, the paper clenched in his fist, summed up their situation: "You're fucked, we are all fucked. God damn it."

Taffy, beet-red and flustered by the doorway, looked at the floor and said quietly, "I don't believe it. I just don't believe it."

Ham recovered first and bolted for the doorway.

"Where you going?" said Phil.

"My bedroom."

Fear crossed each man's face as they followed Ham up the stairs. Howls, expletives, curses, and the crash of furniture filled the farmhouse as each man contemplated the consequences should the photographs and information that detailed their sordid exploits become known to their families or the public. Tyrion, his own package of information squeezed tight in a fist, exited his bedroom and called to the others.

"All right, all right, that's enough, calm down."

Waving photographs, Phil stormed out of his room and shouted at Tyrion, "Calm down, calm down! Have you fucking seen these?"

Tyrion, a calm rage surging, fixed Phil with a cold stare.

"No, I haven't. Would you like me to look at them, Phil?"

Phil, folding the photos closed, said, "No."

"Look," said Tyrion taking charge, "let's go downstairs and think this through. Taffy, put the kettle on, will you?"

Tyrion, Ham, and Phil followed Taffy to the kitchen and watched as Taffy reached for the kettle.

"Hey," said Taffy, his hand pressed against the kettle, "the kettle is warm."

"What?" said Tyrion.

"The kettle, it's warm."

Tyrion, energized by Taffy's observation, addressed the men.

"Right, if the kettle is warm, she can't be far. She probably wasn't expecting us today. Spread out, and find the bitch. Phil, Ham, take the backyard and woods. Taffy, you check the house again. I'm going out front."

Twenty-Three

Without lids, most of the hot tea spilled from the mugs onto their coats and shoes, and they discarded the mugs halfway up Badgers Hill. Sunlight, weak and hesitant, met Krystyna and Anna as they crested the hill. The compulsion to take a last look, or a sixth sense of danger, caused Krystyna to pause and turn toward the farmhouse where she had endured the perverse demands of the men who would now pay for her silence. Krystyna cried out, "Oh no!"

On edge, Anna clung to Krystyna. "What? What's wrong?"

"On the track to the main road, by the gate, Anna. Do you see a white car?"

Anna squinted. "Yes. I see it. Is it the men?"

"Yes. That car belongs to the one they call Tyrion. He is the leader."

"But, but you said they never come on Sundays."

"They don't. Only once, but never so early. I . . ."

A phone sounded inside Krystyna's backpack. Krystyna wriggled out of the backpack, loosened the top straps, and withdrew a phone.

Anna, fearful, whispered, "Who is it?"

Instinctively, Krystyna held the phone at arm's distance. "It's Tyrion"

"Don't answer it, Krystyna."

The ring sounded loud in the open as Krystyna pushed her thumb on the answer button.

"Don't, Krystyna! There is a man in the driveway."

Tyrion's voice, frightening for its cold calmness, hissed from the speaker: "I'm going to kill you."

Krystyna, her own coldness, taking control, remained silent.

"Do you hear me? Jesus, you're there, on the hill. Holy fuck, I'm . . ."

Krystyna ended the call.

"Krystyna, the man in the driveway, he's running toward us."

"I know. He has seen us. We must run, Anna. Run."

"He will catch us, Krystyna."

"No, he won't, Anna. The bus comes in twenty-five minutes. We are well ahead of him, and he doesn't know where we are going. We will make it. I promise."

Over the crest of Badgers Hill, Krystyna led Anna through the bushes and trees on a route she knew well.

Twenty-Four

Ears pricked and nose in the air, like a hunter dog seeking prey, Tyrion stood in the driveway. First, quick, then slow, he turned three hundred and sixty degrees. He reached into his trouser pocket and withdrew his cell phone. With the phone held out in front him, Tyrion peered into the tree line, pressed the speed dial number for Krystyna, and listened.

One, two, three, four, five rings; ears strained, eyes boring into shadow, Tyrion waited. A half-ring, then a shrill, anxious voice, " . . . man in the driveway."

Tyrion, face twisted with malice and hate, pressed the phone to his mouth and snarled, "I'm going to kill you."

In the silence, save the rustle of fabric or wind, Tyrion's mind processed the voice he had heard mention a man in the driveway. His synapses synchronized: they could see him.

"Do you hear me?" shouted Tyrion as he looked up over the tree line to the distant hill.

"Jesus, you're on the hill. Holy fuck. I'm going to fucking kill you right now, you bitch."

Unfamiliar with the area beyond the immediate farmhouse, Tyrion scrambled along the bush and tree line for several minutes until he found a place where the bushes were pressed back. Through the bushes, clear in the wet dirt, footprints marked the way. Adrenalin surged. Tyrion leaped forward and, eyes down, followed the two sets of prints. Under the trees, leaves and twigs, accumulated over many years, covered the ground. Without muddy footprints to follow, Tyrion slowed and searched for other signs. After a hundred metres, the stand of trees thinned and gave way to waist-high bushes before they ended at a wide swath of fallow pasture. Through the trees and bushes, Tyrion stopped at the edge of the field. Depressed grass indicated a faint trail across the field. Aligning the trail with the point on the hill where he had seen Krystyna, Tyrion ran. Across the field, Tyrion forced his way through a narrow strip of bushes that separated the field from the first incline of the hill. Rocks and boulders littered the hillside. To his right, at the base of a small rock, two china tea mugs lay on their sides in the short wet grass. Tyrion, recognizing the mugs from the farmhouse, moved to the right and began to climb the hill.

Out of breath at the top of the hill, Tyrion took his cell phone from his pocket and activated Google Maps. He zoomed in and out of the map until it displayed his location. With the map, Tyrion noted the road down the other side of the hill and a Manchester Transport icon that indicated a bus stop at the junction of Hill Road. Frantic, Tyrion reduced Google, switched to phone, and called Phil. Phil answered on the second ring, but before he could speak, Tyrion shouted, "Phil, get the car."

"What? Where are you? We've been looking for you and . . ."

"Just get the fucking car now, Phil."

"What the fuck? Two of the tires are flat and . . ."

Wary of hitting a rock, Tyrion stumbled as he edged down the slippery hillside.

"I don't fucking care, Phil. Just get it and drive. Turn left out of the driveway, and take the second left, and second right, and . . ."

"You're out of your mind. I can't drive it like that, it'll wreck it."

Tyrion stopped and drew a deep breath.

"Phil, I've found her. She is heading for a road on the other side of the big hill. There is a bus stop at the junction of Hill Road and Higher Road. If she gets on the bus, we have lost her. Now, get the fucking car, and drive it. I don't care what happens to it."

Phil, phone in his ear, called to Taffy and Ham, who both came at a run with questions.

"What's going on Phil?"

As Phil ran, he spoke. "I don't have the fucking key. You have it."

Tyrion, who had resumed his descent, said, "The doors are open. There is a spare key in the pouch behind the passenger seat. Now get a fucking move on, Phil."

Halfway down the hill, Tyrion checked his watch. It was 8:55 a.m.

Twenty-Five

The sisters, hot, sweaty, and scared, crouched behind the bushes opposite the bus shelter. Blood, from a cut left by a tree branch that had slipped from Krystyna's hand and whipped back against Anna, trickled above Anna's left eye. Krystyna poured water from a bottle onto a handkerchief and dabbed away the blood from Anna's brow and cheek. Anna flinched, then grasped and twisted Krystyna's arm to read the watch on her wrist. Krystyna had already checked the time, pulled her arm away, and calmed Anna.

"It's eight fifty, Anna. The bus will be here in ten minutes. We will soon be safe. You must be calm when we get on the bus. We don't want to be remembered."

Anna, the strain unbearable, heaved and sobbed. "I'm sorry. I don't want to be hurt again. I, I'm . . ."

Krystyna reached an arm around Anna. "It's all right, Anna. No one will hurt you ever again."

Anna's sobs lessened and an engine, deep and throbbing, sounded. Breaks squealed as the bus slowed at the junction.

"The bus, Anna. It's early. Come."

Out from the bushes, the sisters straightened their clothes and crossed the road to the bus shelter. The bus engine roared as it rolled through the junction, accelerated and then slowed again to stop in front of Krystyna. The bus doors hissed and creaked open. The sisters climbed into the bus. A jaunty driver, his grey hair short and neat above a pressed white shirt and knotted blue tie, greeted them.

"Good morning, ladies; where to?"

"Manchester. The bus station," said Krystyna.

"Last stop then, eh? That'll be three pounds ten each."

Krystyna held a twenty-pound note to the driver.

The driver regarded the money and said with sympathy, "Sorry, love. I can't make change." He pointed to a metal box with a plastic transparent front and a coin-and-note slot on the top. "You have to put the exact money in the box there."

Krystyna, with no change and in a hurry, went to put the twenty-pound note in the slot.

"Hold on there a minute, love," said the driver with concern. "You're wasting almost fourteen pounds! You can't put a twenty in. Let's see if any of the passengers can at least give you two tens."

The driver leaned out from his seat to address the seven or eight passengers spread out on separate seats through the bus. Anna clutched Krystyna, eyes wide and lips quivering. Krystyna moved her body to screen the driver from the passengers and held his eyes with the wide smile she used hundreds of times to coax men to her services.

"That's very kind of you, but it's all right. We just need to get going. My sister is not well and needs to sit down."

Assured and flattered by the smile, the driver sat back and said, "Listen, keep your twenty for now. When we get to the station, we can get you some change, eh? No need to waste hard-earned money."

With thanks and a radiant smile Krystyna did not feel, she ushered Anna to the empty seats at the rear of the bus. Both sisters wobbled as gears ground and the bus pulled away from the stop toward a curve in the road. Anna fell onto a seat as the front of the bus approached a curve. Through the back window, over Anna's head, Krystyna watched Tyrion jump from the bushes into the road. Tyrion, his arms waving and his mouth wide, ran after the bus. The bus rounded the curve, and Tyrion disappeared. Krystyna turned and looked forward to the front of the bus and sighed with relief as another curve approached. She swivelled to look back again, but all she could see were road and bushes.

As she squeezed up beside Anna, the bus horn blared, and the bus swerved left and brushed up against coarse, prickly hedges that lined the narrow country road. Driver's side, a white SUV flashed past the window, sparks and smoke trailing from the front and rear wheels. Gasps and expletives filled the air from startled passengers, and the bus slowed.

"Everyone all right?" shouted the driver over his shoulder.

Muted responses assured the driver, and he sped up. The bus continued and rounded several more bends.

Anna, hysteria on her face, croaked, "Was that them? Oh no, Krystyna, no."

"I think so, Anna, but there is something wrong with their car. How is the road ahead?"

Anna, who had ridden the bus route several times, said, "The road straightens out soon, and we go much faster. There are no more stops until a small village."

Krystyna, eyes fixed on the road behind the bus, said nothing.

As Anna predicted, the bus accelerated on a straight and Krystyna watched with relief as the asphalt spread out behind them. A half-mile into the straight, Tyrion's SUV, still trailing sparks and smoke, lurched into the road and accelerated toward the bus. Half the distance closed quickly, and Tyrion's face, split with an evil grin, leered at Krystyna over the steering wheel. Less than fifty metres from the bus, the driver's side wheel disintegrated, and the front end of the SUV hit the ground. Losing control, the car pulled left and disappeared through a tall stand of hedges.

Krystyna looked forward. In the large rear-view mirror, the bus driver's eyes fixed on her and Anna. A smile formed across the driver's eyes, and a finger came up to cross his lips as he signalled her to be quiet. An hour later, at the Manchester Central bus station, Krystyna and Anna were the last passengers to the door. Krystyna held the twenty-pound note to the driver.

The driver, sympathy and kindness written on his wrinkled face, closed his hand over Krystyna's and softly said, "You keep it, love. Whatever you're running from, good luck. Now, get going."

Holding on to each other, the driver watched the city swallow Krystyna and Anna.

Part Two

One

From Manchester, Krystyna and Anna travelled separately and randomly: first, via train from Manchester to Leeds, then from Leeds to Newcastle on the east coast. In Newcastle, the sisters stayed in separate hotels for one night before following the east coast via bus from Newcastle to Hull, and then on past Yarmouth until a second night in the port town of Ipswich. On the third day, exhausted, the sisters sat on the banks of the River Orwell eating bread, cheese, and cold meats. Two days and three buses later, Krystyna and Anna stepped off the bus in the seaside resort town of Torquay, on England's south coast.

Luckily, the sisters arrived in early June. The tourist season had begun, and bars, cafés, restaurants, and attractions needed low-cost, unskilled workers to satisfy the hundreds of thousands of holidaymakers that increased the town's population tenfold for four summer months. With enough money to pay first and last month's rent on a small one bedroom flat away from the main town, and with time and determination, they obtained work in the loosely regulated service industry. Within six weeks, the money from Tyrion and the others added to their income, and the sisters settled into a quiet and unobtrusive life. With the exception of an incident with the owner of a small art gallery and restaurant, the sisters prospered and slowly relaxed.

~

At summer's end, property rents declined, and they moved into a two bedroom flat closer to the ocean. Good at their work, reliable and honest, their seasonal full-time service jobs changed to part-time, and the women became integrated into the community. During a Christmas party at the restaurant where Krystyna and Anna worked, two brothers, Mike and David, entered the sisters' lives and by spring, engagements had been announced. Wedding vows were exchanged in the summer, and by the following autumn, just sixteen months since arriving in the small seaside town, both Krystyna and Anna were pregnant with their first child. With marriage certificates based on fake surnames, and ensuing official documentation built on their married names, Krystyna and Anna settled into a secure and anonymous existence with men who treated them well and a community that accepted them.

Babies, two boys, George and Robert, arrived in April. A year later, first birthdays were celebrated and plans were confirmed for the sisters and their husbands to buy a small café with money that Krystyna and Anna had "inherited" from a distant relative in the Czech Republic. By July, three years after their escape from Tyrion and the others, Krystyna and Anna had become established business owners, respected mothers, and desirable wives. Only one thing clouded their otherwise happy lives: the risk associated with blackmail and the files that had to be kept hidden and secure.

The files hadn't been difficult to keep hidden when Krystyna and Anna lived together, but marriage changed that. Now the files were carefully stored in the basement of Anna's house, and the prospect of them being discovered hung over the sisters. In addition, receiving the money from Tyrion had become more difficult and risky. Before marriage, children, and a business, Krystyna had no difficulty in taking a bus to Manchester to collect the money. Now, with mother responsibilities and business duties, getting away from Torquay for a day was more difficult and required the fabrication of a story that Krystyna visited a home for refugees to provide money, support, and guidance to abused women. Unbeknown to Krystyna, the unpredictability of when she made her trips to Manchester had worked in her favour and had gone a long way to preventing Tyrion's attempts to catch or follow Krystyna once the money had been handed over.

The arrangements to collect the money, based on a system used by members of the Roma minority in the Czech Republic to move drugs and guns, was simple and effective. Krystyna would send Tyrion a text with fifteen minutes' notice of where and when he would need to be to hand over the money. The handover point was always on a busy one-way street in downtown Manchester lined with cars which prevented Tyrion from opening his car door or turning around. An envelope would be passed through the window, and Krystyna, in a variety of disguises, would take the money and disappear in the crowds. Despite practice and confidence, the handover was always stressful and dangerous, and the risk ever present. As July drew to a close, Krystyna and Anna walked along the west coast path that paralleled the beach.

"Anna," said Krystyna, "we must talk about the situation with the men and the money."

"Not again, Krystyna. Why now? It's a beautiful day and I don't want to spoil it by thinking about those men. No."

"We must, Anna."

"Why? Everything is perfect. The money from those pigs has brought us our café, and we can keep saving in case anything goes wrong."

"That's the point, Anna. If anything is likely to go wrong, it will have to do with the men and the money."

With a huff and a shake of her head, Anna turned away.

"No, Anna," said Krystyna as she pulled gently at Anna's arm. "Just listen, Anna. For three years, the men have paid. Always on time, always the right amount, and so far our system has worked."

"Exactly. It works, so why stop?"

"Because it can't keep working forever. Someone will make a mistake, our husbands might find out, or Tyrion or one of the others will reach a breaking point and won't care what happens."

Anna, her back pressed against the rail that prevented people falling off the pathway to the beach two metres below, pouted.

"Anna," said Krystyna softly, "we have a beautiful life. Mike and David love us, Robert and George are healthy, and we all have a future. We must protect what we have."

Defiant, Anna pushed off the railing and said, "No, Krystyna, we must keep the money and the men must be punished forever. They are too afraid to try anything."

Krystyna took Anna's hands.

"Listen, Anna, what if one of the wives dies in an accident or if they get divorced or if a wife has an affair and the husband finds out? The point is, something could change, and we wouldn't know about it until they don't follow the rules about the money anymore and somehow manage to find us."

Anna wriggled to move away, but Krystyna held her in place. Anna relaxed and let Krystyna place her hands on her face.

"It's time to end it, Anna. Every time we get the money, we risk being discovered. We will be better without it, Anna."

Anna, eyes fierce, relented, "OK, you're right, but I don't think they have suffered enough."

"Maybe, maybe not, but our part in their lives is over. Tomorrow, I will write to Tyrion and tell him that it is over. You must destroy the files, Anna. Cut everything into tiny pieces, and flush them in small quantities down the toilet. OK, Anna?"

"Fine, I'll do it."

Krystyna looked out to sea, felt the air, and sighed to Anna. "Finally, Anna, we will be free of everything and everyone."

Two

For months, rage at Krystyna, each other, and the world fuelled animosity, insecurity, and accusations between and among the four adulterers. Blame and counter blame tore the friendship in all directions as separate and together the men hunted ineffectually for Krystyna and her accomplice. Visits to known brothels, "red light" districts in Manchester, London, and a few other major cities, as well as furtive and amateurish attempts to try and catch someone during the handover of the money, produced no trace.

Tyrion, the most angry and determined, hired, fired, and rehired a private investigator who, without a photograph, full name, place of birth, or any other substantial identifying information, provided no results. After three years, although resigned to circumstances, their dilemma continued to dominate their lives and sour their Saturday night routine. Like water down a river, the men, unable to change their pattern, sulked in the corner of the Railway Tavern and downed more pints of beer than was good for them or their wallets. Ham, always more focused on money than the others, opened the conversation with his cumulative calculation of how much money they had paid Krystyna to date.

"One hundred and forty-four thousand pounds: That's how much we have paid the bitch so far."

"Yeah, Ham," sighed Taffy, "we know."

Phil, pissed and reflective, added his assessment. "She's a clever bitch too. Not too much to break us; just enough to hurt."

"It's about the same as we paid her plus the expenses of the house," added Ham.

Tyrion, red-faced and bloated from beer, spat at the world. "Almost as though she knew how much and figured if we could pay while we fucked her, we could pay without. Christ, I'll kill the bitch if we ever find her."

"Do we have to go over this again? That's all we do now. Every Saturday night, it's the same shit over again."

"You may not care, Taffy," said Ham, "but every penny of that money eats away at me. There must be something we can do. What's the latest from that private investigator of yours, Tyrion?"

"Nothing. I talked with him again last week. Same shit. Can't do anything with the information we have."

"How long do you think this is gonna go on?"

"Don't know, Ham. If I were her, why would I stop? I mean she's getting almost fifty thousand a year for doing nothing except opening a fucking envelope four times a year. Why the hell would she stop? I wouldn't. It's not as though we can track the money."

"Did you ever tell the investigator about the blackmail and the money?"

"No. I don't want any more people knowing what's going on. I told him I had only met her once and couldn't get her out of my head and that was why I didn't have much information."

"We should try to follow her when she comes for the money next time. Maybe she will make a mistake."

"Doubt she's the type to make a mistake."

"You're right, Taffy. I think we are going to pay for a long time."

"We have to keep trying. We can't give up. When is the next payment?"

"Any time after the fifteenth, Ham."

"Same drill?"

"Yep, I guess. She will call me on the phone she sent and tell me where and when to drop the money."

"You have to hand it to her," said Phil grudgingly. "The system is simple but good."

"It's the timing that's the problem, Phil. She can call anytime after the fifteenth day of the third month. The calls have been all over the map. Remember at first, it was a few days after the fifteenth, then a week, then two weeks, then on the fifteenth. Remember last year, at Christmas, when we all figured she would want the money pronto, and we tried to organize so that one of us could follow the person I handed the money to. She didn't fucking call until the twentieth of January. By then, I'd almost forgot about the money."

Taffy, his glass empty, added, "Not just that though, is it? I mean, you have to carry the money with you all the time because she only gives you fifteen minutes' notice."

"I know, it's impossible to be prepared. We would need three or four people on standby each and every day to follow the money. And because she could call anytime over a ninety-day period, it would cost a shit load of money to keep men on standby."

"What I don't get," said Ham deep in thought, "is, if you're in somewhere you can't get out of, like the swimming pool or whatever, how does she know you can get out to the street to hand over the package?"

"I think someone watches me. Many times, I am called at the office or in my car on the way home. She must just pick a day or two and wait for the right moment."

"It's clever how the drop is always on a busy one-way street."

"I know. Krystyna, or whoever it is, always stands right between parked cars so that all I can do is slow down a bit to hand over the envelope. There is no room to get out, and I can't stop or turn around.

"Even if I did, what the hell would I do? There were two of them that day on the hill. If we get one, and it might not even be one of them, the other could send the stuff. Anyway, the person in the street could be some tosser they offered a tenner to stand on the road and accept a package."

Their dilemma articulated, but still unsolved for another week, the men, once again, drank to inebriation before going home to wallow in their misfortune.

Three

Monday morning, post weekend consumption, Tyrion, like many others, dragged himself to the office. Since the blackmail, Tyrion drank and ate more than he should, exercised less, and, like many victims, experienced a decline in his overall health. Fortunately, business was good, and despite payments to Krystyna, Tyrion still managed a decent lifestyle, not to mention several liaisons with various clients and associates.

Although she was closing in on retirement, Janet, his assistant for the past six years, always opened the office a half-hour before Tyrion arrived at 9 a.m. Set firm in her routine, she would open, scrutinize, and set out typed envelopes for Tyrion only if the correspondence needed his personal attention. Janet would leave handwritten or hand-delivered envelopes on Tyrion's desk unopened.

Tired, Tyrion nodded, greeted Janet, and stepped into his office. He placed his Starbucks coffee on the corner of his desk, took off and hung his coat on the rack by the window, and slumped into his leather, swivel chair. A small stack of typed letters, with the envelopes paper-clipped to the back, lay on the left of his desk. On the right, two outgoing letters waited for his signature. In the middle, a plain white envelope with a yellow sticky note on the front, which obscured the writing on the envelope, announced in Janet's distinctive print "pushed through the office door sometime in the night." Tyrion peeled off the sticky note and sweat burst from his body.

Three years had passed since he had last seen the awkwardly-printed handwriting. Thirty-six months of payments and not a word. Now, set aside on his desk by his assistant Janet, the plain white envelope marked "personal and private" threatened. Tyrion rubbed the sweat from his hands on the legs of his pants and picked up the envelope. The triangle flap on the back of the envelope was sealed tight, and an image of Krystyna's lips entered Tyrion's mind unbiddenly. Shaking away the thought, he pried open the flap and withdrew a plain sheet of white paper folded in three to fit the envelope. Tyrion unfolded the paper. Twelve printed words in blue ink stunned Tyrion:

Pay no more. I am done with you. The material will be destroyed.

Tyrion turned the paper over and checked the envelope. There was nothing else, no signature, no date. His hand shook. He looked around for a hidden camera in case he was the butt of a very sick joke. Disbelief vied with relief. Then anger and irritation contorted Tyrion's face. He had been dismissed. Used and discarded. The whore was done with him! With him! He banged his fist on the table; expletives gushed from his mouth until Janet stepped in to ask if something was wrong. It took a while, but Tyrion calmed down, and he sent an urgent text to Ham, Taffy, and Phil to meet him at lunchtime in the Tavern.

At lunch, Tyrion waved off Ham and Taffy's questions until Phil arrived. With pints before them, Tyrion passed the letter to Phil, who read it and passed it on. Ham, the last to read the terse words, spoke first. "Fuck me. Do you believe it, Tyrion?"

"I don't know. I want to."

"Why would she end it?" asked Taffy, for once not having touched his beer. "I mean, she's getting money every three months for nothing."

Phil, unusually excited and animated, blurted, "Maybe your private investigator was getting close, and she wants to end it before he finds her."

Tyrion, who had more time to contemplate the situation, said, "I don't think so, Phil. That fucking investigator I hired found nothing. He said that without more information on who she is and unless we had help from the authorities, we would never be able to find her."

"Maybe she's got a conscience," said Phil.

A huff exited Tyrion's mouth as he said, "I doubt it. If she can fuck us for months while planning to blackmail us, she's a cold bitch."

"What's more likely," said Tyrion, "is that she has a new life and holding on to the stuff is risky."

Ham, not interested in his beer, pushed the glass away, offered his views.

"Then why bother telling us? She could destroy the stuff and keep getting the money. It must be something to do with getting the money from us every three months. Your investigator is wrong. Perhaps he was getting close, and she decided to quit while she was ahead."

"Either way," said Tyrion, "what do you want to do?"

"What do you mean?" said Taffy perplexed.

"Well, should we believe the letter and stop paying?"

"Fucking right we should," shouted Phil. "God, I could do with the money. Gillian is more suspicious than ever about us being short of money. If it wasn't for the fact that I don't have any money to actually do anything with, she would think I was doing something."

"Of course, we stop," demanded Ham. "Are you for real?"

"No, I mean yes, I'm just suspicious that's all. Who has ever heard of a blackmailer just stopping? I don't get it," said Tyrion as he folded the letter and put it in his pocket.

Phil stood up, smiled, opened his arms, and addressed his friends, "Look, we've paid the bitch for three fucking years, and I don't care why she has decided to stop. Let's just take it as is, get pissed, and go for a curry."

Phil's suggestion won the day. By 11:30 p.m., drunk, full of curry, and immensely relieved their ordeal was over, the men made their blurry way home.

Four

Curry, on top of half a dozen beers, followed by half a dozen more, did not sit well in Tyrion's stomach. In bed at midnight, Tyrion slept until 1:30 a.m. when, mixed and churned by his intestines and guts, the curry and beer made an unwanted appearance. Rushing from his mouth and leaking from his anus, the volatile brew kept Tyrion retching and shitting until 6 a.m. Sleep returned until, at 11 a.m., the incessant ring of his cell phone forced Tyrion to confront the world.

The ring indicated the phone was in his pants' pocket on the floor by the bedroom door. Tyrion crabbed over and bent gingerly down to retrieve the phone. His head swam. Tyrion recognized the number and wondered what the hell Phil wanted. Before Tyrion could ask, Phil's voice screamed from the phone: "God damn it. Fuck. I'm dead. It's the end. Shit. Shit. Shit!"

Startled by Phil's outburst and dulled by the ache in his head, Tyrion spoke slowly, "Phil, calm down. What's wrong, Phil?"

"What's wrong, what's wrong, you fucking moron? This is all your fault. It was your idea. We would never . . ."

Phil's assault sobered Tyrion. "Get a grip, Phil. What is it?"

"That goddamn whore, that filthy bitch. She did it, Tyrion. She fucking went and did it."

Rising panic churned Tyrion's gut. "Did what, Phil? What has she done, for fuck sake?"

Sobs replaced Phil's outburst, and Tyrion had to coax Phil to explain.

"She sent the photographs, Tyrion. To my house. To Gillian. She opened them this morning. Jesus, Tyrion, what am I going to do?"

"What? What did you say, Phil? Phil? Phil?"

The phone was dead. Phil had hung up. Tyrion called three times, but Phil didn't answer. The phone rang, and Tyrion stabbed at the answer button.

"Phil, what the hell did . . .?

"What? It's Taffy, not Phil."

Taffy, less shrill than Phil, reported the same story. Angie had gotten a package this morning. Ham called next and confirmed the worst. Dread, aware of what was happening; Tyrion sat on his bed and waited with his phone in hand. Ten minutes later, the phone rang. As expected, it was Joanne, his wife. Tyrion let it ring and go to voicemail. When the call ended, he listened to the message.

You disgusting pig. Don't bother coming home. Ever. You will hear from my lawyer. How could you? How could you do this to me and our daughter?

Five

It wasn't easy getting them to come. Tyrion had to call, text, and call again before everyone agreed to meet. By 8 p.m., Ham, Taffy, Phil, and Tyrion sat in a dark alcove in the vault of the Railway Tavern. On the small, copper-topped table, four pints sat untouched before them. No one, not even Taffy, wanted a drink.

Phil, a beer mat shredded on the table beside his untouched beer, said what each of them had been asking themselves for the past twenty-four hours. "I don't get it. Why? Why send a letter that it's all over and then the next day send the goddamn photographs to our wives? I just don't get it."

"Simple," said Ham, "she's a sick bitch, and she really hates us. I guess I'm not surprised really."

"What do you mean, you're not surprised?" said Tyrion.

"Well, you know, the way we treated her."

"Treated her! Fuck that. We had a goddamn deal with her. She knew what she was getting into. We paid her, she had a place to live, food, and she was safe. Christ, it was luxury compared to Prague. So don't give me that shit, Ham. It's not our fault."

Taffy, both hands clasped tight around his beer glass, let loose some pent up anger. "Who the fuck cares why she did it? It's done and we're all fucked. All Angie said was 'fuck off Taffy and don't come back.' I stayed over at my mom's last night. What the hell am I going to do? What did Gillian say, Phil?"

"Didn't say anything."

"What? Nothing?"

"No. She just held the photos in her hands and stared at me with those sad eyes that say what a fuck up I am. It's worse than words."

"Did she kick you out?"

"No. I mean, I don't know. I slept in the shed with a sleeping bag last night. When I went in the house this morning, she had gone to work."

"Denial then."

"What?"

"She's in denial. Doesn't, or won't, believe it. She'll probably forgive you and blame herself like she has done for years with your drugs and booze."

"I don't think so, Taffy. I've blown it this time."

Taffy, overcoming his anger and brief abstinence, slurped a long draft of beer before turning to Ham. "What happened at your place, Ham?"

Ham, distant, stirred the foam on his beer with his little finger before pushing the finger into his mouth. Taffy repeated his question. "Ham, Ham, hey, what did Rose do?"

"She laughed."

"Laughed?" Taffy and Phil said together.

"Yes. Anyway, I don't want to talk about it."

"But, are you, you know, still at home?"

"No. I'm in a hotel for a few nights until I find a flat. Rose and I are done."

"Like done, done for good?"

"Yes. What the fuck do you expect, Phil? Rose isn't a do-gooder social worker like your Gillian."

Tyrion, a calm, contemplative expression on his face, downed a long pull on his pint. He stared at each of his friends, in turn, unnerving Phil who said, "What the fuck are you looking at us like that for?"

Tyrion, lips pressed together, fingers interlocked on the table, smiled as he explained, "It's interesting, isn't it, Phil?"

"What is?"

"My wife Joanne. As you all know, she's always been a lazy cow; always late for things and always last minute to get things done, if she even gets around to doing it. How many times have I picked up the pieces for things she didn't get around to or 'forgot'?"

"What are you on about?" asked Ham.

"Motivation, Ham, motivation."

"Eh?"

"Eighteen years of marriage, and I can count on one hand the number of times she has actually gotten herself organized to do what she was supposed to do on time."

"What are you blabbering about, Tyrion? You pissed or what?"

"No, Taffy, not pissed, more amazed. You see, boys, my useless, lazy, always late, disorganized wife, who has bumbled through life without a care, has suddenly become very fucking organized and efficient."

Tyrion paused; his hands unlocked, grabbed his glass, drained the entire pint of beer, and slammed the glass on the table. Done with his beer, his voice grew loud and shrill.

"The locks on the house have been changed. Our joint chequing account is empty. Three suitcases of clothes arrived at my office earlier, my daughter's cell phone no longer responds, and "my" dog Henry, whom she always hated, is in a fucking kennel! Oh, and did I tell you? A fucking divorce lawyer has already called to schedule a convenient time to meet and discuss terms. Discuss terms!"

Ham, Phil, and Taffy, stilled by Tyrion's outburst, fidgeted and waited.

Red-faced and aware of the stares of others in the pub, Tyrion calmed. "So, you see, boys, it's all about motivation. I guess she finally had something to motivate her into action and getting rid of me seems to have been it."

"Jesus," said Taffy, "she really wants you gone then."

"Yes, thank you, Taffy, I think I got that."

"Ham's in a hotel until he gets a flat," said Phil. "What are you going to do?"

"I have a few properties listed where the owners are away. I can bunk down in them for a few days while I get sorted. But first, I'm going to find that bitch, and I am going to kill her."

Three fixed stares locked on Tyrion.

"What? Don't fucking look at me like that. No one, no one, ruins my life and walks away. No one."

"Look, Tyrion," said Phil, "I know it's pretty bad and all, but I don't want any part of it. I'm done with her, it, the whole thing, so leave me out of it, OK?"

"Me too," added Taffy quickly. "I just want to forget it ever happened."

Tyrion turned to face Ham.

"Doesn't matter to me. I don't care what you do."

Tyrion stood, edged his way from behind the table, and slipped his arms into his coat. With the buttons done up, Tyrion bent down, leaned between his three friends, and said with cold certainty, "Well, fuck all of you then. I'll do it myself. Just keep your mouths shut."

Six

Few cars were about at 7 a.m. on Sunday morning as Tyrion's SUV sped along Carrington Road. Phil, his head resting against the rear driver-side passenger window, groaned as Tyrion, moving too fast for the curve, hit the brakes hard. Up front, on Tyrion's right, Taffy lurched forward against his seat belt.

"Jesus. What's the rush?"

"I have a bad feeling, Taffy, that's what."

"What do you mean?"

"It's been two weeks since we saw Ham, right? He didn't come out last week or last night."

"He said he was busy moving into his flat and didn't feel like coming out. I don't exactly feel like socializing much myself these days. I only came out last night to get away from Angie staring at me and muttering under her breath. What's the big deal?"

As the car passed Urmston Meadows on the right, Tyrion slowed and asked, "Phil, where is it again?"

"In about half a mile, take a right on Queen's, left on Manor Avenue, and right on Manor Park. It's a three-story walk-up at the bottom of the street."

The wide SUV tires squealed on the morning-damp road as Tyrion turned right, left, and right again, and stopped in the visitors' parking spot of a plain, brick building. Responding to Taffy's earlier question, Tyrion turned in his seat and said, "The big deal, Taffy, is why the fuck did Ham send us a text last night asking that we come here at seven o'clock this morning?"

"He said he had something to show us, right? He probably has a breakfast ready for us and just wants to show his flat. Come on, I'm starving."

Taffy and Phil, thoughts of breakfast encouraging their step, made for the front door. Tyrion, less certain of what awaited, followed.

~

Through the door, up on the third floor, Taffy and Phil waited for Tyrion.

"What number is it, Phil?" asked Tyrion as he passed Phil and Taffy.

"Number twelve, on the left."

Tyrion halted at Ham's door and knocked. Under the impact of Tyrion's knock, the door moved slightly.

"It's not closed properly," said Phil.

"That's 'cause he's expecting us," said Taffy. "Come on, let's get in."

"Ham, Ham, it's us," called Taffy. "There better be some breakfast."

Through the narrow hallway, Phil, Taffy, and Tyrion froze on the threshold of the small living room. Pressed together, the men gasped in disbelief.

Ham, thin, white electrical wire looped around his neck, hung from a large metal hook in the ceiling. Four inches, the distance between the discoloured toes and the dull grey carpet, separated life and death. Urine, concentrated brown, dripped from the extended toe and pooled under the naked corpse. Tear-sized blobs of black feces, expelled by the limp body, dotted the urine. Taffy and Phil vomited together and on each other as they clamoured to get away. Tyrion, anger overcoming revulsion, held the dead man's eyes.

Tyrion found Taffy and Phil outside in the parking lot dry heaving against the wall of the building.

Phil, between retches and wiping his mouth, said, "Jesus Christ. I can't believe it! Why, why the fuck would he do that?"

"It's fucking crazy," croaked Taffy through soft mucus dripping from his mouth and nose.

"What do we do now?"

"I'm not going back in there, Phil. No fucking way."

"Should we, you know, cut him down or something?" said Taffy.

Tyrion, with detached calmness, spoke softly, "We call the police."

"But, but, they will ask us questions," said Taffy. "Let's just leave and let someone else find him, and then we won't have to . . ."

"And when the police check Ham's phone and see that he sent all three of us a text asking us to come to his flat today, what are you going to tell them, eh?"

Phil, holding his throat and guts, figured he knew what Taffy was worried about.

"That means the police will find out about Krystyna and everything. Shit, me and Gillian are just starting to sort things out. If what we did with Krystyna becomes public, we're fucked all over again. There is no way Gillian will stay with me."

"We don't have to tell the police anything, Phil. Ham's wife, Rose, won't want any of what happened to be public either. All the police need to know is that he and Rose split up, he was depressed, and he topped himself. I'll talk with Rose and tell her she has to make something up about why they separated and to keep us out of it."

"But our wives will know that it's got to do with you-know-who."

"Then we had better make sure they keep their mouths shut. Besides, I don't think Joanne wants details of my sexual activities on the front pages of the newspapers. She couldn't stand the gossip. I think each of our wives and Ham's wife will prefer to keep things private."

"Poor Ham, what a way to go," said Phil.

"Yeah," said Tyrion still calm, "and when I find that bitch, Krystyna, she's gonna go the same way."

~

Eight days after Ham's death, and two days after a verdict of suicide, wet soil thumped down on Ham's casket in the grounds of the Parish Church of Saint Michael in Flixton, on the outskirts of Manchester. The service had been short and Rose, Ham's wife, had not arranged a post-funeral reception. Glum and dejected, Phil and Taffy had hastened to the Railway Tavern.

"Did you get any more questions from the police, Phil?" said Taffy as he slid into the booth beside Phil.

"No. They weren't very fussy really. Most questions were about how Ham got along with Rose and what I knew about any problems in their marriage. They called two days after we found Ham to clarify a detail, but I haven't heard from them since."

"What did you tell them?"

"Like we agreed, I said Ham was a pretty private person, which is true anyway, and all he ever said about his home life was that he and his wife got on each other's nerves a lot. What about you?

"Same as. The police didn't seem all that interested. They did ask about girlfriends."

Pensive, Phil fiddled with his beer glass.

"Not much is it, Taffy?"

"What isn't?"

"Life. I mean, Ham's dead, topped himself, and no one gives a fuck. His wife didn't shed a tear at the funeral, and his son looked fucking bored. Only two people came from his work."

Beer slurped into Phil's mouth for a few moments before he continued. "Just makes you think though, Taffy. What's it all for? How many will miss me when I'm gone? What have I achieved? I . . ."

"Yeah. I know what you mean. I doubt Angie will lose any sleep when I'm gone."

"More likely she'll celebrate, eh?"

"Fuck you!"

"Hey, Taffy, one thing I still don't get is why the bitch sent the first letter. I mean, why would she bother to write she was done with blackmailing us and then send the fucking photographs to our wives?"

"Me either. But I've been thinking about that."

"What about it?"

"Well, we only have Tyrion's word that the first letter arrived when it did."

"What do you mean?"

"Think about it, Phil. What if the letter from Krystyna about ending the blackmail actually arrived months ago or even a year ago?"

"Don't be stupid, Taffy. Then that would mean we have been paying her for no reason."

"No, not paying her. We give the money to Tyrion, and he goes to the drop to hand over the money to Krystyna or whomever. What if the letter is old? What if Tyrion has been keeping the money we give him, but finally decided to stop cheating us at the same time the bitch decides to send the photos and fuck all of us?"

Phil, puzzled, shook his head. "Na. Don't believe it. I mean Tyrion can be a prick, but not that."

"Well, it would explain why there was one letter saying it was all over and then the photographs arriving."

Tyrion, who had entered the pub unseen, greeted Phil and Taffy.

"Hey."

Both looked up, and Taffy spilled his beer.

"What's up?" said Tyrion lightly. "You look guilty. What are you up to?"

Stammering, Phil said, "Oh, hi, Steve, no, nothing. Just, er, wondering about the letter from Krystyna, the one about it all being over and then . . ."

Tyrion pulled a stool to the table and sat down.

"Me too, Phil; I've been thinking a lot about that lately. At first, I thought she was just mean as fuck and wanted to mess with us. You know, give us some hope and then crush us. Then I figured that maybe she had second thoughts, and just said fuck it and sent the photographs to sort of end it once and for all."

"Yeah, you're probably right."

"Perhaps, Phil, but there might be another explanation."

"Like what?" said Taffy.

"Look, we know she had help. The camera had to come from somewhere, and someone was with her on the hill and on the bus. I think the second person might have something to do with it."

"You mean like the other person decided to send us that shit after Krystyna sent the letter?"

"Well, it's a possibility. Do you have any other ideas?"

Guilty and together, both Phil and Taffy responded. "No."

Seven

The Vine Inn, an old-world, low-ceiling, multi-room pub with open-grate coal and wood fires, home cooked meals, and one regular beer, Samuel Smith's Old Brewery Bitter, had been Tyrion's favourite rendezvous pub for many years. Nestled away from prying eyes near the junction of Station Road and Barns Lane in Dunham Massey, Tyrion had begun the seduction of many women in one of the pub's quiet rooms. Over the years, other nearby pubs, the Rope & Anchor, the Swan with Two Nicks, and the Olde No 3, had also featured in Tyrion's merry-go-round of adulterous behaviour, but today, Tyrion waited for a man.

He checked his watch. Tyrion had met the man at the Vine several times. Tyrion scowled his annoyance. Half out of his seat by the window, intent on getting a second pint, Tyrion didn't notice his guest's entrance. As Tyrion straightened, a familiar voice accompanied an outstretched hand.

"Mr. Ennis," said the man as he clasped Tyrion's hand, "nice to see you again."

Tyrion accepted the hand, but responded with less enthusiasm. "For you, maybe, Stringer, but things didn't work out so well last time. Frankly, I'm not sure why I called you again."

Hands released, the men regarded each other as Stringer said, "I was a bit surprised, too. However, I'm sure that based on the information you gave me, no other private investigator would have found your missing person. To be frank back, Mr. Ennis, you weren't very, how shall I put it, polite last time I did some work for you."

"Yes, well, as I said on the phone, I'm sorry about that. I was under a lot of stress at the time, and I had expected better results for the money I paid you."

Stringer, tall and broad, shuffled his feet and took the initiative. "Let me buy you a pint, Mr. Ennis, and you can tell me what I can do for you now."

Tyrion nodded and sat down. When Stringer returned with two fresh pints, Tyrion got to the point. "It's the same woman. I still want you to find her."

Stringer, not a man who rushed things, bought time with a sip of beer before he pursed his lips, inclined his head slightly, and said, "OK, I would too, but like I said before, I need more information than a basic description, nationality, and her 'profession.' Have you been able to establish her DOB or find a driver's licence number or a bank account or . . ."

"No, no, nothing like that, but I do have some information."

Eager, Stringer leaned forward. "Let's have it then, Mr. Ennis."

After a quick conspiratorial glance left and right, Tyrion explained, "First, I have a photograph, or at least I know where one is, but I don't know how to get it. Second, I have the name of a person who knows her very well, and third, I have a postmark on an envelope."

"Well, Mr. Ennis," beamed Stringer, "that's more like it. Now, what do you mean you have a photo, but can't access it?"

"About three years ago, when we first met the woman in Prague, a friend of mine, Ham, took a picture of her on his cell phone."

"Why didn't you tell me that last time and give me the photo? It would have made a difference."

"Ham changed his phone a few months after the Prague visit, and I didn't remember about the photo until recently."

"Are you sure your friend still has the old phone? Most people trade them in, recycle them, or just toss them. Anyway, four years is not that long ago. Have your friend, Ham is it, send me a copy and . . ."

Tyrion squirmed in his seat.

"Ah, well, there is a problem. Ham is dead. He killed himself last week."

Stringer, a patient professional, kept his reaction to raised eyebrows. "I'm sorry to hear that. You have my condolences, Mr. Ennis. What about the phone?"

"I don't know exactly, but if it's around, I guess his wife has it."

"All right, it might be a bit delicate considering he only died a week ago, but surely you could just ask her for it."

"Er, not quite so simple. Did you read the story in the paper about the naked man who hanged himself in his apartment?"

"Yes, I remember. There was some speculation about the man's sexual interests if I recall correctly. I'm guessing the man was Ham?"

"Yes, that was him, and considering the reason for his death, the wife is not on speaking terms with me."

Stringer leaned back and rolled his shoulders. "So, you might have a photograph on a four-year-old phone that may or may not still exist and which is in the possession of a woman who won't speak to you. Well, that's not exactly 'having a photo,' Mr. Ennis."

"Jesus," said Tyrion, as he moved to the edge of his seat. "I expected a little more than sarcasm. You want everything on a plate, I . . ."

"Hold on a minute. I didn't say it was hopeless. Let me think on it a while. Now, you said you have the name of a person who knows your missing woman very well?"

"Yes. His name is Edvard."

"Edward what?"

"No, not Edward-*Edvard*. It's Czech or Polish or something."

"OK, Edvard what?"

"I don't know his surname."

Skeptical, Stringer took a drink. "What do you know about this Edvard then?"

"He lives, or at least did live, in Prague."

The pint glass, small in Stringer's large hand, settled on the wooden table. "I expect then," smiled Stringer knowingly, "Edvard was the girl's pimp?"

Red flush and tiny sweat beads spread up Tyrion's neck.

"All right, all right," flustered Tyrion as he scratched at his neck, "Edvard was her pimp. Krystyna is a prostitute. She mentioned his name when we, I, first met her in Prague."

A notepad, clean and neat, and a disposable pen appeared from Stringer's pocket. After some brief notation, Stringer asked, "You also mentioned 'postmarks' on an envelope. You have the envelope with you?"

Tyrion withdrew an envelope from an inside jacket pocket and handed it to Stringer. Stringer angled the section of the envelope with the postmark into the light.

"It's a little smudged, but it looks like Bo something and the number eighty-eight."

Stringer entered his password on his phone, pushed on an icon for GBSStap.c.uk, waited for it to load, then scrolled down to number eighty-eight.

"Number eighty-eight is the post office stamp code for Bodmin in Cornwall. Well, that's something concrete. Of course, it doesn't mean that the sender lives anywhere near the mailing location, still it's a place to begin."

Tyrion, eyes widened with hope, said, "So, you can find her then?"

"Maybe, maybe not. First, tell me about the money, Mr. Ennis?"

"What money?"

"I'm not a fool, Mr. Ennis. A prostitute, a pimp, postmarked letters, a suicide, one or more middle-aged men, and visits to Prague. How long has this Krystyna woman been blackmailing you?"

Tyrion paused, looked around. "Three years."

"That's a long time, and I assume, a lot of money."

"Yes, damn it. Oh, she was clever. Only asked for what we could afford. Not enough to break us or force us into something desperate. Just enough to bleed us slowly."

More notes flowed from the plastic pen on to the private investigator's notebook. "How do you send the money?"

"She calls me on a cell phone she sent and tells me where and when to drop the money."

"A drop. I assume you've tried to catch her or follow her or have someone take a photo?"

"Um, it's not that easy. The timing is a problem. She calls anytime after the fifteenth of the third month. The calls have been all over the map. I have to carry the money with me all the time 'cause she only gives me fifteen minutes' notice."

As Stringer wrote in his book, he asked another question. "Where does the drop take place?"

"Different places around Manchester city, but always the same routine. She, or someone, stands right between parked cars on a busy one-way street. I slow down, open the window, and hand over the envelope. There is no room to get out, and I can't stop or turn around."

"Ever tried getting a photograph?"

"Actually, I didn't think of it. Besides, she, or whoever it is, always wears a scarf over the face and a hat. I can't even be sure if it's a man or a woman."

"What about having someone in another car who gets out near the one-way street and waits to see the drop, then follows the person. Have you tried that?"

"Even if I did, what the hell would I do? There are two of them and . . ."

"Excuse me, Mr. Ennis, two of them? That's the first time you've mentioned a second person. Who are you talking about?"

"Oh, I don't know who it is. I think it's another woman. The day Krystyna esc— I mean left, I saw her with another person, so I assume they are in it together. So, even if we managed to follow or catch the person who gets the money, and it might not even be one of them, the other could send the stuff. Anyway, the person in the street could be some tosser they offered a tenner to stand on the road and accept a package."

There was a long pause while Stringer made more notes. Then he said, "How many of you?"

"How many what?'

"Being blackmailed."

"Four."

"Why now, Mr. Ennis? Why are you, as you say, doing something desperate to find her?"

"Because the bitch sent the photographs to our wives."

"What? Did you stop paying?"

"No. It's fucking crazy. One day, I get a letter from her saying it's all over and to stop paying and that the evidence will be destroyed. Then she sends the photos and everything to our wives. I don't get it. She's an evil, sadistic bitch."

Stringer eyed Tyrion. "Perhaps, but it confirms to me that, as you say, there is a second person involved."

"Well, I thought that also. Look, I don't want to go into details. Let's just say that she had compromising details of our meetings, and she held us to ransom for three goddamn years, then she shit all over us for no reason."

"I assume your friend Ham's death is connected to his wife receiving the details?"

"Yes. His wife. Well, let's just say his wife ended it and Ham topped himself a few days later."

"Are the police aware of the blackmail?"

"Christ, no, I don't want them involved and neither do our wives. No publicity or anything. It's got to be kept quiet."

"And what about your wife and the other two? What's happening?"

"Joanne, my wife, has been very efficient in arranging our separation and forthcoming divorce. Given the evidence she has, I don't have a leg to stand on, and I won't be contesting it."

"And the others?"

"Don't know yet. It's still up in the air for them. Anyway, what does it matter? I want the bitch found. Can you do that?"

"If I find her," said Stringer, "what are your intentions, Mr. Ennis?"

"I'm not entirely sure. I haven't worked it through yet, but I want her to pay for what she has done. She practically murdered Ham."

"I won't undertake anything illegal or be a party to any crime. Do you understand?"

"Yes, of course. I don't want any trouble. I just want to know what happened to her and where she is."

"How serious are you, Mr. Ennis, about finding this woman?"

"Look, Stringer, she's bled me dry for three years, ruined my marriage, and killed my friend. How bloody serious do you think I am?"

"All right, how much are you willing to pay?"

"I'm not stupid. How much will it cost?"

"I still need to get a photograph of the woman and some details about her birth and citizenship. Based on what you have told me, there are only two ways to get that information. Either the phone from your friend's wife, assuming it still exists and I can get a hold of it and extract the files, or I need to find and speak to this Edvard person in Prague, assuming he still exists. In fact, I probably need both to have a good chance of finding her. In terms of cost, the first thing will be a trip to Prague. While I am there, you can try to figure out a way to get the phone."

"You want me to pay for a trip to Prague!"

"Do you see any other way? Like I asked, how badly do you want this woman?"

His glass empty, Tyrion fidgeted before answering. "OK, I want her, but I'm not made of money."

"Understood. How about I give you an estimate of costs to visit Prague? If you agree, I will go and try to find Edvard. If I find him, and if he wants to help, we can take it from there. How does that sound?"

Tyrion, unaware of the chain of events he would set in motion, nodded.

Eight

Customers at the café had been plentiful in the early morning hours, but by 9:30 a.m., business had slowed and Krystyna and Anna had left the running of the café to their part-time waitress, Jill, and their husbands. After a short drive to Krystyna's house to collect their children, George and Robert, from Phyllis, Krystyna's mother-in-law who watched the children in the mornings, the sisters and their offspring headed for Torwood Gardens.

Having turned one, both children had inherited their father's blue eyes and coarse brown hair. From their mothers, high Slavic cheekbones and thin noses set the boys apart from local children. Content children, loving husbands, a supportive mother-in-law, and a welcoming community rounded out Krystyna and Anna's new lives. Torwood Gardens had become symbolic of their domestic bliss. The gardens, a short walk from Krystyna's house on Braddons Hill Road, had become a favourite place for the sisters to take their children for fresh air and sunshine. Mature trees, well-maintained flower beds, clean benches, and lots of grass with no 'keep off' signs soothed and relaxed both parents and children.

Entering the gardens from a narrow passage between two houses on Torwood Road, Anna slowed and turned her head skyward to feel the sun's heat. Content, Anna sighed and called to Krystyna, "My God, Krystyna, what a beautiful day. I can't believe we are here and what we have."

Warm air, softly swirled by a light breeze, rustled the leaves on the trees and released petals from flowers. Krystyna gulped the air, unfurled her long hair, and squeezed Anna's hand.

"Me too, Anna. Every day I am thankful for our new lives, our children, and our husbands."

"We would have nothing without you, Krystyna. We would still be in Prague with Edvard spreading our legs for . . ."

"Hush, Anna, that's all over. We will never have to live that life again."

Not far from the entrance to the gardens, Krystyna stopped at a bench speckled with shade by a tall oak tree.

"Let's sit here. Do you have the tea, Anna?"

"Yes. And cake."

Krystyna, her voice tightened by concern, whispered to Anna, "But nothing else, Anna?"

"No, nothing else, Krystyna. I haven't touched any for weeks."

Silent, eyes narrowed in exaggeration, Krystyna waited.

"Honest!" said Anna, crossing her heart like she did when they were kids.

Anna poured tea, already milked and sweetened, from a thermos and handed a cup to Krystyna.

"Pass me the paper too, Anna."

From under the stroller, Anna withdrew a fresh unread copy of *The Sun*, one of England's national tabloid newspapers.

"I don't know why you read this paper, Anna. It's all gossip and trash."

"Yes, but it helps with my English. Anyway, that's what people read, and it's good for me to keep up with the TV soaps that everyone watches. Anyway, don't mess it up. I haven't read it yet."

Away to the left of the bench, several kids, about five years old, chased and kicked an oversized football, their shouts and squeals adding to the idyllic scene. While Krystyna turned pages and snorted at the outlandish and innuendo-laden headlines that typified *The Sun's* journalistic style, Anna absently stared at two sleeping babies. A snap of paper and a sharp gasp from Krystyna jolted Anna from her absence.

"What? What is it, Krystyna?"

"Oh no, it can't be."

Anna, eyes widened by anxiety, faced Krystyna.

"My God, Anna, it is him. One of the men. It's the one called Ham, Graham Williams."

"In the paper," asked Anna. "What's he done?"

"He's dead, Anna. He killed himself."

"What?"

"Yes, Anna, listen. 'Naked Man Hung Self By Electrical Cord - Kinky Sex Suspected.'"

Together, Anna and Krystyna read the article. Done reading, Anna said quietly, "Wasn't he the one that strapped on the . . .?"

"Yes, yes, I don't want to think about it."

"I'm sorry, Krystyna. Anyway, he was horrible and deserved to die."

Krystyna nodded and placed the newspaper on her lap. Across the park, the children had stopped chasing the ball and sat in a group eating. Pensive, Krystyna said to no one, "I wonder why he did it."

"What?" said Anna.

"I wonder why he killed himself."

"Hmm, maybe because of what he was really like inside. You know. The stuff he liked. Maybe his wife found out."

"It's a strange coincidence, though, Anna. You know that I delivered the letter to Tyrion's office last week, telling them that it was all over, and we would destroy the photographs and files."

Anna stood, fussed with the light cotton blanket in the stroller and said quickly, "Yes, yes, I remember. We should go now or we might be late for the lunchtime rush at the café."

Krystyna remained seated and fixed on the question. "Then why would he kill himself now?"

Anna rubbed her palms, looked away, and leaned into the stroller to check on her son, Robert. Anna lingered over Robert and breathed in his scent. Back in Prague, between the demands of Edvard and clients, Anna had dreamed of motherhood and wept that it would never happen. Robert gurgled and grasped for Anna's finger as she withdrew from the stroller. When she straightened up, Krystyna eyed her anxiously.

"I, I don't know Krystyna. It must have been for another reason. Nothing to do with those photographs."

Krystyna, tense, leaned into Anna. "Anna. You destroyed the photographs and files like I told you to?"

Anna, tears welling, gripped the handle of the stroller.

"Anna, what did you do?"

"I, I, I'm sorry, Krystyna."

"No, Anna, please tell me you didn't."

A sob burst from Anna.

"I didn't mean to, but when I opened the file and saw the photographs again, I got so angry for the way they treated you. The way men have always treated you and me. I tried to do what you said, but the more I looked at them, the more I hated them, and the more I wanted to punish them."

Krystyna, her eyes soft and understanding, stared at Anna.

"Please, Krystyna, please, don't look at me like that. The men are animals; they deserve to pay, to die. Oh, oh, I'm sorry, I'm sorry."

Anna fell into Krystyna's open arms. With her head pressed against Krystyna's chest, Anna could not see her sister's taut, worried face.

Through sniffles, Anna sought assurance. "What does it matter anyway? We don't have the files anymore, so there's no need for them to find us. It's over and we are safe. Right?"

"I don't know, Anna. I don't know," said Krystyna as she stroked Anna's hair.

"Anna," continued Krystyna, "where did you mail the packages from, and how did you pay?"

"Oh, don't worry," cried Anna with confidence. "I took the bus to Bodmin. It's miles from here. I brought tons of stamps and put them in a mailbox in the town centre."

Krystyna, who had protected Anna from others and herself since she was little, hugged her sister close and allowed Anna her naivety.

Nine

Intense pain, low, left of his spine, directly on his kidney, cut short his open leer at the thin blond-haired woman and her oversized pink lips that pouted with promise. A second blow, low and right, hit his second kidney as the woman's lips briefly pulled back over crooked teeth before closing tight as she turned and disappeared into the bustling crowd of Wensceslas Square.

His shoulder sockets ground as strong hands wrenched and twisted his arms backward and up over his aching kidneys. Unable to resist, men pushed him down an alleyway and slammed his face and body against a rough brick wall. Quick, experienced hands searched his body, emptied his pockets, and spun him around to blink into the harsh beam of a flashlight. From behind the light, words, accented and rough, got to the point.

"You look for Edvard. Why?"

"I want his help to find a woman."

"Plenty of women in square. You don't need Edvard to find a woman."

"No, not that kind of woman. I am looking for a particular . . ."

"All kinds of women in square."

"Look, I don't want a prostitute. I'm looking for information about Krystyna."

The men's grip tightened. Unintelligible words bounced between the men until one addressed their captive. "You have make mistake to ask for her. Now you will come with us."

His arms still held and pinned up his back, his captors forced the man to walk as he protested, "No. No, I'm not going anywhere. Look, I just wanted some information."

Afraid of what might happen, the man struggled and began to shout for help.

The men stopped. A gun appeared, its cold barrel pressed against the bound man's nostril. A man spoke slowly. "You will walk now, or never walk again."

Flanked front, back, and side, Stringer, a private investigator from Manchester, walked.

Unsteady on the slippery cobbles, the ache in his back that had pushed bile to his throat, and a constant twist of his head in search of an escape or assistance, Stringer kept reluctant step with his captors. After a few minutes, the alleyway narrowed, and the men stopped at a scratched and dented metal door recessed in a brownstone archway. One of the men withdrew a cell phone, pressed a button, waited. After speaking a single word, the man held the phone to conduct a three-sixty pan of the alleyway, Stringer, and the other three men. Done, the phone beeped off, and the metal door opened.

Pushed, Stringer entered a dimly lighted hallway and followed the back of a man with the telltale straps of a shoulder holster cinched across his back. Down stone steps and through two more steel doors, each guarded by another holstered man, Stringer entered a large, low-ceilinged, windowless room.

Inside, the air, hot and humid, smelled of onions and meat. Seated behind a solid wooden table, a man, his face twisted and crooked, pushed a food-laden spoon into a partially open and toothless mouth. Juice or sauce leaked from the mouth and dripped onto an already stained, off-white paper napkin.

The spoon, animated by the seated man's hand, gestured for Stringer to sit in a wooden chair in front of the table. Stringer sat and spoke. "I'm just looking for . . ."

A fist, tight and hard, jabbed Stringer's right jaw and ended his speech. The man behind the table, an ugly scar connecting his chin to his left ear, used the spoon to stem the actions of his henchman. Stringer waited as the man slurped and spilled several more spoonfuls of food before he wiped his mouth, belched, and leaned forward to expel gas. Done eating, the man sort of smiled as he spoke. "You search for Edvard. Why?"

Moving his tongue to clear the blood in his mouth, Stringer answered. "My name is Stringer. I am a private investigator. I have been hired to find a woman named Krystyna who used to work as a prostitute here in Prague. I was told that Edvard used to be her, her, er manager."

"Who told you these things?"

"My client."

Another jab, to the same jaw, and Stringer got the message.

"A Mr. Ennis. He lives in Manchester, England. A woman called Krystyna blackmailed him and some other men. He hired me to find her, but he has no picture or details except that she used to work in Prague for a man called Edvard. I came here to ask Edvard for help."

The interrogator stood, placed his hands on the table, and leaned toward Stringer. "If Edvard was here, what kind of help would you ask for?"

Not wanting to offend, Stringer swallowed hard to suppress a gasp brought on by the stench of the man's breath before he responded. "A photograph, date of birth, any kind of official documents that I could use to help find her."

"Why should this Edvard help you?"

Pensive, uncertain about the situation, Stringer said hesitantly, "For money."

"How much?"

"I don't know. I would have to ask my client, I mean Mr. Ennis, how much he could pay. But I don't think he has much left after three years of paying blackmail."

"The blackmail," said Edvard, "it still goes on, yes?"

"No. She, Krystyna, sent the pictures to the wives of the men and now Mr. Ennis wants to find her."

Edvard lifted his hands from the table and pushed something into his mouth. The jaws closed slowly, then opened quickly. Food flew out of his mouth and across the table, small bits landing at Stringer's feet.

"So," cried Edvard, "the bitch lives. For three years, I search for her. Her and her little bitch sister, Anna."

Edvard walked around the table and leaned his head close to Stringer. "This," said Edvard pointing to his face, "is what Anna, the sister of that bitch Krystyna, left me with the day she disappeared from Prague."

"Her sister did that?" asked Stringer with surprise.

"No, you idiot. A man she was fucking for money in the square caught me unaware and broke my jaw in eight places. It did not heal, and it became infected. I lost my teeth, and, as you can see, my mouth does not open far."

"You are Edvard?"

Ignoring Stringer's assertion of the obvious, Edvard continued. "Does the whore sister, Anna, live too?"

"I'm not sure, but I think so."

Edvard gestured to a man out of Stringer's sight.

"Bring us vodka. Me and this private investigator have much to talk about."

Three shots of vodka and twenty minutes later, Stringer had told all he knew, and Edvard returned to his seat behind the table. He signalled and spoke to the men in what Stringer assumed was Czech, and they returned Stringer the contents of his pockets. Edvard waited while Stringer reloaded his pockets. When he was done, Edvard said, "You will return to Manchester. You have a card?"

Stringer handed a business card over, and Edvard studied it for a moment. "I will contact you when I have some information."

"What about money? I'm not sure that Mr. Ennis can, you know, pay very much. I should really call him before we reach any agreement."

Malice and hatred, made worse by his injury and scar, filled Edvard's face. With a half-smile, Edvard provided a not so cryptic answer. "We have an agreement. I do not want money. Finding Krystyna will be payment enough."

Ten

Tyrion arrived at the Bird I'th Hand pub at 2:30 on a bright afternoon. Eager for news, Tyrion was a half-hour early for his appointment with Stringer. Tyrion knew the pub well. The large, red-brick Victorian-era building on the corner of Flixton Road and Brooke Road had been one of his watering holes for more than twenty-five years. Tyrion thought the recent refurbishment in late 2015 had removed some of the pub's warmth. Tyrion, Phil, Taffy, and Ham had continued to keep the pub on their Saturday night drinking route.

With a pint of Theakston's keg beer, Tyrion fixed his eyes on the pub entrance and waited. When Stringer had called late the previous night, the investigator had been tight-lipped about what he had learned in Prague preferring, as he had said, to "explain in person." Perturbed by Stringer's secrecy, Tyrion gulped beer. At 2:55 p.m., Stringer, stiff-legged, entered the pub and made straight for Tyrion's table. For a greeting, Stringer pointed to Tyrion's three-quarter-empty glass.

"Need a refill?"

"Yes. Theakston's."

Kneading his lower back with the knuckles of his right hand, Stringer leaned on the bar and ordered two pints of Theakston's bitter. Transaction complete, Stringer joined Tyrion at his table. Tyrion, impatient, made to speak, but Stringer held his left hand up while his right lifted his glass to his lips. Several gulps and half the pint consumed, Stringer placed the glass on the table and exclaimed, "Christ, I needed that."

Tyrion, fingers tapping his glass, nodded at Stringer and said, "What happened to your face?"

"I'll tell you what happened, Mr. Ennis. I found your Edvard character, that's what happened. Or I should say, he found me."

"He did that?"

"Actually, no. Edvard munched on a late supper while one of his thugs punched my head to keep me focused on the question at hand."

Concerned, Tyrion leaned forward and put his pint down.

"Jesus, I'm sorry. What happened?"

More beer passed Stringer's lips before he replied.

"I was asking around in Wensceslas Square for Edvard when I got punched in the kidneys, slammed against a wall, frog marched down a dingy alleyway, and forced into a basement where men with guns plopped me down in front of a disfigured man eating meat and onions."

"Bloody hell."

"Exactly, Mr. Ennis. I thought I was going to die."

Tyrion sat back and drank, as did Stringer.

After a polite amount of time, Tyrion got back on track.

"Well, you're back and alive. Did you get what we need?"

"Yes and no, and possibly much more than we wanted."

"What the fuck does that mean?"

Stringer finished his pint, wiggled the empty glass, and pushed his chair back from the table to stand. As he stood, Stringer smiled at Tyrion and said, "I need another if you don't mind, eh?"

"Stop fucking me around. I'm not paying you to drink beer."

"And you're not paying me enough to get beaten up and almost killed by some lunatic in Prague. So, let me get a goddamn pint if you want the rest of it."

Not waiting for Tyrion's permission, Stringer walked slowly to the bar. When he returned, he had two beers and placed one in front of Tyrion, who snorted a grudging acceptance of the peace offering. Seated, Stringer picked up where he had left off.

"What I mean is that Edvard, who I must say is a very bad piece of work, told me he will get what we need and contact me when he has it."

"That's good then," said Tyrion with enthusiasm. "How long will it take him?"

"He didn't say how long, but more importantly, I'm not so sure involving Edvard is a good idea."

"Why? What can a lousy pimp in Prague do?"

"I don't know, but I suspect, from what he told me, that finding Krystyna is personal. Incidentally, she has a younger sister called Anna whom Edvard believes is with Krystyna. That would perhaps explain why you think Krystyna had help and might explain the two letters."

Widened eyes and raised eyebrows conveyed Tyrion's agreement with Stringer's assessment, but Tyrion wanted to know more. "What do you mean personal? Does he want the bitch back in Prague to work for him?"

"I don't think so. Did I mention that Edvard is disfigured? His face is a mess. His jaw is off to one side, he can't open his mouth properly, and he has no teeth. Ugly as sin he is. Anyhow, he said that Krystyna, or someone she paid I think, did it to him. I think Edvard wants revenge."

Tyrion hid his own thoughts and expression behind his glass as Stringer continued. "Anyway, maybe we don't need Edvard. What about the phone from Ham's wife?"

Tyrion scowled. "Not a chance in hell. She said everything Ham owned has gone to the dump. And on top of that, she said that now she knows I'm looking for his phone, she will smash it to pieces if she finds it."

"I take it she doesn't like you," smirked Stringer.

"Hmm. She blames me for everything. Anyway, no phone, so I guess we're stuck with Edvard for better or worse."

"I suspect worse. And remember, I won't be a party to anything illegal."

A large group, five men and six women, entered the pub noisily. Dressed in "work casual" clothes, they made for the bar and ordered a round of half pints and shots. With drinks in hand, the group of co-workers moved to the far side of the pub and set the glasses in a line in front of each person. Tyrion, having participated in his fair share of drinking competitions, shook his head and addressed Stringer.

"What do we do now?"

"Well, the only lead we have so far is the postmark on the envelope. As you saw, the stamp was a little smudged, but it looks like the letter was posted in Bodmin. Do you know it?"

"As a matter of fact, I do. It's a small town in Wales near the west coast. I used to drive through it on the way to Newquay with the wife and kids."

"Yes, I think I may have driven through it as well. Can't recall it, though."

"Neither could I, so I looked it up on Wikipedia," said Tyrion waving his phone at Stringer. "Population about fourteen thousand. Not known for much except churches, a castle, and a moor. Can't see a whore from Prague fitting in there."

"I'm sure there is a market for her services everywhere, but I would have thought she would want to keep a low profile and stay away from that business. Especially with the money she got from you. No need to work really."

"Don't remind me," said Tyrion.

His glass empty again, Stringer placed it on the table, but made no pronouncement about wanting another. Instead, Stringer jutted his chin out and challenged Tyrion.

"Today is Friday. What plans do you have for the weekend?"

"Nothing I can't change. Why?"

"I suggest we take a trip to Bodmin. It's about what, a five or six-hour drive? If we leave first thing Saturday morning, we can spend the afternoon, evening, and most of Sunday asking around. You never know, you might sight her."

"You mean just show up and look around? She could be anywhere in the town."

"Yes and no. I mean, she's young, single, has money, and not exactly a nun. We have a name, a general description, and you would recognize her. In addition, we know she has a sister called Anna. People, bars, pubs, clubs, they might remember sisters, especially attractive ones with accents."

Tyrion pursed his lips and narrowed his eyes at Stringer.

"I know it's a long shot, and it's your call," said Stringer in response to Tyrion's skepticism. "We can wait for Edvard, or we can take a chance."

"I suppose you will travel at my expense?"

"Yes, at least for the hotel room and meal allowance, but I'll buy my own booze."

"That's big of you."

"Well, Mr. Ennis, do we wait on Edvard or get on with it?"

A decision-maker and risk-taker by nature, Tyrion responded quickly. "We'll take my car. No need for me to pay your mileage and gas. I'll pick you up at 6 a.m."

Eleven

After Krystyna's escape, Edvard had taken all forms of official identification from the twenty or so prostitutes for whom he euphemistically provided "protection services." What he hadn't done until after Anna's departure was take photocopies of the documents and keep them in a safe rather than a locked cupboard. If he had done so, Edvard and his two henchmen, Petr and Boris, would not be using time and money to travel to Usti nad Labem in search of photographs of Krystyna and Anna.

Edvard had visited Usti nad Labem once before. It wasn't a pleasant memory. Ten years earlier, as a young punk, Edvard had visited Usti nad Labem's active river port. The port, situated on the Elbe River, facilitated trade among the Czech Republic, Germany, the Benelux countries, and Northern France. The river also brought drugs. Edvard, after trying his hand at extortion, theft, and fraud, trawled the port area for a drug dealer to supply his intended drug business in Prague. Instead of encountering a drug dealer, Edvard received a severe beating and a message that port drug trade was a closed business with no room, no need, and no interest in a scrawny, inexperienced kid from Prague.

Five kilometres out from Usti nad Labem on Route 261, Edvard's driver, Petr, asked for a destination.

"Where to?"

The only reference Edvard had for the home of Krystyna was when she had mentioned her memories of the wall on Maticni Street. He had heard of the wall, most Czechs had, but it meant nothing to him now except a starting point.

"Maticni Street."

Beside the driver, Boris, Edvard's blunt instrument, stabbed the street name into the Sat Nav with calloused fingers. Twenty-five minutes later, Edvard's black Mercedes diesel stopped, engine running, at the junction of Maticni and Pristavni.

Houses, dilapidated and abandoned, lined Maticni, while Pristavni still held on to life with a sprinkle of inhabited homes and a few businesses. On the corner of Maticni and Pristavni, a Portraviny convenience store clung to life. Getting out of the car, Edvard told Petr: "Wait here. I'm going in the store. Boris, come with me."

Five minutes later, Edvard, followed by Boris, who rubbed the knuckles on his right hand, exited the store and climbed in the car. Seated, Boris entered a new street address into the sat Nav. Six hours, four stops, and more bruises to Boris' knuckles provided the last destination Edvard needed.

More directions than an actual address, the black Mercedes bumped along a narrow dirt track that ended at the bank of a small stream. Set back, off the track and in the woods, a small rustic cabin leaned to the left. Weak, white smoke leaked from a metal chimney. Secured by frayed rope, the ubiquitous, scrawny dog of isolated rural life barked at the unwelcome visitors.

As Edvard and Boris approached the door, a window creaked open, and the double barrel of a shotgun poked out. A voice, raspy yet strong, called out: "Stop there. What do you want?"

At the challenge, Boris drifted to the right away from Edvard. Petr, Edvard's driver, who had remained in the car, silently opened his door and crept out.

Edvard, biding time, called back, "Only information. We mean no harm."

"What information? We know nothing. Leave."

Aware that Petr and Boris would act, Edvard played for time. "I'm looking for someone."

"There is only me here," replied the voice behind the shotgun, "and no one needs to look for me."

Edvard, straining his peripheral vision, could see that Boris stood next to the cabin within five feet of the protruding gun barrel, and Petr had almost worked his way around to the rear of the building.

"I can pay for the information."

Silence hung for a moment. The barrel receded a little, then returned. "How much?"

"That depends on what you can tell me. Why don't I come in, and we can talk?"

"No," shouted the man, "stay where you are, and tell me what you want."

Boris nodded to Edvard that he was ready, and Edvard assumed Petr would be in place.

"I am looking for Krystyna and Anna."

The strong voice broke a little as the man replied, "They are not here. They left many years ago, and we have not heard from them. Why do you want them?"

"I know they are not here. They are in England."

"England!" exclaimed the unseen man. "Then why are you here?"

"I told you, I am looking for them and I need something from you to help me find them."

"What? Why? What you want with my daughters?"

Edvard pushed a smile across his distorted face and spoke calmly. "Because I'm going to kill your little bitches. But first, I will fuck them, beat them, and make them suffer."

As the gun extended through the window to take a shot, Boris covered the five feet, grasped the barrel, and yanked the gun through the window. Then Boris stepped away from the cabin, levelled the gun at the cabin door, and pulled the trigger. The door splintered and fell inward.

A man, thin and wiry, filled the doorway. His hand grasped a long, serrated knife. Boris tossed the shotgun aside and withdrew a gun from his shoulder holster. From the rear of the cabin, a woman screamed.

In response to the scream, Edvard called out: "Petr, you have the woman?"

"Yes."

"Now," said Edvard to the man, "put the knife down and come outside."

The dog, aware of the danger to its owner, barked and strained at the rope around its neck.

"Petr," called Edvard, "bring the woman here. Boris, shut that dog up."

Forced to their knees beside their blood-soaked dog, Krystyna's parents, beaten down by years of discrimination and poverty, awaited their fate as Edvard entered the cabin. Within a minute, Edvard reappeared. A photograph, 4 x 8, worn at the edges, hung between thumb and forefinger. He waved the picture in front of the kneeling man and woman who had instinctively linked arms.

"You see," said Edvard waving the photo in front of his captives, "that was easy. I see the photo was taken in Prague in Wenscelas Square. I recognize the statue of the king in the background."

Despite his situation, Krystyna's father raised his head defiantly at Edvard and spat harsh words. "Why do you want them? What have they done that brings an ugly man and his dogs from Prague?"

The insult earned a kick to the head from Boris, who stood over the man eager to dispense more pain. Blood leaked from the man's mouth as his wife held him up.

"Your daughters," said Edvard, "the offspring of filthy Roma, the whores of Prague, have become very bad girls indeed. Many men search for them, and when they are found, they will suffer."

Recovered enough to speak, the man defended his children.

"They have done nothing except survive. You, people like you, are responsible for what they might have become and what they had to do. You are pigs, animals."

Boris, anger mounting, gestured to Edvard with his gun and pointed it at Krystyna's parents.

"No, Boris," barked Edvard, his hand grasping Boris' arm. "Too many people know we have searched for them. Even Roma deaths will be investigated. Give them money. We will tell people they sold their own daughters. They will believe this of Roma. Besides, it will be more painful for them to know what is to come for their daughters than ending it now."

Boris inverted his gun, and after using the butt to hit the man unconscious, tossed a wad of bank notes over the man and woman.

Coughing in the diesel exhaust of the departing Mercedes, the woman watched her tears drip onto the limp body of the man she had loved and stood with for over thirty years.

Twelve

As promised, Tyrion collected Stringer at 6:00 a.m. Twenty minutes later, after a fifteen-minute drive on the A5103 and a short hop on the M6, Tyrion joined the M5 motorway for the 234-mile drive south-west to Devon. Stringer fell asleep five minutes onto the M5. He didn't wake until Tyrion slowed to take Exit 31 off the M5 to the A30. Through a yawn, Stringer asked Tyrion where they were.

"Just got on the A30. It's about an hour from here. Should be in Bodmin by noon unless you need to piss?"

"No, thanks, Mr. Ennis," said Stringer as he pushed his feet hard against the car under the dashboard to stretch out his legs.

"Now that you've had your beauty sleep," chided Tyrion, "what exactly will we do when we get there?"

"First," said Stringer with a grin, "we check into a hotel."

"I've already done that. I booked online last night. We're staying at the Westberry Hotel. It's in the centre of town."

"Right, good job, Mr. Ennis. That will save some time."

Tyrion, business-like and serious, glanced at Stringer and told him what else he had done. "I also checked the tourism and visitors' websites. There is not much to talk about in Bodmin, unless you like museums, trains, an old courtroom, and jails."

Stringer, sleep rubbed away from his face with the palms of his hands, smiled mischievously. "As a matter of fact, Mr. Ennis, museums are my favourite, and trains are the best. Steam train, I expect."

An indignant expression lit Tyrion's face as words formed. Before he could speak, Stringer smiled wide and said: "I'm kidding. Besides, I doubt a woman from Prague with limited English will have found a job explaining the intricacies of English and Welsh history. What we need are pubs, restaurants, cafés, maybe hair salons, small stores. Places people can work for cash and under the table."

"Well," said Tyrion placated by Stringer's assurance, "there aren't many pubs, but there are plenty of small cafés and tea rooms. Also a couple of Indian restaurants, a Chinese place, and a wine bar."

"You have been busy, Mr. Ennis. I'm impressed."

A curt nod and an accusing eye fixed Stringer.

"No point showing up without some information and a plan is there, eh?"

Stringer pulled a two-page document from his pocket and waved it in front of Tyrion.

"What's that?"

"This," said Stringer, "is a list of all the potential places that might provide work on a no-questions-asked cash basis. All the pubs, cafés, restaurants, bed and breakfasts, hotels, etc. Also, I have arranged them on a map in the most effective way to visit each one on foot. What's more, the list is organized into mornings, lunchtime, afternoons, and evenings."

A harrumph leaked from Tyrion before he said, "Oh. Why mornings, lunchtime, afternoons, and evenings?"

"Not much point going to a pub at 8 a.m. or a tea shop at 10 p.m. is there?"

"Ah, I see. I guess you've been busy too."

Steady traffic slowed their pace, and it was 12:30 before Tyrion slid his SUV into the parking lot at the rear of the Westberry Hotel in what passed for "downtown" Bodmin.

~

After an efficient check-in at the hotel, Tyrion met Stringer in the hotel reception area. Ready to begin, Tyrion quizzed Stringer. "OK, where to first?"

"It's time for lunch," said Stringer, "so we will start with the small cafés and tea shops. Weavers, The Green Frog, Folly Tea Room, and Waffles Coffee Shop are all grouped together, so we will try them first. Then we will try a place called Bosvena. It sounds Eastern European, so you never know."

As they left the hotel and began the short walk to their first tea shop, Tyrion had another question. "What do we do exactly? We can't just walk in and ask if they know or have seen a tall, blond, blackmailing whore from Prague."

Laughing at Tyrion's description, Stringer answered: "Of course not. First, we order tea, coffee, or whatever, we sit, read the paper, and we watch. We look at notices on bulletin boards for anyone either offering to work, or anyone seeking work, for unskilled jobs like cleaning, child minding, or gardening, or the like. We take note of the details for later. We also listen to the conversations around us. Gossip is what we want. Talk about two women who arrived in town and whatever. While we are watching and listening, I will decide which employee to approach and what to say."

"How will you ask?'

"Depends on the situation and the opportunity. Might be something in the place that looks or sounds European like a photo, an ornament, a menu item, an accent, background music, the way someone is dressed. Anything that would allow me to segue into a comment and a conversation about Europeans, immigrants, workers, jobs, terrorism, whatever. From there, I simply note that there aren't many in Bodmin. That is usually enough to loosen tongues either for or against foreigners, and from there, it leads to who is who in town. Especially in a small town like this."

"It's really that easy?"

"No," said Stringer sounding disgruntled, "it's not easy at all, Mr. Ennis. The trick is to ask without the person realizing they have been asked. The person needs to offer the information during a conversation and not in response to a direct question. We don't want the town talking about two men asking questions about foreigners."

"Sneaky bastard, aren't you?"

"A professional, Mr. Ennis. That's what I am."

"How," said Tyrion impressed by Stringer's plan, "did you become an investigator in the first place?"

Reluctant to share the real reasons with Tyrion, or any client for that matter, Stringer explained the process that all investigators followed.

"First, I passed the 'fit and proper person test' with the Association of British Investigators Training Academy. After that, I obtained the IQ Level 3 Award for Professional Investigators and then there were several other professional courses until I got my Security Industry Private Investigators Licence."

"That's not what I meant."

Stringer ignored Tyrion's dissatisfaction and said, "Let's get started, shall we?"

~

By 4:30 p.m., Tyrion had had enough.

"My God, Stringer, it's like being in a nightmare. How do people stand it? How many tea and coffee places have we been in? All this walking, sitting, and pissing out tea and coffee for nothing."

"Not as many as you think. And not for nothing. In fact, only eight. But the good news is, there is only one left. It's called Potts. And, based on what we have learned so far, there are very few foreigners in Bodmin, which is good news."

"Good news how?"

"If Krystyna and her sister Anna are here, or hereabouts, they will have been noticed. We just need to try another demographic."

"Demographic?"

"Yes. That was round one. After Potts, we can call it a day for the tea and crumpet crowd. I don't know about you, but I need a nap."

"A nap," cried Tyrion. "I'm not paying you to take a fucking nap, for God's sake."

Stringer stopped dead in the street and rounded on his employer. "Listen, Mr. Ennis. You may be able to go all day and all night, but I need a rest to keep my wits about me. It's already been a long day, and we have a lot more ground to cover."

Tyrion made to interrupt, but Stringer cut him off.

"After my, our nap, we have a long night ahead. We have to trawl the beer and pie crowd. We will begin with the Blisland Inn and the Lanivet Inn. They are both pubs a little out of town, and we will drive to them. When we get back, we can walk to the Masons Arms, Chapel-an-Gansblydhen, and the Hole in the Wall. If we have any energy left and it's not too late, we can try a couple of hotel bars. Same drill as before, but try not to get too pissed."

~

Although Tyrion didn't tell Stringer, he too had a short nap and felt much fresher for it. Stringer was waiting for him in the reception area at 5 p.m., and by 5:20, after the short drive to the Blisland Inn, Tyrion relished his first pint of the evening.

Despite Stringer's instruction not to get too pissed, habit got the better of Tyrion. By 10:30 p.m., after downing multiple beers in each of the first four pubs Tyrion was well on his way to the sweet spot of drunkenness. Tired, happy, and momentarily relaxed about why they were in Bodmin, Tyrion hummed as he and Stringer walked to their last stop for the night—The Hole in Wall pub.

In the pub, Stringer summarized their evening. "Well, Mr. Ennis. I confess that we achieved little this afternoon and even less tonight."

"Ah well," replied Tyrion, his slur progressively thickening, "at least we discovered some fine beers and excellent whiskey."

Reaching an arm around Stringer's shoulder, Tyrion leaned in and said, "Why don't you stop working now and have a proper drink with me? You've been on tomato juice and pop all night. Come on, relax a bit. I don't like drinking alone."

Stringer, the day's work weighing on him, offered only a token protest before he doubled up on the next round of drinks. Despite his earlier consumption, Tyrion, happy to have a drinking partner, kept pace with Stringer. Unfortunately, for Tyrion, Stringer was never really off the job. After plying Tyrion with several more whiskeys, Stringer employed his trade-craft to elicit from Tyrion what he and the other men had done to Krystyna, what they had planned to do the Sunday morning she had escaped, and more disturbing, the truth about what Tyrion intended to do when they found Krystyna.

~

Tyrion woke at 11:45 a.m. He had no recollection of the last hour at the bar with Stringer, except that in his memory, he had had a good time. On his way to the bathroom, Tyrion noticed a piece of paper on the floor by the door. It was a short note from Stringer explaining that he had gone for breakfast at local hotels and B and Bs and would return around one.

It was 2 p.m. before Stringer returned to the hotel to find Tyrion slumped in a chair in the reception area. Stringer had checked out earlier and, after collecting his bags from the storage area, nudged Tyrion awake. Groggy, but aware, Tyrion asked, "Any luck?"

"No. Nothing. I don't think she is in Bodmin."

"Oh," was all Tyrion could manage.

Stringer looked down on Tyrion and held out his hand.

"Maybe I should drive."

"Yeah, OK, but what now?"

With a reluctance that Tyrion did not notice, Stringer replied, "Guess we will have to wait on Edvard."

Thirteen

Until Edvard stepped on to Ryanair flight 463 to Manchester, his international travel had been limited to Continental Europe. Trips east, to find and coerce vulnerable girls to bring to Prague for promised, but non-existent "respectable" employment. Trips west, to seek clients for "trained" girls, who could be trafficked into ever seedier and cruel environments until, physically and emotionally used up, they were cast aside in whatever city or country they found themselves in.

Most of his international travel had been via car or train; Edvard took few flights because he often used drugs in support of his activities. Aware of the vigilance of the UK Border Services, and the prevalence of sniffer dogs at all international airports, Edvard had bathed several times, wore and brought with him only newly purchased clothes.

Clean, well-dressed, and eliciting sympathetic avoidance due to his disfigured face, Edvard sailed through Manchester Airport's passport and customs controls. Outside the terminal three arrivals area, Edvard, in response to the driving rain, flicked up the collar on his lightweight summer coat.

Rain in July. Only in England, thought Edvard as he squeezed into the shelter with other lightly clothed travellers as they waited for a bus, friend, or taxi to take them from the airport to their destinations. While Edvard waited, he consulted the business card that Stringer had handed over in his basement stronghold in Prague a week earlier. After his cell phone synchronized and joined the UK cellular network, Edvard dialled Stringer's office number. A voice answered the call before the second ring.

"Hello, Alliance Private Investigations. How may I help you?"

"You are Stringer, yes?"

Hesitant, the voice answered, "Yes, I'm Stringer. Who are you?"

"This is Edvard. You remember me?"

"Yes, how could I forget? Do you have something?"

"Of course, yes. I have a photograph of the bitch and her sister. It is good quality."

Stringer, surprised, mumbled, "Thank you, that was, er, very quick. I didn't expect . . ."

"It was no problem. I can be very persuasive. Perhaps you remember?"

"Yes. Well, thank you. Perhaps you could email it to me at the address on the card I gave you?"

"No. I think not, Mr. Stringer," said Edvard lightly.

"Oh."

"I will deliver the photograph to you myself."

"That's really not necessary," stammered Stringer. "I can easily print a copy and . . ."

"You do not understand, Mr. Stringer. I am not giving you the photograph. We shall use it together."

"You mean," said Stringer's strained voice, "you will come to Manchester?"

A distorted chuckle bled through the phone.

"I am already in Manchester. I am at the airport. I will come directly to your office. We must talk and share if we are to find my girls. You will be there, yes?"

"Um, yes, I'll be here."

Satisfied he had established control, Edvard entered a taxi and handed the driver the card.

"How long?"

"About half an hour," replied the taxi driver. "Depends on traffic. You in a hurry?"

"No, not at all," said Edvard as he settled back into the taxi's rear seat.

~

Stringer paced his office. At only eight and a half feet by nine feet it didn't take long. Stringer rarely engaged with clients at the office, and when he did, he had to explain that the size and decor of an office did not equate to the ability and success of the office occupant. In fact, as he told many clients the office was mostly a mail drop, a place to keep physical evidence and supplies. With modern technology, private investigation, like many industries, did not require brick and mortar structures. Nevertheless, the office did house a small desk and two chairs. The pacing area, from the window to the door between one chair and the desk, only required four steps. Four steps, stop, turn, four more.

Edvard's arrival in England was unwelcome. Prague had told Stringer all he needed to know about Edvard, and the prospect of actually working with Edvard was not something he wanted to do. Lost in apprehensive thought, the knock on the office door startled Stringer. When he opened the door, Edvard entered, surveyed the sparseness, and proclaimed, "Not much of an office. More like a shoe box. Where can we go to talk?"

Not wanting to give his speech on the irrelevance of office size, Stringer said, "We can go to the Slug and Lettuce pub. It's not far."

Stringer ushered Edvard out of his office and into the street. Five minutes later, Stringer led him to the pub. Inside, needing to establish control, Stringer gestured for Edvard to find a table while he got two bottles of Old Speckled Hen. With the beer in hand, Stringer joined Edvard at a table deep in the interior of the pub. Determined to take the initiative, Stringer started the conversation.

"I didn't expect you to come to Manchester. You could have emailed the photograph and . . ."

Edvard cut Stringer off. "Of course, I come. How else am I sure everything is done? You, me, we work together, and we find them."

As he spoke, Edvard pulled a photograph from an inside pocket. "We begin now," said Edvard as he passed the photograph to Stringer.

Stringer took the photograph and studied the image. Two girls, fresh-faced with knee-length cotton dresses, long neat hair and playful, bright smiles filled the foreground. Looking up, Stringer asked, "The statue in the background. It's the one in Prague, right?"

"Yes."

"When was this taken?"

"About five years ago."

Edvard sipped his beer, took out a cigarette, and tried to read Stringer's face.

"They look so young."

"Young," said Edvard, "yes, they were young when they came to work for me. Is good for business. You like them, yes?"

Disturbed by Edvard's suggestion, Stringer avoided answering by pointing at Edvard's cigarette.

"You can't smoke in here."

Unlit, Edvard rolled the cigarette between his thumb and forefinger. "You've seen the photograph. Now what have you got?"

Stringer explained the postal code on the envelopes, the visit to Bodmin, and the lack of results.

Edvard listened, snorted, and asked, "The money. How was the money given to the girls, and why did you not catch them?"

Stringer began to tell Edvard what Tyrion had said about the one-way streets, the last minute phone call, but Edvard interrupted him.

"Ah, she is a clever bitch. That is the system the Roma have used for years to receive and deliver drugs and money. Yes, I understand why you would not be able to follow or catch the person."

Edvard, using his sleeve to wipe beer from his cheek and chin, continued, "This town, Bodmin. It is our only chance."

"But I told you, we've been there and found nothing."

"Perhaps," Edvard said through a toothless grin, "you don't ask the right questions, or you don't ask the right way. Now, we have photographs. It will help people remember, yes?"

Stringer, thinking of the methods Edvard used in Prague to elicit information from him, twitched. Before Stringer could respond, Edvard asked about Tyrion. "Your client, Mr. Ennis. How do I contact him?"

Sensing the initiative slipping away, Stringer bristled and snapped back, "Mr. Ennis is my client. I will keep him informed."

Edvard broke the unlit cigarette in two and watched as the tobacco fell to the table. "Very well, Mr. Stringer, you may keep Mr. Ennis to yourself for now. Now, how long will it take to get to Bodmin?"

"Five or six hours."

"Then we leave tomorrow morning. You have my number in your phone. I stay at the Radisson Hotel. You pick me up at 7 a.m., yes?"

Reluctant to commit, and more reluctant to accompany Edvard, Stringer tried to stall. "I need to check with Mr. Ennis. He may not agree to another visit to Bodmin and the expenses. I will call you later."

Edvard stood abruptly, locked eyes with Stringer, and pronounced: "You may come or not. But I go tomorrow, and I will find them. Tell that to your Mr. Ennis."

Edvard turned and left without waiting for an answer. With Edvard gone, Stringer called Tyrion.

"Mr. Ennis, it's Stringer."

"I've just met with Edvard from Prague."

"He's here, in Manchester."

"No, I didn't know he was coming. He just showed up."

"He brought a photograph of Krystyna and her sister, Anna."

"Yes, it's good news."

"He wants to go back to Bodmin and try again."

"Yes, I told him we had tried everywhere and that it was a dead end, but he still wants to go."

"Tomorrow morning."

"Well, he didn't actually say he wanted you to go. Just him and me."

"It's a very, very long shot, Mr. Ennis. I mean we covered Bodmin very well and not one person . . ."

"Yes, the photograph might help, but . . ."

"I think Edvard is dangerous."

"Well, based on what he did to me in Prague, I'm worried what he might do to get information and . . ."

"Yes, I suppose he might, but as I made clear, I won't do anything illegal."

"All right. You want me to go with Edvard and you authorize the expense?"

"Er, no, I don't have his contact details. He said he would call me later and tell me where to collect him in the morning."

"Yes, I will give you his details when I get them."

"OK, I'll call you."

Stringer, his palms sticky with sweat, ended the call. A young waitress, short, trim, with cropped black hair and pale white skin, scooped the empty bottles from the table.

"Would you like another?" asked the girl with a sunny smile.

An image of the two young girls in Edvard's photograph blurred unbidden with an image of his younger sister Mandy. Mandy, or more precisely the memory of Mandy's nightmare, rarely strayed from Stringer's thoughts.

Twelve years earlier, a rapist had attacked Mandy on her way home from Manchester University. She had been nineteen, full of life, hope, and plans. The police investigation lasted two years, but no arrest materialized. A re-enactment, four years after the incident, yielded no response, and the man had never been caught.

Frustrated by the inability of the police, Stringer had undertaken his own amateurish and clumsy investigation until, after several weeks and repeated warnings from the police that his blundering about could actually make things worse, he had stopped searching.

A few months later, as Mandy developed all the classic symptoms of a victim living with the fear that her attacker would return, Stringer had contacted the Association of British Investigators and taken his first step toward his chosen profession. Shaken by the thought, Stringer declined and quickly left the pub.

Fourteen

At 7:10 a.m., Stringer steered his three-year-old black Ford Escort up the ramp to the front doors of the luxury Radisson Blu Hotel on Elm Street in Manchester's historic Free Trade Hall. Built in 1853 to commemorate the end of the Corn Laws, the Free Trade Hall has been at the centre of life in Manchester for over a hundred and sixty years.

Edvard, a cigarette hanging from his twisted lips, stood nonchalantly on the step in front of the revolving door. Arrogant confidence oozed from Edvard as he acknowledged Stringer's arrival with a curt nod. Ignoring the "butt out" sand-filled bucket, Edvard flicked his cigarette over Stringer's car, grabbed a small-sized black holdall from his feet, and climbed in the front passenger seat.

"Good morning, Stringer. No rain today."

Not wanting to talk, Stringer turned up the radio and concentrated on the hectic morning traffic. He followed the same route as he and Tyrion had taken two weeks earlier, but the traffic was much heavier on a weekday, and it took almost seven hours before they arrived at the Westberry Inn in Bodmin. They had not made reservations, but the Inn had plenty of room.

After separate check-ins, Stringer and Edvard met in the reception area. Stringer, eager to get it over quickly and confirm that the women were not in Bodmin, spoke first.

"How do you want to do this?"

"We will show the photograph and ask if they have been seen."

Surprised by Edvard's direct approach, Stringer frowned and cautioned Edvard. "I don't think that's a good idea. It will make people suspicious, especially in a small town. Once word gets around . . ."

"That depends on how we do it, yes. In my home, people talk for three reasons, sympathy, money, and fear. Fear, while very useful and good for quick results, will not be best way here, I think. So, we use sympathy and money."

"You mean a reward or something?"

Edvard opened his arms and hands like a minister about to impart a revelation.

"We will tell the following story. My sisters, Krystyna and Anna, left the Czech Republic for new life in England a few months ago. A week ago, we had fire in home that killed our parents, and I lost all information about where my sisters were staying. All I have from fire is a letter mailed from Bodmin two weeks ago to say they had found work. The funeral for our parents is in three days, and I am desperate to find them in time. After we tell story, I will add that there is small reward for anyone who can help find them."

Reluctant, Stringer acknowledged the plausibility of Edvard's approach. "OK, I guess that could work. Here is the list of places we visited last week."

"Thank you."

"You know, they will probably remember me and be suspicious."

"That is no problem. If someone asks, I will explain that you are a private investigator, and I asked you to help, but now I am so desperate that I wanted to check for myself. People will understand."

Edvard used a finger to guide his eye down the list. His finger stopped. "The place called Bosvena. What is it?"

"A café and restaurant. We checked there."

"It sounds European. I think . . ."

"Yeah, I know it sounds European, but it's not. Bosvena is the Cornish name for Bodmin."

"What is Cornish?"

"It used to be the language of peoples who lived in this area about a thousand years ago. The restaurant is one hundred per cent local foods and nothing to do with Europe. Like I said, we checked."

Edvard walked away from Stringer and passed through the front door of the hotel. He stopped in the parking lot, withdrew and lit a cigarette, then said, "Yes, maybe you did, but I thought it might be European, and if I did, then Krystyna and Anna might have thought the same. We will check again. We go now, yes."

Twelve minutes later, Edvard and Stringer paused in front of an immaculate, white stucco building. A solid black door, flanked by bright white pillars, stood partially open. Accepting the invitation, Edvard entered. Inside, surprised by the crisp elegance, Edvard hesitated and blinked. Drawn by a chrome-and-red vintage espresso machine mounted on a wooden bar-high counter, Edvard stepped farther into the café/restaurant. A moment later, heels clicked on the black-and-white tiled floor and a well-dressed middle-aged woman smiled and greeted them.

"Good afternoon, gentlemen. Welcome to Bosvena. A table for two?"

Edvard, one hand covering his mouth and scar in feigned embarrassment, bowed slightly. Words, soft and gentle, to mask the lies, began to flow from Edvard's mouth. "Very kind, but thank you, no. I come to ask for help."

With grudging admiration, Stringer listened as Edvard spun his story of the fire and the death of his parents. The woman didn't stand a chance.

"You see, your lovely restaurant, its name, it sound European, and I thought maybe my sisters find work here."

A kind laugh and a knowing smile accompanied the woman's well-worn response. "Well, you're not the first to think we sell European food."

"Oh," said Edvard, disappointment and fragility in his voice, "I'm sorry to waste your time, but you see I am desperate to find my sisters."

Taken in, the woman put the menus down. "Your sisters, what do they look like?"

"I have a photograph. It is a little worn, but it was all I could save from the fire."

The woman held the photograph and took her time. Moments ticked by before she smiled hesitantly and said, "I'm not sure. There was a young woman a few weeks ago, I think. She thought we served

European food as well. Wanted some kind of fruit pudding. I can't recall what it was called."

Edvard, genuine excitement raising his voice, seized on the woman's recollection. "Could it have been ovocné knedlíky she asked for?"

"Yes, that sounds like it. I mean, I didn't really understand what she said, but your words sound the same."

"Ah, that makes sense. Ovocné knedlíkymy is my sister's favourite. It is fresh dumplings filled with strawberries, apricots, plums, or plum jam."

"Well," said the woman as she held the photograph closer and under the light, "I can't be absolutely certain, but the woman who came looks a bit like the one on the left."

"That is Anna, my youngest sister. She always had a sweet tooth."

The woman handed the photograph back to Edvard.

"I'm sorry I can't be more help. Are you sure you won't stay for something to eat?"

Edvard, eager for more information, but not wanting to linger, declined and tried another question. "Thank you, no. You have been good help. Just one thing, do you think my sister Anna might live here in your town?"

"Oh, I doubt it. Everyone knows everyone else and everyone's business. If a foreigner . . . Oh, I'm sorry I didn't mean anything by it. Well, everyone would know. Especially two pretty things like your sisters."

Apologetic and embarrassed by her gaff, the woman smiled wide as Edvard and Stringer left.

~

~

Outside, Edvard smirked at Stringer.

"You see, Edvard's way it works. First try, yes."

"All right, maybe, but one possible sighting a few weeks ago of a girl wanting a dessert doesn't mean they are here. It's a waste of time."

"Maybe, maybe not. But I know Anna, and she is stupid enough to look for a Czech dessert in a small English town. Yes, Anna is stupid, yet she is probably smart enough to go away from her home to post the letters. We need the post office, yes."

The post office, as Edvard expected, was very close to the Bosvena Café. Less than five hundred metres up Fore Street, Costcutter, a discount convenience chain store, held the franchise with the Royal Mail to provide postal services to the residents of Bodmin. Inside Costcutter, a clerk, ink- and nicotine-stained fingers, glasses perched on head, with dandruff speckled on a stained black waistcoat that hung lopsided on round shoulders, represented the customer interface for the Royal Mail.

Talkative, in the way some service people can be, the man remembered everything except the two young women in Edvard's photograph. Frustrated, Edvard turned to Stringer who, unable to stem his professionalism, asked the clerk, "The woman would have mailed four identical packages to Manchester."

The mention of packages, the things the man understood more than people, jogged the clerk's memory.

"Ah, now that rings a bell. Yes, about two weeks ago or so. I remember 'cause I had to weigh them and the woman insisted on stamps instead of just letting me run through the machine for the postage. This was odd because she was in a hurry."

"A hurry?" interjected Edvard.

"Yes, she said she had a bus to catch."

"Oh, a local bus then?" added Stringer.

"Nah, wrong time of day," mused the clerk. "Must have been one of the intercity buses that pass through on the A30. You can get to any city up and down the coast on them buses."

Done with the clerk and outside the store, Edvard conveyed his excitement to Stringer. "You see, my friend, we have found our first trace of my girls. Soon, I shall have them."

"All we have found," said Stringer with a tone of deliberate defeatism, "is two possible sightings. Hardly conclusive."

"You do not look at bright side. They were here. I don't think they live here, but they came here. Probably to mail the letter to your client and the others."

"They could be anywhere."

A cigarette flamed as Edvard inhaled deeply. Releasing the smoke, Edvard asked Stringer if he had a map of the area. Stringer nodded. He tapped his iPhone, entered Bodmin in Google Maps, and zoomed out until the blue waters of the English Channel to the southeast, and the Atlantic Ocean to the southwest, surrounded England's southern peninsular. Edvard took the phone from Stringer and toggled in and out for a few moments.

"I do not know this area," said Edvard, handing the phone back to Stringer. "What are the biggest towns around fifty kilometres from here?"

Studying the map, running finger to make crude estimates, Stringer said with disbelief, "You're not suggesting we visit all the towns within fifty kilometres of Bodmin, are you?"

"No, it is not possible. And there is no need. You need to think like a whore, Mr. Stringer. They are lazy and stupid. They would not go too far from their home. We need small- to medium-sized towns, the ones that people would know or that would be in travel brochures or tourist magazines. Places where a person could get unskilled work. Where there are tourists and people come and go."

After a moment's thought, Stringer offered some suggestions: "There are quite a few, but I'd say four largish towns worth looking at would be Exmouth and Torquay to the east, and maybe St. Austell to the south, and Newquay to the west. They are popular tourist destinations that need seasonal and casual workers if that's what you mean. But, come on, they could be anywhere in England. They could have been riding the bus to and from anywhere."

Decisive, Edvard flicked his cigarette into the street.

"I think not. The two letters. One to say it was over and one to deliver the blackmail material. These speak of two people with different ideas of what should be done. The more I think, the more I am right."

"What do you mean? Right about what?"

"The first letter informing that the blackmail is over. This sounds like the older sister Krystyna. She is the smart one. She plans and thinks. The second letter, to punish despite the men paying for years, is impulsive and speaks of revenge and hate. This, I think, was sent by Anna, the younger sister. She does not think. And if I am right, she did not think too much, or travel too far, when she decided to travel to Bodmin to post the letters."

"I don't know. It's a bit of a stretch," offered Stringer.

"Yes, but you do not know these women. I know them. That is my advantage and why I will find them. Now, we will search in the four towns you identified. We will take two each. If we get nothing, then I think of something else."

"All right, but I will have to check with my client first."

"Very well, and before you do, please do give me his contact details now."

Reluctant, Stringer gave Edvard Tyrion's phone number. After he entered the number in his own phone, Edvard became business-like. "When you talk to Mr. Ennis, you may tell him that you will search, how you say them, Exmouth and Torquay. I will take St. Austell and Newquay. Two days for each, I think."

Fifteen

Back at the Westberry Hotel, Stringer told Edvard that he would leave for Torquay right away so he could get a fresh start the next day. Edvard, who needed time to arrange a rental car, watched Stringer leave the parking lot before he called Tyrion.

"Mr. Ennis, I am Edvard."

"Edvard? From Prague?"

"Yes."

"What? Why are you calling me? Where is Stringer?"

"Never mind. Where is Stringer? I call you to talk about your private investigator."

"What's happened? Is he all right?"

"Yes, for now."

"What do you mean? Look, I heard what you did to him in Prague. I don't want anything to . . ."

"I don't call to discuss what you don't want, Mr. Ennis. I call about what you do want. You want the bitch Krystyna, yes?"

"Yes, you're damn right I do. What's going on?"

"I am worried about Stringer. I don't think he has, how I say, the balls for what is needed. Also, I don't think he understands or agrees with what our intentions are when we find our girls."

Tyrion, cautious, paused, but Edvard out-waited him.

"I, don't know what you mean."

"Let us be clear with each other. This woman and her sister have caused me much trouble. They have cost me money and one, Anna, is responsible for what happen to my face. You, you have been blackmailed for three years, you lose your wife, children, and Stringer tells me one of your friends kill self because of the bitch. Is that right?"

"Yes, yes, but I, er . . ."

"I don't search for them to have happy reunion. No, Mr. Ennis, our reunion will be short, painful, and final. Do you understand?"

"Yes, no, I mean, I don't know anything about . . ."

"Do not worry. I have experience and will show you how. It is not as hard as people think. Also, I believe there should be time for some personal fun, yes."

Tyrion's hesitation was short, yet long enough for the hate to win. "All right, but if we get caught?"

"We won't," assured Edvard. "There will be no trace. Believe me. Now your Stringer. He is not the person to be part of our plan. He will be useful for a few days, and I have sent him to search in two towns near Bodmin."

"I know. He called me earlier. He thinks your plan is a long shot."

"Perhaps, but I think not. The girls are close. I can feel it. Anyway, when he is done with the two towns I send him to, you must end your arrangement with him. Understood?"

"But what if he finds them? What then?"

"It is not problem: You pay him and tell him the job is done. You will handle from there."

"All right, but are you sure we can find them without him?"

"I am sure."

Sixteen

There were two ways to get to Torquay from Bodmin. Both routes had to skirt around, rather than pass through, Dartmoor National Park. The A38, northeast, had several toll roads, the other, the A30, southeast, didn't. Despite a twenty-mile difference between the two routes, Google Maps indicated that either way would take one hour and thirty-one minutes.

A memory of a school trip to visit Britain's famous Port Plymouth, and a whim that he might stop to view the ships in the harbour, prompted Stringer to choose the A30. But Stringer didn't stop. Instead, his mind wandered as it tried to hide from his conscience. Past Plymouth, and touching the most southerly edge of the national park, Stringer's cell phone, positioned on a holder fixed to the dashboard, rang.

Caller ID indicated that Marc Corey, his sometimes partner for investigations, wanted to talk. Marc, pudgy with a large bald head, was a slightly dishonest investigator who was not above stringing clients along to extend the investigation and pad his expenses. His moral compass was also a little off. However, he could and did ferret out information others couldn't. Stringer, not really wanting to talk, relented and answered the call on the speaker function. Marc didn't bother with introductions.

"What's going on, Stringer? You haven't been around for a few days. Got yourself a nice earner, have you?"

"Hey, Marc. I'm working on a missing person. The one where the client is on and off and always pissed when I can't find anything 'cause he has no information for me to go on. Are you on a case, Marc?"

"No, not really. You got some new info, have you? Where are you anyway?"

"On my way to Torquay."

"Nice. Wouldn't mind a bit of sunshine and bikinis myself, you lucky bastard. I suppose your hotel and everything is being paid for as well?"

"What do you want, Marc?"

"Oh, nothing really. I've time on my hands and wondered if you needed anything doing. I might even do it for free, if it gets me a trip down south, eh?"

Stringer thought for a moment, wondering if he could actually use Marc's help.

"Hey, Stringer. You still there?

"Yes, just thinking, but no, sorry, I don't have anything.

"Oh well, I guess I'll just have to keep my feet up. Thanks, though. I'll see you when you . . ."

"Wait a minute, Marc. I, don't have a job for you, but I do have a hypothetical."

"Gawd, not another client that wants to fuck you, is it?"

"No, Marc, nothing like that."

"Go on then, shoot."

"This case I'm working on, the missing woman. I'm worried about what will happen to the woman if I find her."

"Come on, Stringer. We've talked about this sort of thing before. Our job is to find people, not determine what happens to them. That's the terms of our business. If you can't live with that, you shouldn't be an investigator."

"I know, I know, but this is more serious than a bit of a beating or being turned over to the authorities."

"Yeah, what's up then? Is your client going to kill the person you're looking for?"

"Maybe not my client exactly, but another person has joined the search. His name is Edvard, and he is a pimp from Prague. The woman I am looking for used to work for him, and I think he wants her back or worse."

"You're looking for a hooker! I didn't know that. Well, I'll tell you this, you don't want to get mixed up with these Eastern European fuckers. They're all crazy druggies, and from what I've heard, violence is their first option."

"Exactly, Marc, that's why I'm worried. The woman, well, she and her sister, I really think their lives are in danger."

"Pimps, whores, Eastern Europeans, leave them to it, man. These women, I'm sure they're not innocent. There must be a reason."

"What reason could be enough to kill them, Marc?"

"Look, do you actually know that this Edvard person and your client are going to harm the women?"

"No, but I've got a feeling if you . . ."

"Listen, Stringer, if you really think something bad will happen, the answer is simple. Don't find the women."

An hour later, after getting a room at a bed and breakfast a few blocks from the Torquay harbour, Stringer decided on a walk to clear his head. He soon found himself rooted to the spot on the very end of Princess Pier. Dusk had come and gone, and the darkness of the English Channel pulled at Stringer's mind and body. Unable to fight the fatigue and uncertainty that suddenly overwhelmed him, Stringer returned to his room at the bed and breakfast to sleep and hope things would be better in the morning.

~

The breakfast part of Stringer's bed and breakfast had been served and cleared away by the time he descended from his second-floor room to the dining room. It was 10:40 a.m. and breakfast, which began at 7:30 a.m., had ended at 9 a.m. Refreshed and very hungry, Stringer found a small café that served all-day breakfast. At 11:30 a.m., fortified with a full English breakfast and several cups of tea, Stringer set off to search for two needles in a haystack.

Back on the ocean front, Stringer ignored Princess Pier and instead chose to walk the South West Coastal Path along the beach. In the bright warm sun, blue sky, and a gentle onshore breeze, hundreds of people milled and strolled. Families, content and happy, meandered without a care. Asian tourists, conforming to the stereotype, snapped endless photographs. Elderly people walked dogs and each other, and joggers dodged everyone.

When the path dead-ended at Torbay Road, Stringer retraced his steps until he arrived at the Pier Point Restaurant and Bar. The patio was full, but a tiny metal table with one chair soon became available. The table, squeezed up against the low wall that served as the barrier between patio and path, overlooked Princess Pier and the bay beyond.

Thirsty from his walk, Stringer ordered a bottle of Peroni lager and a glass of water. After draining the water, Stringer sipped his cold beer and did what most people sitting on the patio seemed to be doing: people watching. Lulled by the calm flow of a content populace, Stringer drifted and gazed through, rather than at, the people who sauntered back and forth. Relaxed, Stringer didn't recall ordering a second beer and was surprised when it arrived.

Beer number two was extra cold, and he tilted his head back to savour a long swallow. As he did, from the right, two women came into view. Each woman, animated and laughing, pushed a stroller. When the women entered Stringer's direct line of sight, momentarily blocking the ocean, a child's toy fell from one of the strollers, and the women stopped. The shorter of the two women picked up the toy and handed it to an unseen child. Silhouetted against the shimmering ocean, the women resumed their exchange and their walk.

Stringer, struggling to remain calm, placed ten pounds under his half-full bottle of Peroni and stepped over the low patio wall. Tempering his initial rush,

Stringer slowed and fell in behind women and children. As he followed, Stringer took a photocopied version of Edvard's photo from his pocket. Certain he had found the women, and equally sure they wouldn't move too fast with children, Stringer fell farther back.

The women stayed on the south-west path until it rounded Torquay Marina and joined Cary Parade Road. Two hundred metres later, at a junction marked by a clock tower in the middle of a roundabout, the women turned left onto Torwood Street. After about five minutes, Stringer watched them enter Brothers & Sisters Café, a small café next to a real estate agent office.

Conspicuous in the street, Stringer crossed the road and entered McColl's newsagent and bookstore. Inside, Stringer randomly selected a bestseller paperback from the book stand by the front window. He glanced at the title, *Some People Deserve to Die*, and flipped the book over to read the back jacket.

As he read the blurb about another tale of revenge, the café door opened and, one after another, the two strollers, this time pushed by two older women, entered the street and turned left away from the harbour. Stringer replaced the book, bought a newspaper and, with the paper tucked under his arm, crossed the road and entered the café.

~

The Brothers & Sisters Café was busy. The only available place was a lone wooden chair wedged under a table by a door that, according to the sign on the adjacent wall, led to the washroom. Stringer made for the chair and sat. Before he could unfold his newspaper or consider the menu, a voice startled him.

"Hello, I get you something?"

In front of him, the one Edvard had called Anna in the photograph waited expectantly with a pen and notepad.

"Er, yes, please," said Stringer flustered, "a tea and a ham and cheese sandwich."

"Brown or white bread?"

"Brown please."

"And you would like small salad also?"

"Er, no, thanks."

"OK, will not be long."

Anna, moving quickly, slipped the notepad and pen in the front of her white apron, gathered used dishes from a nearby table, and disappeared through a two-way door at the rear of the café beside a glass-fronted counter. Over his newspaper, Stringer observed the bustle of the café.

~

For the next half-hour, as Stringer nursed his tea and sandwich, he concluded that Krystyna and Anna ran the front of the café while two men worked in the back. The two men, who looked like brothers, had come through the swinging door several times, either with plates or with a question. Both men were fair skinned with short brown hair, plain features, slight paunches, and wide smiles. One, a little broader in the shoulders than the other, and perhaps older, gently brushed hands with Krystyna, while the narrow-shouldered man blushed when Anna smiled at him.

Deducing the obvious concerning the café's Brothers & Sisters name, Stringer smiled to himself.

Concerned about lingering too long, Stringer finished his now cold tea, the crust from his sandwich, and signalled Anna for his bill. A one-page promotional flyer, stapled to his bill, listed daily specials. On his way out, Stringer noted on the front door that the café closed at 6 p.m.

Stringer walked left from the café and took two more lefts until he had located the back of the café. He checked his watch; 2:30 p.m. Satisfied, Stringer walked back to the harbour area and sat on a bench facing the ocean. Using his iPhone, Stringer web searched the café. On the café website, a link directed him to a small article in the food section of the *Torquay Herald Express*. The article featured a photograph of the café, noted the grand opening of Brothers & Sisters Café in 2014, and highlighted the uniqueness of sisters marrying brothers and entering business together. The owners were listed as Mike and Christina Mills, and David and Annie Mills. A couple of follow-up articles noted the café's success.

At 6 p.m., Stringer parked his car a quarter block down the street from the back entrance to the Brothers & Sisters Café. At 6:45 p.m., Krystyna/Christina Mills and her husband Mike came out of the café laughing and got into in a blue Volkswagen Jetta. Stringer followed the Jetta, and five minutes later, the Jetta turned onto Braddons Hill Road, in a small residential suburb.

Stringer passed Braddons Hill Road, turned around, and drove onto Braddons Hill Road as the Jetta stopped in a driveway on the left. As Stringer passed by, he noted the address on the monthly specials paper next to where he had already noted C & A Mills.

~

Confident he had found Krystyna's home and that through her he could also find Anna, Stringer returned to his B&B, parked his car, and walked to a nearby pub. Swallowing large quaffs of beer, Stringer fingered the monthly specials paper in his hand and thought about Tyrion's drunken description of what he and the other men had done with Krystyna. One beer turned into many, and images of Prague, prostitutes, pimps, and Edvard blended and mixed with Tyrion and his perversions. Thoughts of his sister Mandy, her life as a victim, and his failure to find her attacker clawed at his conscience and morality. Somewhere between his fifth and sixth pint, Stringer recalled his conversation with his sometimes investigative partner, Marc Corey.

"'. . . if you really think something bad will happen, the answer is easy. Don't find the women. Simple.'"

Swilling the last of his beer, Stringer mumbled to himself, "But it's not simple. I found them."

Seventeen

The White Hart Inn, built in 1520, was the oldest pub in Bodmin and had served as a magistrate's court during the sixteenth century, and a debtor's court in the eighteenth century. In 2015, the family-run pub billed itself as relaxed, unpretentious, and friendly.

Seated in the corner farthest from the bar, and out of earshot from accidental or intentional observers, Stringer asked Edvard if he had found anything in St. Austell and Newquay.

Edvard checked his watch as he replied, "Another is joining us anytime. We will wait for him."

On cue, Tyrion entered the pub, saw Edvard and Stringer, and joined them at the table.

Surprised and confused, Stringer stood to address Tyrion.

"Mr. Ennis, I didn't know you were going to be here."

Nodding to Edvard, Tyrion replied casually, "Edvard suggested I join you to get the information first-hand."

As Tyrion sat, a waiter took their drinks order. After he returned with three pints, Edvard began.

"As you know, Mr. Ennis, I am certain that Krystyna and Anna, or at least one of them, came to Bodmin to post the letters. I don't think they live in Bodmin, but as I told Stringer, whores are lazy and stupid and would not have travelled far to make the post. I decided to search small and medium tourist towns within a short distance from Bodmin. Places where a person could easily obtain unskilled work. Stringer suggested four towns."

As Edvard took a long drink and opened a packet of cigarettes, Tyrion and Stringer inched their chairs closer to the table.

"I went to Newquay and St. Austell," continued Edvard. "Several Eastern Europeans were working in bars and restaurants and a few driving taxis. In Newquay, an old whore from Poland tried to play me for money for information. But she knew nothing."

"So, they are not there?" said Tyrion.

"Maybe, but I did not find them or any sign of them. Of course, two days is not long time to search a town. They might be there, but there is limit to how long I can stay."

Edvard turned to Stringer. "So, my friend, you did not call yesterday. Are you saving the good news for a personal presentation?"

Edvard's joke unnerved Stringer, who slurped to cover his nervousness. "Like you," said Stringer, the faintest crack in his voice, "I found some Europeans working in the service industry in both Exmouth and Torquay, but I didn't find any trace of the women."

"Any whores?" asked Edvard toying with his open cigarette package.

"Um, no. Well, I didn't actually meet any. Like you said, two days is not very long to find someone in a town. I told you it was, well, a bit hopeful."

Tyrion, who appeared unusually relaxed, said, "What's Torquay like these days, Stringer?"

"Torquay? Why?"

"Oh, me, the wife and kid used to go there years ago. I always loved the place. Happier times back then. The marina and the boats. Always said I would get a boat someday. My daughter, Beth, she loved the beach and the pier. Is the Paignton Zoo still there?"

"I guess so. I didn't really notice it."

"It's a bit away from the main centre, so you probably wouldn't have seen it. Beth loved that too."

Tyrion signalled the bar for another round of drinks and Edvard summed up: "I don't like to lose. That bitch is somewhere in this area, but is not good to be away from my business too long. People get ideas."

"So, I guess," said Stringer, a bit too eagerly, "that's it then?"

"For now," mused Edvard, "but I am not finished. Maybe I send one or two of my boys for vacation. Let them look for a while."

Tyrion, taking a pint from the waiter, looked at both Edvard and Stringer. "I really thought we would find them. Well, as I am down here, I think I will take advantage of the good weather."

"Going to have a little holiday in Bodmin, Mr. Ennis?" asked Stringer.

"Bodmin? Christ, no. I think I'll take a drive to Torquay and stay for a night or two. You know, think about the good times for a change. My wife and I used to walk up and down the streets, stopping in cafés and shopping. Strange to think that that sort of thing used to make me happy once."

The prospect of Tyrion sauntering around Torquay's waterfront and marina, just a short walk from Krystyna and Anna's café, constricted Stringer's throat, and he involuntarily choked on his beer.

"You all right?" said Tyrion.

"Yes, I'm OK. It's about Torquay, Mr. Ennis."

"What about it?"

"Well, when you asked about it, I didn't want to spoil things for you, but to be honest, it's a bit run down these days. Everything needs a coat of paint, and once you get off the main drag, the back streets are awful. I even had trouble finding a decent B&B. You might want to hold on to your memories, Mr. Ennis, and give Torquay a miss."

Still coughing, Stringer excused himself to use the washroom. When Stringer left, Tyrion lamented to Edvard.

"That's too bad about Torquay. I'm a bit surprised really."

"Why? Is not usual for small tourist town to become worn and dirty with time."

"Yes and no. I mean Torquay used to be called the English Riviera. I can't believe it has gone downhill."

Edvard, thoughtful, whispered quickly to Tyrion, "When Stringer returns, it is time to tell him you are done with his services and he can go. You will pay him later. We will stay. We need to talk."

Stringer returned, but before he could sit, Tyrion said bluntly, "Well, Stringer, I guess you're done. I'm not happy with the outcome, but there seems little else to do. You can send me your bill, and I'll pay it next week."

Stringer, happy to get away, downed the remainder of his pint, wiped his mouth, and offered his hand to Tyrion.

"Well, I'm sorry we didn't find her for you, Mr. Ennis, but we tried our best. I'll send you my bill next week."

Nods ended their meeting and Stringer left. As soon as the door closed on Stringer's back, Tyrion questioned Edvard.

"What's going on? Why did you want him to leave?"

"Because he lies," hissed Edvard.

"Lies, about what?"

"Torquay. I think he found something, maybe someone."

"What? Why the hell would he lie? Why do you think that?"

"In my business, you learn how to read a person. If you read them wrong, you might be dead. I still live, and he is hiding something. As you say, it is hard to believe your Torquay has become down."

Tyrion shrugged. "Well, it's a bit thin. What do you want to do?"

"Perhaps you do Internet search on your phone about Torquay while I go smoke. If, as Stringer says, the town is declined, there will be news. If there is news, Stringer tells truth. If no news, he lie and we go to Torquay."

Tyrion searched the Internet, but instead of waiting for Edvard to return, joined him outside.

"Well, my friend, does your private investigator lie?"

Angry red and blue veins bubbled on Tyrion's neck as he held up his cell phone and showed it to Edvard.

"I think he does. According to the Torquay Tourism website, Torquay has never been better. But why lie?"

"I think he cares about what we will do."

"The bastard. It's none of his business. I paid the fucker good money to find the bitch. We need to get him and find out what he knows."

"In time, yes. But I expect Stringer will be hard to find for a few days. At least until he thinks I have returned to Prague. He can wait. I will deal with him later. Now we go to Torquay. If Stringer can find them, we should have no trouble."

~

Two hundred metres away, screened by parked vehicles, moving traffic, and distance, Stringer observed Tyrion and Ennis outside the pub. Stringer knew dishonesty and deceit. His father, and older brother Paul, had exemplified both. Stringer Senior had been a career criminal, mostly petty theft and buying and selling stolen goods, until his premature death of cancer at fifty-five. Paul, always their father's favourite, followed in his dad's footsteps, and with equal success, passed more time in than out of prison. Indirectly, his father and Paul had both shaped Stringer's moral compass, and in addition to what had happened to his sister Mandy, Stringer had begun to realize he had to do the right thing.

~

Unable to hear or read lips, Stringer relied on body language as he watched Tyrion's body bounce with energy as he spoke to Edvard, waved, and pointed at his cell phone.

Edvard, calm, spoke to Tyrion and a moment later, they walked to the parking lot where Edvard transferred two bags from his rental car to Tyrion's SUV. Edvard re-entered the pub for a few minutes, then came out and got in Tyrion's car. Tyrion pulled out of the parking lot and followed the A389 toward the A30. Stringer, apprehensive, started his engine and followed Tyrion.

At the A389/A30 junction, to Stringer's relief, Tyrion took the A30 North ramp toward Exeter. Just after Exeter, the A30 ended, and drivers had the choice of taking the M5 north to Bristol, Birmingham, and on up to Manchester, or the A38 south to Newton Abbot and Torquay. Stringer, a half-dozen vehicles behind, watched Tyrion's break light turn red as he slowed his approach to the M5 junction. To Stringer's horror, Tyrion eased right instead of left and joined the A38 south to Torquay and to the women he had found.

Ten minutes later, Stringer pulled off the A38 near Kennford and stopped in the large parking lot of a Partridge Cycles Superstore. From the passenger seat, Stringer took the photocopy of Krystyna and Anna and pressed it against the steering wheel. Bright, hopeful eyes had held the camera's lens, and now they bored into Stringer. Ten years of private investigative work had taught Stringer that innocence, like guilt, could not be seen in a picture. He hadn't seen it all, and hoped he never would, but he had seen enough to believe his instinct and his gut. And his gut told him he had to do something.

Decision made, Stringer reached for the promotional flyer that Anna/Annie had given him and ran his finger under the phone number for the Brothers & Sisters Café.

Eighteen

On the Besigheim Way Bridge, a few miles north on Newton Abbot, the A30 changed from two to four lanes as it crossed the River Teign. Named Teng in pre-Roman times until listed as Teign in the Anglo-Saxon charter of 739, the river flows fifty kilometres from its source on Dartmouth Moor to its English Channel outlet at Teignharvey. With light traffic, Tyrion pushed his SUV to sixty miles an hour over the bridge. Edvard, exhaling cigarette smoke in short puffs to the gap at the top of the partially opened passenger side window, nodded to the river scene below the bridge.

"Beautiful. Reminds me of the Vltava River that runs through Prague."

Tyrion, unmoved by the scenery, grunted acknowledgement as he steered the car around a slow moving truck. A mile farther, Tyrion banged a fist on the steering wheel and shouted, "I can't believe Stringer lied to me."

Jolted by Tyrion's outburst, Edvard pushed the butt of his cigarette through the window. "I said from beginning that Stringer has no balls. We deal with him another day. How long to Torquay?"

"About an hour from here."

"Good. We will begin when arrive. You visited many times before with family, yes? You know town. Take us to centre, and we start there."

"OK."

Construction and a diversion greeted Tyrion and Edvard when they joined Riviera Way, the main connection road from the A30 to Torquay. Slowed to a crawl behind a long line of traffic, Edvard smiled as Tyrion fumbled for the right words.

"Edvard, when we find them, what . . . will we, you know, do?"

"What you want to do? What was your plan? You must have thought about it many times."

Hands tightened their grip on the steering wheel as Tyrion shared his plan.

"First, I thought I would destroy her life with the same photos and information she used against me. Even without her face in the photos, it would be enough. I would show the photographs to the people she is with, who care for her. Then I would beat the shit out of her. What about you?"

Amused by his own thoughts and imaginings, Edvard's smile widened.

"Best would be to take back to Prague. I would work them until no one would pay, then I would give them away for free. When no one wanted them free, there are men who like to hurt women. When done with them, if they still lived, I would give them to the white slavers who take women to the Middle East. That would be the end of them."

Tyrion shuddered. Edvard continued.

"But, my friend, it is not possible to take to Prague. Krystyna is the tough one. Anna is weak. We will take both, use Anna in front of Krystyna, kill Anna, then kill Krystyna."

The car lurched as Tyrion mis-timed a clutch change.

"You are good with this, yes?" said Edvard without emotion.

Tyrion, through gritted teeth, looked ahead and whispered,

"Yes."

"Good, we have understanding."

Nineteen

Customers, eager for refreshment and a respite from the hot July weather, had swamped the Brothers & Sisters Café from 11:30 am until 1:30 p.m. With the lunch rush over, Krystyna tidied the main counter area while Anna, along with Jill, a part-time helper, cleaned and reset tables. Anna, sweat sucking her shirt to her back, spoke quickly to Krystyna as she squeezed behind her to reach a package of napkins under the counter.

"What a day. Thank God it's quiet now."

"Yes, we were very busy, but it's good for business, Anna."

Anna's squeeze pressed Krystyna against the counter, and a grimace flashed across Krystyna's face.

"Are you all right?" asked Anna.

"Yes, but I haven't had a chance to use the bathroom since this morning. Can you stay at the counter for a few minutes?"

"Yes, of course."

As Krystyna disappeared through the swinging door to the kitchen and the staff bathroom located at the back of the café, the phone on the counter rang. Expecting a customer enquiry or a question from a supplier, Anna picked up a pen and answered the phone as she and Krystyna had practised.

"Hello, Brothers & Sisters Café. Annie speaking, how can I help?"

An unmistakable hum and buzz that accompanies a call from a vehicle filled the phone, but no one spoke. Anna asked again.

"Annie speaking, how can I help?"

Over the hum and buzz, a strained male voice whispered,

"Anna? Is that Anna?"

The phone slipped from Anna's hand and fell on the counter. Heat surged through Anna and stole her breath. Light-headed, she leaned her elbows on the counter and held her head. From the phone, the quiet voice continued. "Anna, Anna, answer me. Please, Anna."

Across the café, Jill, laying out napkins on the clean tables, paused and focused concerned eyes on Anna. Forced to act, Anna picked up the phone.

"No, no, this is Annie. There is no Anna here. You have the wrong number."

The background hum and buzz of the traffic faded as though the speaker had pressed his phone to his mouth. A strong voice replaced the whisper. "Listen to me, Anna. I know about your sister Krystyna, the men in Manchester, and about Prague."

Unable to stand, Anna slid to the floor behind the counter and pushed breathless words into the phone. "You're wrong. I am Annie. I have no sister. Go away."

"Anna, you are in danger. Please listen, there isn't much time."

"Are you there, Anna? Please."

The use of the word please and the tone of the request quietened Anna. Hesitant, Anna answered. "Yes."

"They are coming for you, Anna. They will be there in about an hour. I'm sorry, it's my fault. I found you, but I didn't mean to tell them."

Anna swallowed and asked what she already sensed. "Who comes?"

"Edvard and Mr. Ennis."

Anna cried out no into the phone and threw it to the floor. Up on her feet against the counter, Anna staggered and knocked a plastic charity contribution box over. A lone customer, startled by the thump of the heavy plastic box, stepped away from the counter. The café fell silent for a moment until the customer offered help and asked if Anna was all right.

Krystyna entered from the kitchen, reached for Anna, and held her up. Anna, ghost-white and trembling, clung to her sister.

"Anna, what's wrong? What happened?"

"He's coming, he's coming! We have to get away."

With arms wrapped tight around Anna, Krystyna steered her to the kitchen. In the kitchen, David, Anna's husband, stopped washing dishes and rushed to Anna and Krystyna.

"What's wrong? Is Annie all right?"

To avoid unwanted questions and attention, Krystyna, who knew David would want to care for Anna, diverted him.

"It's fine, David. Annie is feeling faint and tired. She needs some fresh air. Go watch the front with Jill for a few moments while I help Annie."

David, loving and trusting like his brother, Krystyna's husband Mike, held open the rear door to the alleyway. Outside, Anna sagged to the concrete and cried. Krystyna, frightened, shook Anna.

"Anna, what is it? Tell me now!"

Through tears and sobs, Anna explained the call.

"We must run, Krystyna. Edvard will kill us."

"How long did the man say until they come?"

"He said about an hour."

Hardness, formed by years of abuse and humiliation, boiled from within Krystyna as she held Anna's face in her hands. Squeezing harder than intended, Krystyna pulled Anna close.

"We will not run, Anna. We have too much to lose."

"But what can we do?"

"We will prepare, Anna. We will go home, change our clothes, and we will wait for them."

Twenty

Reflecting on his agreement to commit murder, Tyrion didn't speak until they turned off the A38.

"This is Riviera Way. It takes us directly to Torbay Road, which follows the ocean into Torquay and the main harbour. My wife and I used to come this way."

"When was last time you come here?"

"Oh, I don't know. Ten years, I guess."

"Has changed, you think?"

"Mm, not so far. But, that McDonald's over there is new. Bloody things are everywhere."

"Yes. Even in my country, there is McDonald's. Even where people have very little money, there is a McDonald's to take what they have."

Past the new McDonald's, Riviera Way changed to Newton Road, but Tyrion didn't mention it. Through the haze of another cigarette, Edvard asked, "Riviera Way? I thought the French had the Riviera."

"Yes, lots of people say that. This is the English equivalent. You know, a fancy place by the sea."

"Then it is for rich people, yes?"

"No, not really. Maybe during Victorian times. Now it's a seaside town for everyone."

Newton Road changed again to Avenue Road and finally The King's Drive before it dead-ended at Torbay Road. Left onto Torbay, a childlike expression burst from Tyrion's lips, "Look, there is the English Channel! On a clear day, you can see France."

Unimpressed, Edvard responded tersely, "We need somewhere to stay."

"I know a place. It's on Babbacombe Road. We used to stay at the Kingsholm Hotel."

"The hotel is near the water?"

"Oh yes, less than half a mile. We used to walk to the harbour twice a day, and then we would take my daughter . . ."

Tyrion, Edvard's disinterest clear, ended his reminiscence of better days and concentrated on his driving.

Pedestrians, heading for the harbour walkway and the beach, dodged between the cars that choked Torbay Road. Frustrated, Tyrion honked his horn several times, but could do nothing to improve their crawl along the waterfront. A circle, centred with a large Victorian-era clock, marked the junction of Cary Parade, Victoria Parade, and Torwood Street.

Tyrion exited the circle first left on Torwood and continued until it changed to Babbacombe Road. A quarter mile up Babbacombe, Tyrion stopped in front of a large Edwardian-era house with three floors and well-tended gardens. A tasteful sign indicated vacancies and free guest parking. With the car parked and engine off, Tyrion turned to Edvard. "I, er, think two rooms would be best?"

"Yes. I wait here."

"You don't want to come in and see the place? It's very nice and . . ."

"This is not a holiday. Get room and key and come back while I think."

~

Tyrion returned to the parking lot and found Edvard seated and smoking on the car hood. As he approached, Tyrion reported his success. "We have two rooms on the third floor overlooking gardens at the back."

Handing over the key, Tyrion continued. "You're in room fourteen. What now?"

Edvard pushed off the car, flicked his cigarette butt to the ground, pocketed the room key, and said to Tyrion, "Now we walk."

"What? Where to?"

"You will go to the harbour. I will walk the main streets and side streets."

Tyrion's face pinched and his shoulders hunched upward. Confused and skeptical, he challenged, "You think it will be that easy. There are thousands of people, and they could be anywhere."

Edvard spoke with quiet confidence.

"You are right. It will not be easy, but I don't expect us to find them today. I want to get a feel of the town. To understand how it works and where people go and what they do. On the other hand, Stringer, your private investigator, he visited for only two days, and he found them. Perhaps you or I will get lucky. As we say in Prague, Kdo hledá, najde, he who look, finds."

Unmoved by Edvard's assertions, but without a better suggestion, Tyrion accepted.

"OK, I'll take a tour then and meet you somewhere?"

"The hotel," said Edvard, "it has a bar?"

"Yes, inside the front door to the left. See that window," said Tyrion as he pointed. "There is a table and two leather chairs."

"Good. In one hour, at four, we will meet. Then I will make more detailed plan."

Edvard turned right and strode up Babbacombe Street and Tyrion, without an option, turned left toward the harbour.

Twenty-One

Krystyna and Anna wore conservative sun dresses, practical hats, and large sunglasses. Krystyna opted for lightweight, white slip-ons, while Anna preferred open-toed sandals. Their hair, no longer cut short and practical for their former lives in Prague, was un-tucked and flowing from beneath their hats. Dressed like carefree tourists, the two women walked away from the car they had parked a few blocks from their café. On the corner of Montpellier and The Terrace, a short walk from the harbour, Krystyna stopped and said, "Your cell phone is charged?"

"Yes, I checked it two times, but I don't want to go alone."

"You must, Anna. They will be searching for two women, and together we will attract attention. Also, if we separate, we can cover two times the ground."

"But I'm afraid, Krystyna. What if Edvard recognizes me and takes me?"

"This is England, Anna, not Prague. If he tries to get you, scream and someone will help."

"I, I don't know if I can."

A transparent tear trickled from under Anna's dark sunglasses and spread down over her flushed cheeks caressed by the yellow light of the low afternoon sun. Krystyna gently dabbed the tear with the tip of a finger and stared at her young sister.

"I love you, Anna, and I won't let anything happen to you. With the hat, glasses, and your long hair, Edvard will not recognize you. Take this bag, and go in and out of shops buying small items for gifts as though you were on vacation."

The bag, off-white cotton with two stick figures seated under an umbrella on a beach, hung limply in Anna's hand.

"OK. But where should I go?"

"You search the main streets in town. I will go to the harbour area. If you see Edvard, stay away from him and call me. I will come."

"What will we do if we see him?"

"I, I don't know."

Krystyna adjusted her hat and glasses and cinched the straps on a small bag that hung across her chest.

"Look, Anna, we must do this. We must do it for our children. What will become of them if we let Edvard take us or worse? What of David and Mike? They are good men, Anna. They do not deserve the pain of losing us or of finding out about our past. What of all we have built here? No, Anna, I cannot begin again."

Anna, trembling despite the warmth of the sun, reached for Krystyna and clung until Krystyna eased her away.

"I will call every fifteen minutes, OK? It will be all right, Anna. I promise."

Krystyna stopped at the circle at the bottom of Torwood Road. Three roads, Torwood, Victoria Parade, and Cary Parade, converged at the circle. In the centre of the circle, the Mallock Memorial Clock, built in 1902 to commemorate the life and works of former Member of Parliament Richard Mallock, silently marked 4:15 p.m. To the left, Victoria Parade, populated with numerous restaurants and bars, led south along the harbour. Cary Parade, to the right, followed the more scenic, walking route. Krystyna chose right.

Between lunch and dinner, most tourists and many locals walked the Cary Parade Road to the South West Coastal Path. Content and relaxed, as they digested lunch to make way for dinner while gulping crisp sea air, people meandered without purpose. Conscious of the gentle pedestrian flow, Krystyna slowed her pace and took the time to view the ocean and feel the breeze.

Three years ago, when Krystyna and Anna first arrived in Torquay, the serene waters of the bay had stilled their fears and calmed their nerves. Arriving in the early afternoon, they had sat until the sun set before finding an inexpensive bed and breakfast far from the main drag. Since then, the coastal path had become a regular favourite for Krystyna and Anna, and each step along the path increased their resolve to keep all they had achieved.

A scream jolted Krystyna from her memories. Moisture burst on her skin and her throat contracted. A few steps from Krystyna a teenage girl jumped up and down as she pulled her t-shirt away from her back and chest. Three boys and two girls surrounded the yelling girl and laughed as they squirted water from plastic bottles. When the water was spent, one of the boys embraced the girl and they kissed as their friends whooped and hollered encouragement. Calm returned as the boisterous kids departed and Krystyna sighed with relief.

After twenty minutes, Krystyna turned and retraced her steps along the coastal path. Many walkers had done the same from the other direction, and Krystyna noted several people she had already seen. Concrete and wooden benches, impervious to the changing seasons, faced the ocean like sentinels. Krystyna joined an elderly couple on a bench and withdrew a magazine from her bag. Over the magazine, as Krystyna searched for Edvard and Tyrion, Krystyna noticed the tide had turned, and the ocean had begun its early evening retreat.

~

Time did not stand still, light did not blaze, and there was no fanfare when Tyrion entered the narrow field of vision above Krystyna's magazine. Krystyna's hand did shake momentarily until Tyrion walked within four feet of Krystyna without any indication of recognition. Certain that Tyrion had not seen her, Krystyna waited several moments before she followed him. Overdressed for the warm evening with trousers, shirt, and jacket, Tyrion was easy to keep in sight.

Krystyna checked the time on her phone as she called Anna.

"Anna."

"Yes."

"I've found Tyrion."

"Oh God, no. They are really here. What do we do now? Oh . . ."

"Calm down, Anna. He walked right past me without recognizing me. He has never seen you, so don't worry."

"Where are you?"

"I am on the coastal path heading back toward the main circle where the clock is."

"Oh no, that's on the way to our café. What if he . . .?"

"Where are you, Anna?"

"I'm near the Meadfoot Inn."

"OK, stay away from the café."

"Krystyna, Krystyna."

"Anna, everything will be all right. I will call you. OK, Anna?"

"Yes. OK."

Tyrion, to Krystyna's horror, turned up Torwood Road. In a few minutes, he would pass their café. Steps from the café, Tyrion twisted his wrist to view his watch and sped up. Krystyna looked back at the clock on the circle. It was 4:15 p.m.

Torwood Road changed to Babbacombe Street about two hundred metres past the café, and Tyrion kept on walking. Several hotels fronted Babbacombe Street, and Krystyna suspected one of the hotels was Tyrion's destination. The pedestrian traffic thinned, and Krystyna held back, but remained close enough to watch Tyrion enter the Kingsholm Hotel.

Slowed by a desire to turn and run, Krystyna edged closer to the hotel entrance. Shielded by roadside bushes, Krystyna scanned the ground floor doorway and windows. To the right, two human shapes appeared through a large rectangle window, withdrew chairs from a table, and sat down. Acrid bile rushed up Krystyna's throat and swamped her back teeth as she saw Edvard glance toward the window. Teetering with nausea, Krystyna retreated from the hotel. Fifty metres from the hotel, Krystyna stopped and steadied herself against the plastic wall of a bus shelter. Tears welled in her eyes, but she did not let them fall. Instead, Krystyna called Anna.

Twenty-Two

The bar promised by Tyrion was no more than a narrow seven-foot L-shaped counter with three white wooden chairs pressed together on the long and short side of the white-fronted, black-topped counter. Behind the counter, a limited selection of spirits and wines dotted sparse shelves that looked more suited to books than bottles. Despite appearances, the hotel proprietor managed to produce decent drinks for his guests.

Edvard, a double vodka over ice sweating moisture on the polished wooden table before him, gestured for Tyrion to move his pint to the side of the table as he unfolded a tourist street map of Torquay.

"I picked up two of these maps. We shall divide the town and make an organized search."

"You didn't find them?"

"No. I didn't expect such luck, but now I understand the area, and I am certain this is the kind of town the bitch and her sister would hide in."

"What makes you think that?"

"Tourists. Many unskilled and part-time jobs for cash. Foreigners would not be noticed here. Many visit, and many work in bars and restaurants as well as stores. While I walk, I observe window signs for workers to wash dishes, wait tables, clean hotel rooms, and serve in stores. That is the kind of work whores will do if they don't want to spread their legs."

Through slurped beer, Tyrion acknowledged Edvard.

"I guess that makes sense. So what do we do then? Check out every restaurant and bar in Torquay?"

"Yes. But not all. They have no experience, and their English will not be so good, so don't bother with expensive restaurants, the best hotels, or fancy stores. Look at smaller places, which will have less rules and like to pay less taxes, yes."

"OK, I get it. How do you want to divide the town?"

Edvard swallowed his double vodka in two gulps and set the glass on the window ledge. Smoothing the map on the table, Edvard pointed and drew a rough line that dissected the town in two.

"Same as before. I will stay in main town roads while you search waterfront area. Only this time, we keep track of where we look. Here is pen for you to mark areas you look."

"Do I just look, or do I ask questions like we did in Bodmin?"

"Both. But you will need a story to tell."

"Yes, right. What about you?"

"I think as I go. You need make story and stick with it. Can you make one?"

"Um, yes. I could be an insurance person. You know, hired by a lawyer to find girls because of some money left to them back in Prague. I will show the photograph to people and . . ."

An open palm slammed on the table and Tyrion spilled beer on the map as Edvard barked, "No. Your story is stupid and no photograph."

"Well, fuck you! What do you mean no photograph? And what's wrong with my story? Do you have a better one?"

Edvard, anger giving way to experience, demonstrated his superiority.

"The photograph is old and unofficial. It is not what an insurance agent would use. Also, many would ask you for business card and company name. Then they use phone to check Internet. In one minute, they know you lie. A man showing photograph of two young foreign girls and asking questions would make suspicion."

"What then?" mumbled Tyrion, "I just look?"

"No. You talk about your holidays to Prague and how much you like. That the clock by the water reminds you of one in Prague and how the boats and harbour remind you of the rivers. To men, you nod and wink and talk of the girls and their beauty and accents. To women, you talk of the hardship for women in Prague. You decide what to say based on who you meet. That is how you search for persons, yes."

"Fine, I get it, but I've never done this kind of thing before."

Edvard ignored Tyrion's whine, placed a bag on the table, and took out two cell phones. He passed one to Tyrion.

"I pick up these. The number is on the back. Memorize and give the number to people to call if they have any information. I have written my number on your map. We will only use these two phones, not our own. They are untraceable. Understand?"

With the map and phone in hand, Tyrion asked, "Yes. But what do I do if I find them?"

"You call me, of course. You watch. You make sure they do not see you. When I come, we will find where they live. Then we make plan."

Edvard folded his map and sucked an ice cube from his glass. As Tyrion rose from the chair, a dark expression filled Edvard's face.

"One more thing, Mr. Ennis, when you and your wife visited, do you remember a quiet place away from people but where car can be driven?"

"Not really. I mean, we didn't, you know, go to places like that."

"Well, you need to think, my friend. I do not know this place. We will need a private place. That is your job."

"What time do we come back?"

"When everything is closed. Even then, we will walk the streets. Perhaps the bitch and her sister have not closed their legs and look for customers."

Walking to the door, Edvard caught Tyrion's arm and leaned in to whisper, "One last thing: beside Stringer, does anyone else know about me?"

"Er, no. I thought it best to keep all this 'and you' secret."

"That is good."

Twenty-Three

Three hotels down from the Kingsholm, Krystyna met Anna as arranged in the driveway of the Hotel Barton. Anna, eyes wide like a cornered rabbit, twitched with stress as she croaked hoarse words at Krystyna. "Is he really here? Are you sure it's Edvard, Krystyna?"

Taking Anna's hands, Krystyna nodded and said, "Yes. It is Edvard, but he looks different."

"Different, what do you mean?"

"Edvard's face. It's twisted and crooked, and I think he has a big scar on one side. Anyway, it was him and the one called Tyrion. They are together in the Hotel Kingsholm. I saw them through a window."

"What! The Kingsholm. Are you crazy? It's right there. What if they saw you? What if they come out right now? We must get away from here."

"They didn't see me, Anna. I wouldn't be standing here if they did."

"What? What were they doing?"

Krystyna released Anna's hand and stared up the road.

"I saw Edvard unfold some paper. I think they had a map. Probably of Torquay. They will search the town for us."

"Oh God, we must leave. Leave now and never come back."

"And what of our sons, Anna? Our husbands? What of the lives we have made here? No, Anna, we cannot run anymore."

"Then we must hide until they give up. They can't stay here forever."

Anna moved away from Krystyna and peered left and right. Krystyna pulled Anna back and held her tight.

"Yes, Anna, you are right. They can't stay forever. Especially Edvard. But we cannot hide."

Tears began to form, but Krystyna had had enough.

"No, Anna. No more tears. It is time for you to be strong."

"But what can we do?"

"We must watch them, Anna. We must know where they are and what they do."

"That's crazy," said Anna becoming more agitated. "They will see us. Let's go home. We won't go to work at the café. We will be sick for days."

"No, Anna, we must know what they do. Listen, Anna, I've been thinking. It will be like in Prague when one of us had a bad customer."

"You mean when we followed each other and, if something happened, we called Edvard?"

"Yes, but this time we will both follow and watch. We will take turns and switch. Besides, they will not suspect that we will be watching them."

Anna wrung her hands and moved her head side to side in dismissal. "It's no good. Edvard is too smart. He is an animal with animal instincts. Always, he finds people in Prague. You know how many have tried to hide from him."

"I know that, Anna. I don't mean for us to follow Edvard. We will follow the Englishman, Tyrion. As long as we have him in sight, we know they cannot find us."

"But they will be together."

"I don't think so, Anna. Edvard works alone. They will split up like they did earlier when I saw Tyrion."

"But when they meet, what then?"

"The hotel is their meeting place. When Tyrion heads to the hotel, we stop following. We will know where they are."

Anna, unable to stop shaking, sobbed, "This is all my fault. I should not have sent those photographs. You were right to stop and forget them."

"Yes, Anna, it is your fault. I will not hide that from you. But it doesn't matter. It is done, and now we must deal with it."

"I'm sorry, Krystyna, I'm sorry."

"It's OK, Anna. I know you did it because you love me. I love you, Anna. We can do this. We will survive."

Anna straightened up, and Krystyna helped dry her eyes.

"Anna, I will go first. You will follow me. Stay back. I will send you a text or call you when it is a good time to switch."

"A good time?"

"When he enters a shop or café or somewhere."

"Krystyna?"

"Yes."

"What, what if he goes in our café?"

"We close in two hours, at 6:30. He won't have time today."

"But it's right here. What if he begins as soon as he comes out of the hotel? What if . . .?"

"I don't know, Anna. We have to hope."

The sisters stood facing each other. Out of time and choices, Krystyna took charge. "Go to the clock and wait. I will remain here. When he comes out, I will follow and call to tell you which street he is on and his direction."

Anna pressed Krystyna's hand and hurried away. With Anna out of sight, Krystyna left the hotel driveway, crossed the road, and entered a souvenir shop. Inside, pretending to study trinkets, Krystyna watched the front of the Kingsholm Hotel. Moments later, Edvard and Tyrion appeared on the sidewalk. Krystyna watched the two hunters exchange a few words, smile, and set off in opposite directions. Tyrion folded paper in one hand, turned toward the harbour, and walked past the store on the opposite side of the road. Behind Krystyna, a soft voice sounded. "Hi. You're one of the sisters who owns the café, right?"

Startled, Krystyna turned and knocked a plastic cup with a printed map of Torquay on one side off a display stand. Flustered, Krystyna apologized. "Oh, oh, I'm sorry."

"No problem. I'll get it. I didn't mean to startle you. It's my fault."

"I was just thinking, not paying attention."

"You do work in the café, right?"

Krystyna strained to see out of the window. Tyrion passed out of sight and Krystyna hurried to the door.

"Yes, yes, that's right. I'm sorry, I must go. I will come back later."

Krystyna exited the store and searched for Tyrion. He had not gone far. She could see him stopped outside Bianco's, a fine Italian restaurant. He peered in the window for a moment before continuing on his way. Krystyna watched as Tyrion paused outside Jingles, a Tex-Mex diner. He studied the menu in the window, then entered. Ten minutes later, Tyrion came out, paused to make a mark on his map, and then resumed walking toward the harbour.

Krystyna followed. Her heart stopped as Tyrion paused again, this time in front of McColl's newsagent. He stared across the road at her café. She sensed him reading the café name 'Brothers & Sisters Café.' *No, no,* she screamed in her head. Tyrion held his map, and Krystyna watched as he made a mark. Done with the map, Tyrion continued walking down Torwood Road.

Next, Tyrion stopped at the Pizza Express on the corner of Torwood and Cary Parade, directly opposite the circle clock. Krystyna texted Anna to stay out of sight. Tyrion exited the Pizza Express in moments with a distraught and angry expression. Lebanese immigrants owned the Pizza Express and employed many illegal workers, and Krystyna expected they had not been friendly to someone asking questions.

Around the corner from the Pizza Express on Cary Parade, Tyrion entered the London Inn pub and stayed for almost half an hour. Krystyna knew the area well and that many more restaurants and pubs fronted

Victoria Parade rather than Cary Parade. If Tyrion had a tourist map with restaurants and hotels indicated with little icons, he would likely cross the circle and head along the harbour front and Victoria Parade. Krystyna called Anna.

"Anna, he is in the London Inn. I think he will come your way next. He is searching in restaurants and bars. Tiger Bills is the first bar on Victoria Parade. Stay behind the clock on the water side. I will text you when he leaves the pub. You can take over for a while. Just stay back and watch him. I will keep further back. Remember, Tyrion has never seen you, so you will be safe."

"You will be close, Krystyna?"

"Yes, I will be close and will come if something happens. Here he comes now. Stay back."

Krystyna was thankful now that when they had first arrived in Torquay, they had told people they were from Warsaw, Poland, and never mentioned Prague and the Czech Republic. If Tyrion and Edvard asked for girls from Prague, they would not find any.

Anna observed Tyrion enter and exit Subway, Burridge's, Alporto, and Ella before Krystyna took over. Six more stops, and Anna relieved Krystyna. With Anna watching Tyrion, Krystyna's phone rang.

"Hi, David."

"Yes, Annie is OK. She's feeling much better."

"Oh, er, we are getting some fresh air by the harbour."

"Yes, I know. Yes, we will try to be back in time to help close."

As Anna's husband, always chatty, continued to talk, a beep indicated an incoming text.

"I'm sorry, David. Have to go. Will meet you at the café."

Anna's text demanded Krystyna call.

"Anna."

"He's not going into restaurants anymore. He is walking past them and heading up Beacon Hill. What is he doing?"

Krystyna thought in silence.

"Krystyna, are you there?"

"Oh no, Anna. He must be going to Reflections. You remember that is where we had our first job when we came. Someone must have remembered us and sent him there."

Twenty-Four

Lies, deception, and power punctuated Edvard's life. Enlightened by his first beating and real life lesson in Usti nad Labem's river port at the hands of the local drug gang, Edvard had applied himself to honing his manipulative and deceptive skills. Skills that had made him a mid-level crime leader in Prague and enabled him to survive and prosper where many had died or failed.

His casual movement and unhurried step concealed a sharp mind and cruel intentions as he disarmed and charmed the employees, owners, and customers of the many cafés, restaurants, and stores that dotted the streets of Torquay's inner-town area. Even Edvard's disfigured face became an asset as he eased people's discomfort with self-deprecating remarks.

Despite stories of Prague, lost sisters, and an interest in finding work for young women seeking a new life, Edvard received no useful information about two women from Prague. Even posing as a freelance reporter searching for people from the Czech Republic to learn of their experience for international employment and travel publications brought no relevant information until he entered AMF Bowling.

A multi-lane bowling alley, AMF Bowling boasted an American-style diner and a small bar. The bowling alley manager, a fat, greasy man with eyes that lingered far too long on the younger bowlers, told Edvard about some Polish girls who had arrived in town a couple of years ago, and he thought they had a shop or something in town.

Outside the bowling alley, encouraged by the fat man's recollections, Edvard consulted his map for directions to his next call, The Hole in the Wall Pub on Park Lane. Instinct told Edvard that Krystyna was smart enough to present themselves as Polish rather than Czech, and he chided himself for not thinking of that himself. His newly purchased cell phone buzzed, and Edvard answered without waiting.

"You have found something?"

"It's Tyrion."

"I know. Only you have my number. What you have found?"

"In one of the pubs on the front, Harvesters, a barman remembers two girls who used to work at a place called Quay Reflections a couple of years ago. He remembered them because they were a bit rough, which he seemed to like. Thing is, though, he thought they were Russian. What do you think?"

"It is worth to check. I also have mention of two girls, but the man thought they were Polish."

"Polish, eh? Well, maybe they tell people different things."

"Perhaps, but I think it is more that to you English, we from the Eastern Europe are all the same."

"Oh, er."

"Never mind. I am not offended. You are all same to me. You will go to this place Reflection. Call me after with news. I will continue and work my way to the harbour, yes."

"OK. I can't wait to see her face when I . . ."

"No! I told you; do not let them see you. We find where they live, then we take them. Understand?"

"Yes."

Edvard ended the call. A lopsided smile broke his face, and warm salt-laden ocean air rushed to fill his lungs through flared nostrils. His movements and steps became more purposeful as the certainty of capturing his quarry neared.

Checking his map for directions, Edvard had two options. One route would take him via Parkhill Road, which, according to the map icons, had only one other point of interest, The Orange Tree Restaurant, and that was close to the Hole in the Wall Pub. The alternative route, via Torwood Street and Park Lane, would take him past six or seven potential enquiry points.

Opting for efficiency, Edvard made for Torwood Street. On the corner of Parkhill and Torwood, Edvard paused to peer in the window of Simla Spice, wriggled his nose, and moved on. Indian restaurants only employed family members. Next, the Ephesus restaurant, which was closed, and then Amici, an Italian pizza and pasta restaurant. Through the window, Edvard could see no empty tables and noted the frantic pace of the servers. Too busy to engage staff, Edvard moved on two doors farther down Torwood and looked up at the sign above the door. A gasp leaked from Edvard's twisted mouth: Brothers & Sisters Café.

Stunned by the possibility this was the café the man at the bowling alley mentioned, Edvard paused on the doorstep. The door swung open and cut short his indecision as an elderly lady exited, held the door, and said, "You'd better get in there, love, if you want something. They close in twenty minutes."

Decision made, Edvard entered the Brothers & Sisters Café.

Twenty-Five

Excited by his discovery and Edvard's news about two Polish girls, Tyrion jammed the cell phone in his pocket and folded the map, which he didn't need for direction. The bartender in the Harvester Pub had told him to turn left out of the pub and head up the hill. He couldn't miss it. As he walked, Tyrion web searched Reflections, which was listed as a coffee shop and gallery featuring local artists including jewellery, ceramics, and original prints. Situated on Beacon Quay waterfront, the café boasted indoor and outdoor exhibits and encouraged visitors to stroll the harbour wall while savouring their coffee.

Eager, Tyrion strode the hill quickly. Halfway up, waterside, a large car park opened up. Beside the car park entrance, a sign invited customers to enter Reflections from the far side of the lot. Anna, familiar with Reflections from the few weeks she and Krystyna had worked there almost three years ago, hung back and watched Tyrion stride toward the café entrance.

~

"Anna, has he gone in yet?"
"Yes, just now."

"The owner, Heston, he will remember us, Anna."

"It wasn't my fault; you know what happened with the man Heston."

"I know."

"Do you think he will remember enough to link us with our café?"

"I don't think so. The café is under our husbands' names, and we have gone by Christina and Annie for years now. I think he will recall us, but not know what became of us. We were only there for a short time."

"Krystyna, I forgot to tell you that he made a call when he came out of the Harvester Pub. He seemed excited. Do you think he called Edvard?"

"Yes, I expect so."

"Oh God, then Edvard will come."

"Maybe, Anna, but Tyrion knows nothing yet."

"I'm going closer. I want to see what he does and if he makes another call right away. If he does, then he knows something."

"No, Anna, don't. It's too dangerous."

"It's OK, Krystyna. Like you told me, he has never seen me, and I have my hat and glasses."

"No, Anna, stay back. I'm at the bottom of the hill. I'll be there in two minutes."

~

Inside, Tyrion stilled to adjust his eyes from the early evening hue to the bright, indoor, gallery-style lights. Business was good, and Tyrion needed to turn sideways several times as he made his way past the displays to the coffee counter. Three people tended the coffee counter, and all appeared under twenty years old.

Tyrion ordered a latté to go and asked the young woman who took his money who owned or managed the café.

"That would be Mr. Heston. He's the one over in the corner by the desk. White hair and a blue cravat."

Tyrion turned and saw his man. Four people, two couples, were engaged in an animated exchange with the man Heston and Tyrion crabbed his way toward them. As he closed in on the group, the men exchanged handshakes, and the people moved away. Heston, a satisfied grin on his face, moved behind the desk and moved something from the desktop to a drawer. Taking the opportunity, Tyrion moved in.

"Mr. Heston?"

"Yes. How may I help you, Mr.?"

Flustered, Tyrion responded lamely.

"Jones, Mr. Jones."

A skeptical, mischievous smile opened Heston's face as he replied lightly.

"Ah, I see. We get many Joneses visiting the gallery. Are you seeking something specific? A painting or jewellery perhaps?"

"Well, yes, I mean, not exactly."

Heston, open palmed, raised an eyebrow.

"Do go on."

"It's a little delicate. I'm, um, looking for two women."

Heston's face widened more as he toyed with "Mr. Jones."

"Two women. I must say that's brave of you. I usually limit myself to one. Easier at my age."

Crimson spread up Tyrion's neck and into his face. Embarrassed, Tyrion said, "No, no, I don't mean like that. I mean, two women who used to work here a few years ago."

"Ah, so many come and go. It is the nature of the business and the young ones, so beautiful. Now you have the curiosity of an old man. Which women do you seek and why?"

~

"Anna, where are you? Are you all right? I'm in the parking lot, Anna."

"Yes, yes, I'm good. I'm by the main gallery window. I can see him. He's talking to that bastard, Heston."

"Come away, Anna. Heston won't know anything about us now. Besides, after what happened, I doubt he would want to tell a stranger about it."

"I don't know. They are talking a long time. They are the same kind of man."

"Anna, you must not stand still and stare. You will be noticed."

~

Tyrion, recognizing perhaps the predator's glint in Heston's eyes, decided on honesty.

"The two women are from Prague. They are whores, and they have done bad things. We think they worked here two or three years ago and that they are still in Torquay."

Heston, with an exaggerated gasp, held up a hand to his mouth and mocked. "Well, it's not every day a pimp comes looking for his whores. I . . ."

"I'm not a pimp, I'm . . ."

"Ah, an aggrieved customer then? I myself have never paid for the pleasures of women. No need, you see."

Tyrion, pissed off by Heston's manner, tensed and stepped up to the desk.

"Do you know who I'm looking for or not?"

A soft laugh accompanied a snide smile as Heston opened his arms wide.

"My dear chap, I don't. Even if I did, I wouldn't tell some trumped up little man from up north who needs to pay to get his jollies."

"But, but you seem . . ."

"Don't confuse me with being like you, my dear man. Oh no, what I want, I take. Like a man. Now get out."

Tyrion moved toward Heston and said, "You bastard. You think you can mess with me? I'll . . ."

At Tyrion's threat, Heston looked past Tyrion and greeted two men. "Ah, good evening, gentlemen."

"Sorry, we're late. I hope we're not interrupting."

"Not at all. This man is just leaving. We don't sell the kind of thing he is looking for."

Tyrion, anger rising, stormed away from Heston and crashed through the main doors. Tyrion's sudden movement startled Anna, who was still peering through a large glass window by the entrance. When Tyrion burst through the doors, Anna froze. Anna, to see better through the glass, had taken her sunglasses off. Tyrion, seeking someone to vent on or at, saw Anna. Their eyes locked.

"What the fuck are you looking at?"

Unable to speak, Anna gaped at Tyrion.

Tyrion stopped dead and stared at Anna. He didn't need to look at the photograph in his pocket to see the resemblance and he shouted at Anna.

"Hey, what the fuck?"

Anna turned and ran.

Twenty-Six

Two people, man and wife, who looked to be in their seventies, exchanged tourist pleasantries with the young women behind the counter. While they talked and ordered tea, Edvard studied the woman and quickly confirmed that she was not Krystyna or Anna.

Jill, filling in for Krystyna and Anna, steered an elderly couple toward a window table and assured them their tea would be along soon and they wouldn't be rushed to finish before the café closed at 6:30 p.m. After she placed the order stub on the ledge of the pass-through window to the café's kitchen, she turned to greet Edvard.

"Hello. Welcome to Brothers & Sisters Café. What can I get for you?"

Edvard pasted a lopsided smile on his face and nodded to the daily specials listed in neat cursive writing on a chalkboard. With a heavy accent, Edvard asked, "Is there time for a tea and some of the Devon cream pie?"

Ever happy and eager to please, which is why Krystyna hired her in the first place, Jill returned Edvard's smile and said, "Yes, there's time, and you're lucky, that's our last piece. If you take a table, I'll bring it over in a few minutes."

~

Edvard chose a two-person table away from the old couple and studied the café. White walls, small tables, wooden chairs, a glass display case beside the counter, two ceiling fans, a child's highchair, salt, pepper, and sugar shakers, an exit sign, and a finger sign pointing to a door to the washroom passed without importance through Edvard's consciousness.

Only two items grabbed Edvard's attention and distinguished this café from thousands of others. Attached to the wall beside the entrance, Edvard fixed on a faded poster of Warsaw. A small Polish flag, the kind attached to short sticks that are often seen waving in the hands of small children as they stand roadside in support of some unknown dignitary, hung by one staple to the poster.

Jill approached Edvard and transferred tea, sugar, milk, and pie to Edvard's table. Before Jill could withdraw, Edvard pointed to the poster on the wall and remarked, "I am surprised to see pictures of my homeland in your café."

"Oh, the poster. That's the owners. They come from Poland."

"I see. And the owners, they are really brother and sister?"

As though asked all the time, Jill smiled over a small sigh and replied, "Yes. I mean, yes and no."

Edvard, puzzled, waited.

"Well, yes, the owners are brothers and sisters, but not you know, brother and sister."

With an idea forming, Edvard thickened his accent even more. "I sorry, but my English, I don't understand."

"Well, there are two sisters and two brothers, and they are married to each other."

"What! Sisters marry each other and . . ."

Laughing at Edvard's deliberate tactic to put her at ease, Jill explained, "No, no. I mean each sister married a brother. So brothers and sisters. Kinda cute, don't you think?"

Jill turned away, cleared a nearby table, and placed a "closed" sign on the door.

Edvard lingered over his tea and pie until the old couple left and only he and Jill remained. Edvard checked his watch. It was 6:37 p.m., and Jill had begun to place chairs on tables in preparation for mopping the floor. A table over from Edvard, Jill paused and said, "Excuse me, I'm sorry to hurry you, but we are closing now if you don't mind."

Edvard, feigned apologies, stood and said: "Of course, of course. The poster of Warsaw, it got me to think about my homeland. You know, I am here to look for a place to live for myself and my wife and children. I like much this Torquay, but I don't know anyone or where might be good place."

Jill, wrestling with another chair, suggested, "You should come by and ask Annie and Cristina. They're the ones from Poland. You could talk with them, and they could give you some information."

At the mention of Annie and Christina, Edvard's eyes glinted. "Ah, Annie and Christina, yes. Have they been here long?"

"I'm not sure. I've only worked here for about six months, but I think they came here around three or four years ago."

Edvard, skilled in asking indirect questions, asked, "And they live here at the café?"

"Oh no, of course not. Christina-she's the real boss, but don't tell Annie I said that-lives up on Braddons Hill not far from here. It's a real nice place, all white with grass all around and a wooden play structure out front."

"A play structure. Then Annie and Christina have children, yes? And will know of schools?"

"Yes, they both have a son, but they're only a year old or so. How old are your kids?"

"Oh, mine are ten and twelve."

"Anna lives there also?"

"Who? You mean Annie, not Anna. No, she lives a bit farther out near Warberry Road, I think."

"Ah, too bad they are not here now. I could ask them to dinner."

"They usually are, but Annie got sick all of a sudden this afternoon, and Christina took her home.

Their husbands, David and Mike, are in the back. I could ask them to come out, and you could talk to them and . . ."

Inside Edvard's pocket, the disposable phone, for which only Tyrion had the number, buzzed. Edvard moved quickly to the door, pointed to the phone he had withdrawn from his pocket, and said, "No, no, that's all right. I'm in town for a while. I'll stop by tomorrow. Maybe you keep me as a surprise. That might be fun, yes?"

"OK. I can do that. Thanks for coming by. See you tomorrow."

Outside the café, Edvard listened to Tyrion, ended the call, checked his map, and set off toward the harbour and the wharf.

Twenty-Seven

Anna made the wrong choice. She should have turned right, through the car park, out to the road, and into safety among the tourists heading down Beacon Hill to the main harbour area. Instead, Anna ran left onto the concrete walkway that topped the harbour wall and stretched out into the English Channel.

On the walkway, a few people, who had watched the sun dip to the horizon, stepped back as Anna ran through them. Glad of her lightweight slip-on shoes, Anna moved quickly and crouched behind a small, wooden storage shed used by local fishermen to store tackle and bait. Fifty metres away, Anna watched Tyrion slow, stand still, and take out a cell phone. Anna realized her mistake. He had stopped because he had trapped her.

Panic surged. Anna fumbled and dropped her phone as she dialled Krystyna. On the floor, the phone rang. Anna grasped the phone.

"Anna, I'm outside the gallery. Where are you?"

Behind her, Tyrion had resumed walking.

"Oh God, he's coming for me, he's coming for me. Help me, Krystyna, help me."

"What? Who's coming? Where are you, Anna?"

Anna un-crouched, stood, and began to back up along the harbour wall.

"Anna!"

"I'm on the wall. The harbour wall. He, Tyrion, he's following me. I can't get away. What should I do?"

"I'm coming, Anna. Keep walking to the end. Stay calm."

Unseen behind Anna, the salty air and water had worn away parts of the concrete. Anna, her open-toed sandals snagging, tripped, fell, and cried out as her elbows connected with the concrete. Pain rippled through Anna's arms, and the impact knocked the phone from her hand. Another cry pushed out when the phone bounced, slid, and dropped harbour-side into the water. Rolled over onto her knees facing inland, Anna winced as a cruel smile spread on Tyrion's face. Less than twenty metres away, he moved unhurriedly toward her.

Anna scrambled to her feet and searched for people or a way out. Only seagulls. No people and no way out, Anna kept pace with Tyrion's advance and edged farther along the wharf. The wharf narrowed, angled right, then left, and ended with a knee-high wall to separate walkers from the ocean. Anna reached the wall and looked back.

Tyrion, who had paused ten metres away at the left angle of the wharf, started toward Anna. Desperate, Anna ran to the right, harbour-side, and gazed into the dark ocean water two metres below. Anna ran left, ocean-side, and gasped at the rocks and boulders that formed the outer breakwater of the wharf. Tyrion closed the distance to five metres before he stopped. He spoke into his phone, put it in his pocket, and then spat at Anna. "Where's that whore sister of yours, bitch?"

"What, what are you talking about? Leave me alone. I'm going to call the police."

"Don't bullshit me. I know who you are."

"Get away. I'll scream."

"Go ahead. It's too late for that, Anna. You should have screamed before you got out here. No one will hear you over the seagulls."

Tyrion moved closer. Anna felt the top of the wall press against the back of her knees.

"I'm Annie, not Anna. Get away. What do you want?"

"Annie, Anna, I don't give a fuck what you call yourself. You're Krystyna's sister. I've seen you in the photograph. You may have put on a couple of pounds and your hair is different, but it's you. Your old friend Edvard will be here soon, and then you're gonna tell us where that bitch is."

Relief and hope lit Anna's face as she looked past Tyrion and saw Krystyna race around the angle of the walkway.

"Do you think I'm stupid? Sure, there is someone behind me. Jesus, can't you . . ."

Krystyna slammed into Tyrion from behind. Surprised and winded by the impact, Tyrion staggered but did not fall. Past Tyrion, Krystyna grasped Anna, pulled her away from the wall, and together they faced Tyrion. Seagulls, perched on the wall, scattered and screeched as they peeled away over the ocean. Recovered, but wary, Tyrion pulled a heavy cosh from his jacket pocket and slapped it against the palm of his hand. Hatred-filled eyes glared at each other. Tyrion, ever the one to lead, spoke first. "Ah, the bitch arrives. It's good to see you again, Krystyna."

Krystyna, eyes darting left and right, said nothing.

"What? Can't talk? That was never a problem when we had you at the house, eh? Well, your talking days are over now. In fact, when Edvard gets here, all your fucking days are over."

Krystyna placed her lips against Anna's ear and whispered. On an unspoken count of three, the sisters rushed Tyrion. Tyrion, instead of retreating, stepped into the women and crashed a full swing of the cosh on Krystyna's chest. The force of the swing, her own momentum, and the focused force and weight of the cosh laid Krystyna flat on her back breathless. While Tyrion had flattened Krystyna, Anna had slipped by and stood, land side, three metres from Tyrion. Tyrion turned and mocked Anna. "Go on, run, you bitch. I got what I wanted. But say goodbye to your sister first because you won't be seeing her again."

Krystyna, up on one elbow, screamed at Anna, "Go, Anna, run. Run!"

Anna burst into tears and cried as she walked to her sister. "I can't leave you. I can't live without you."

Tyrion smirked and waved the cosh at Anna. "Try anything, and I'll crush the bitch's head with this."

Past Tyrion, Anna knelt beside Krystyna and held her in her arms.

"I'm sorry, I'm sorry, I'm sorry, Krystyna."

More recovered, Krystyna sat up and spat at Tyrion. A glob of phlegm landed on his face. Enraged, Tyrion lunged and swung the cosh at Krystyna, but

Anna's arm came up and deflected the blow. Up on one knee, Krystyna tried to grab Tyrion's arm, but he was too quick. Tyrion drew his arm back for another swing. Anna, holding her limp arm, could not help, and the cosh arched and began to fall at Krystyna's head.

A man's hand caught Tyrion's arm mid-way through the killer downstroke and wrenched Tyrion backward and away from Krystyna. Grunting profanity, Tyrion turned. Disbelief and anger filled Tyrion's words. "What the fuck? What the hell are you doing here?"

Stringer had let go of Tyrion's arm and faced Tyrion. "I told you from the beginning that I wouldn't be part of something illegal, and what you are doing to these women is wrong."

"Wrong, wrong? You fucking dipshit. I'll tell you what's wrong. This bitch ruined my life, my friend's life, and she killed Ham. That's what's wrong. Now fuck off, and leave it alone."

While Stringer and Tyrion faced off, Anna had helped Krystyna to her feet. With the men between them and no escape, Krystyna motioned Anna to remain silent and follow her lead.

"I can't do that, Mr. Ennis. Whatever you feel these women have done to you, I won't stand by and watch you murder them."

Tyrion edged up on the balls of his feet.

"What do you propose then? Just let them go? These two bitches have blackmailed me for three years."

Stringer turned sideways to lower his profile. "You will have to go to the police. It is the only way."

"The police? Are you mad? I don't want this getting out. My marriage has gone, but this would ruin my business, my life. No, they are coming with me and Edvard when he gets here."

"Then you'll have to deal with me first, Mr. Ennis."

Tyrion and Stringer jockeyed for an opening while Stringer tried to talk Tyrion down.

"Look, Mr. Ennis, I know you have been through a lot, but murder is not the answer."

"You know nothing, Stringer. And I don't care what you think."

"It's madness, Ennis. You'll never get away with it. Do you want to spend the rest of your life in prison?"

Unresponsive to Stringer's pleas, Tyrion moved to keep Krystyna and Anna seaward.

"Look, just stay calm. I'm going to call the police, and they can sort it all out. If these women have done something wrong, then the police will take care of it."

Stringer took his cell phone out and looked down to find the number nine. The glance was all Tyrion needed. A quick step, and his cosh swung and connected with the side of Stringer's head.

Stringer didn't fall but staggered, dropped his phone, and fell hard against the wharf wall. Tyrion took another swing, missed, and hit the wall instead. Between Tyrion's swing, Stringer pushed himself away from the wall, grasped Tyrion with one hand and plunged a fist into Tyrion's stomach. Winded, Tyrion swung again, this time connecting with Stringer's neck. Stringer, falling back against the wall, grabbed Tyrion's arm, pulled him sharply, and cracked his forehead into

Tyrion's face. As the men punched, kicked, and grabbed, Stringer, bigger, stronger, and younger, edged ahead, and Tyrion faded and sank to his knees.

"All right, all right, stop," gasped Tyrion. "I'm done. Call the police."

Exhausted and groggy from the cosh blows to his head and neck, Stringer knelt down to retrieve his phone. On his way up, with cell phone in hand, Krystyna and Anna screamed together.

"Look out!"

Stringer looked; straight into the thick end of Tyrion's cosh as it smacked into his forehead. The impact thrust Stringer backward, and his upper body hung half over the wall. Without pause, Tyrion dropped his cosh, grasped Stringer's legs, lifted them up, and pushed Stringer head-first onto the rocks below. Satisfied, Tyrion turned back. Krystyna and Anna stood before him.

"You, you killed him," cried Anna.

Weakened by his struggle with Stringer, Tyrion stammered as he held onto the wall for support.

"He tried to kill me. You saw it. He attacked me first."

Krystyna, wary, spoke quietly. "If you let us go and take Edvard away, we will tell no one about this."

Tyrion edged himself up off the wall.

"It's too late for that. Edvard is on his way. Besides," snarled Tyrion, bloodlust in his eyes, "you won't be around to tell anyone anything."

Tyrion lunged, grabbed Anna by the hair, and pulled her backward to him and crooked an arm around her neck. Anna squirmed until Tyrion tensed his arm and began to choke her.

"Stop, stop. She has done nothing. Let her go. You can have me," cried Krystyna.

Tyrion squeezed a little more.

"No need. I can have both of you. Besides, Edvard wants Anna too. And I can't disappoint him, can I?"

Unaware of how tight he held Anna's neck, Anna slumped unconscious in his arms. Fearing Anna's death, Krystyna jumped at Tyrion. In her hand, Tyrion's cosh, which he had dropped when he lifted Stringer over the wall, crashed down on Tyrion's skull. Like a light switched off, Tyrion buckled to the ground with Anna on top of him. Krystyna pulled Anna from Tyrion and gently patted her face until she woke with a splutter.

"What happened?" asked Anna.

"You fainted, and I hit him with this," said Krystyna holding Tyrion's cosh.

"Is he dead?"

Krystyna leaned over and held the back of her hand to Tyrion's mouth.

"No, he's breathing."

"What do we do now, Krystyna?"

Krystyna looked around the empty wharf. "What we must to survive. Help me get him up."

"What? Let's leave him. Get away before he wakes and Edvard comes."

With her hands under his armpits, Krystyna began to pull Tyrion up. "Help me, Anna. Take the other side," instructed Krystyna as she shifted her hold.

As Krystyna edged Tyrion forward against the wall, Tyrion mumbled, "What are you doing?"

Krystyna pushed Tyrion's upper torso until he leaned over the wharf wall. As Tyrion teetered, Krystyna grabbed one leg and motioned Anna to get the other. Helpless, as his own body weight provided momentum for the lift, Krystyna and Anna lifted Tyrion up and over the wall to join Stringer on the rocks, his neck snapping on impact.

Twenty-Eight

Fighting Anna's and her own urge to run, Krystyna led Anna back along the wharf, across the parking lot, and out onto Beacon Hill Road. Krystyna, to avoid the evening crowds heading down to the harbour, turned right on Beacon Hill Road and then left on Parkhill Road to take a slightly longer, but much quieter, route to the café. Halfway to the café, the blare of emergency vehicles polluted the night air. Krystyna and Anna walked head down and silent. Twenty-five minutes later, outside the back entrance to their café, Krystyna pulled Anna into the shadows and faced her nose-to-nose.

"Anna, how are you?"

Anna, who for the first time appeared calm, nodded.

"You are in shock, Anna, but we must act normal. We have to help close the café and pretend nothing has happened. Do you understand, Anna?"

"Yes, my sister," said Anna vacantly. "I understand."

Wedged open to allow ventilation, Krystyna and Anna entered the rear of the café.

Mike, Krystyna's husband, arms loaded with clean plates, greeted them with a concerned smile and an enquiry. "Hi there. Oh, you both look like you ran a mile. Are you all right?"

"Hi, Mike, yes, we're good. We lost track of time, and we were hurrying to get back in time to help."

"Well, no need really. Things slowed down a lot around five. Aside from an old couple and a funny looking man from Poland, we didn't have much to do. David and I cleaned up in the back, and Jill got most of the front done before the last customer left. So there's nothing for you to do really."

"Where's David?" asked Anna.

"It's our darts night tonight, remember? He left around six to go to the pub. I'm going to join him soon as we're done. You sure you're OK, Anna? You look a bit worn."

Krystyna, worried for Anna, but also concerned by what Mike had said, answered for Anna. "Oh, she's OK. A bit of an upset stomach and a bit tired, but Anna's OK. What was that you said about a man from Poland?"

"Not sure. Jill said something about it and being a surprise. Oops, I think I wasn't supposed to tell you. Now I'm in it."

Anna, who had sat on a stool by the door, hadn't registered the conversation, but Krystyna, gripped by a sudden fear and dread, fought to control herself as she hurried past Mike to the front of the café. Through the swing door that separated kitchen from café, Krystyna met Jill.

"Oh hi, Christina. Did you and Annie have a good afternoon? Is Annie feeling better?"

"Yes, yes, thank you. But Annie is still a little unwell."

"That's too bad. Well, we're pretty much done here, so . . ."

Krystyna touched Jill's arm lightly. "Jill, Mike said that a man from Poland came into the café today?"

"Oh, that Mike of yours. He wasn't supposed to say anything."

"It's OK, Jill. Who was the man, and what did he want?"

"He saw the poster on the wall; the one about Poland. He said he was from Warsaw, and he became very chatty. He told me he and his family were looking for a place to settle. I told him about you and Annie, and he asked about when you had come and where you had settled. He has kids, and he was glad that you settled down with your kids and all. He asked about houses, schools, and areas to live, so I mentioned that you live up on Braddons Hill. He said he would come in the café tomorrow to chat, but he asked me not to mention anything because he thought it might be a surprise to, you know, talk with someone from your own country."

Thoughtful and relieved by Jill's description of events, which seemed harmless, Krystyna let go Jill's arm. As she did, Jill added: "One thing though-if the man does come back, his face is pretty messed up. His face is kind of twisted, and there is a big scar on his right side."

Krystyna froze. The image of the Edvard she had seen through the window of the Kingsholm Hotel flashed through her mind.

"Are you sure, Jill?"

"Yes, course I am. Couldn't miss it. Why?"

Panic surged through Krystyna as she fumbled for her cell phone. Speed dial number one called her home on Braddons Hill. Her mother-in-law, Phyllis, was home with George and Anna's son.

Phyllis, in her early seventies, moved a little slow and didn't answer the phone until the fifth ring.

"Phyllis, thank God you're home."

"Of course, I am. Where else would I be?"

"The children, they're OK?"

"Yes, yes, what's going on?"

"Oh nothing, I was just thinking of you, and I'll be home in . . ."

"Just a minute, Krystyna. There's someone at the door."

Through the phone's speaker, Krystyna listened to Phyllis' slow footsteps on the wooden floor and her voice calling to the door, "I'm coming."

"Phyllis, no, Phyllis . . ."

A man's voice, muffled and calm, slipped from the phone speaker and mixed with Phyllis' shout.

"You can't just come in here. Who the bloody hell . . ."

The phone, its harsh tone signalling the end of the call, rested in Krystyna's shaking hands. Frantic, Krystyna re-pressed the speed dial. No one answered. Two more calls without answer, and Krystyna knew.

Jill, who had watched confused, asked if anything was wrong.

Without answering , Krystyna marched to the kitchen, ignored Mike's questions, grabbed Anna, and ran to her car.

Twenty-Nine

Physical fitness and dietary care hadn't figured much in Edvard's life as one of Prague's pimps and mid-level gangsters. Going downhill on Torwood Road, past the clock, and along the level ground on Victoria Parade, had rendered Edvard winded, and he stopped to recover at the base of Beacon Hill Road. Up the hill, against the downward flow of tourists on their way to dinner at harbour-side restaurants, Edvard struggled for speed. Unfamiliar with the area, Edvard paused at the car park. The wharf jutted out from the far side of the car park, and Edvard strained in the fading light to glimpse Tyrion and his prey.

Ten steps along the wharf, Edvard stopped and stared. Confused by the empty wharf, Edvard consulted his map and noted that the line depicting the wharf angled right and then left before it ended. Relieved, and pleased that Tyrion had the sense to trap the women out of sight, Edvard hurried.

As he approached the wharf's narrowed right-angle turn, Edvard's survival instinct kicked in, and he slowed before edging his way onto the short stretch of concrete that led to the next turn. Unable to see around the second angle, Edvard strained his ears to hear expected voices, but only seagulls, their high-pitched screams spoiling the soft rhythm of ocean waves, spoke.

~

A gun, obtained from a contact of a contact in Manchester, nestled under Edvard's left armpit. Edvard scanned the wharf before he slipped his left hand under his jacket and withdrew the gun. Prepared and confident, Edvard marched around the angle.

Nothing. Nobody. Edvard, his face contorting from triumph to disbelief, swept his gun left and right and called out, "Ennis! Ennis, where the fuck are you?"

Cautious steps took Edvard to the knee-high wall at the end of the wharf. He stood beside the wall and looked over into the grey water. He turned back and studied the area for a clue as to what had happened. To his right, ocean-side, by the base of the wharf wall, Edvard noticed a slim black form about ten inches long. He picked the object up and nodded with knowledge. It wasn't the first cosh he had held. Apprehensive, Edvard stashed the cosh in his pocket, took out his phone, and called Tyrion.

A breeze, stiff and cool, swept over the wharf wall, and Edvard pressed the phone to his ear. After five rings, the call disconnected. Edvard tried again. As Edvard listened to the ring tone, he scrunched his gun hand over the phone to mute what sounded like a distorted echo caused by the wind. Another disconnect. A third call, this time, Edvard crouched beside the wall out of the wind. Edvard held the phone away from his ear and tilted his head. On the fourth and fifth rings, Edvard stood up to follow the echo. Edvard called again. This time, he held the phone by his side and listened to the air. Caught on the wind as it blew up and over the wharf wall, Edvard heard Tyrion's phone ring. With his gun leading, Edvard peered over the wall.

Even from four metres away, the red was vibrant. Drizzled over rocks like a dessert sauce on ice cream, or splashed in thick blobs like an artist's frenzy, blood leaked from two heads. Side by side, Stringer and Tyrion lay twisted over the boulders of the wharf's ocean-side break wall. Saltwater, leaving the scene as the tide ebbed out, lapped at their feet like weak fingers trying to claim the corpses. Unmoved by the deaths, but angry at Tyrion's failure and the absence of Krystyna and Anna, Edvard stared out at the ocean.

In the near distance, about five hundred metres offshore, a medium-sized yacht bobbed on the water. Stern end, by the wheel, a woman stared back. Binoculars, big and black, obscured her face and a cell phone hung on her ear. Eager to be out of sight, Edvard stepped away from the wall. The wail of emergency sirens sounded, and Edvard walked briskly along the wharf.

Lights, red and blue, flashed on Beacon Hill Road, and Edvard hesitated. On his right a shed, the same one Anna had hidden behind, provided Edvard cover. Behind the shed, Edvard, in an attempt to confuse anyone who might have seen him on the wharf, took off his jacket, emptied the pockets, and stuffed the jacket beside the shed. His wallet and cell phones fit in his trouser pockets. Loathing to give them up, Edvard weighed the gun and cosh in his hand. If the authorities stopped him with either weapon, the questions would be bad enough and even worse after the police did some background checks. Without the weapons, Edvard would be vulnerable. Opting for security, Edvard tucked both in the back waistband of his trousers and loosened his shirt over them.

Voices of paramedics and police officers mixed and competed with a crowd that had followed the emergency responders on to the wharf. Where the wharf narrowed, just past the shed Edvard hid behind, the police made a stand and blocked the crowd from going farther. Taking his chance, Edvard entered the swell of people. When the police began to clear the entire wharf of people, Edvard, head down and silent, walked calmly away.

Through the car park, Edvard turned right and headed up Beacon Hill Road. At the junction with Parkhill Road, Edvard flagged a passing taxi and climbed in the back.

"Where to then?" asked the driver as he flicked the metre on.

Edvard, recalling the information given by the woman in the café about where Krystyna lived, said: "Braddons Hill. I've forgotten the number. I met some people this afternoon who invited me for a drink this evening. I do remember that they said it's all white with lots of grass and a play structure out front."

"Ah, that's not far. I might know the house. A lot of houses are white, but not too many with a play structure. What was the person's name?"

"Christina. She works at the café Brothers & Sisters."

"I know the café, but can't say I know the woman or where she lives. Anyhow, Braddons Hill is not that long a street. I'll drive slowly, and we can take a look."

Eight minutes later, the cab stopped.

"Reckon this is the place. Want me to wait while you check?"

"No, thanks. If it's wrong, I'll just walk and look."

Edvard waited on the street until the taxi passed out of sight. Confident he had the right house, Edvard walked to the front door, withdrew his gun, and rang the bell.

Thirty

Toys, plastic and brightly coloured, lay upright or on their sides, under and around the wooden play structure. At the base of the ladder, and the bottom of the slide, brown patches of worn grass told of many parent and child trips up and down the structure. Edvard, with little recollection of toys in his own childhood, stopped and stared at a small, plastic brown horse positioned to lean against the base of the play structure. At the sound of a phone ringing in the house, Edvard gently nudged the horse upright with his foot. The phone's ring ended as Edvard reached the front door of the house. Edvard knocked. A moment later, a woman's voice called, "All right, I'm coming."

The door opened, and Edvard stepped in. An elderly woman, a phone in her hand, retreated involuntarily, raised an arm, and shouted.

"You can't just come in here. Who the bloody hell . . ."

Edvard snatched the phone from the woman, pressed the end button, and closed the front door with the heel of his foot. When the door closed, the woman saw Edvard's gun. Her first scream rushed out between breaths, floundered hoarse and dry. Her second, fortified by a deep breath, rattled the walls. She didn't make a third. Edvard's gun, its barrel hard and cold, thudded against the old woman's temple, pressing the arm of her glasses into her head. Instantly inert, the woman crumpled to the ground. Indifferent, Edvard stepped over the woman and followed the sound of a child's cry into the kitchen at the back of the house.

The children sat in two identical high chairs. Yellow and green globs of food spotted both white trays, the children's faces, and their clenched hands. For a moment, Edvard's sudden appearance silenced the children until an innate sense of danger propelled them to wail simultaneously. Edvard moved to the nearest high chair and held the muzzle of the gun inches from the child's face. A sticky hand gripped the gun, and a finger entered the end of the barrel. Edvard wiggled the gun gently and the child laughed. The second child laughed too.

To the left, behind the high chairs, a large flat-screen TV hung on the wall. Using the remote on the counter, Edvard turned the TV on and channel surfed until a cartoon appeared. Mesmerized by the movement, bright colours, and funny sounds, the children quieted. With the children occupied, Edvard searched the kitchen and a small workshop area off the back of the kitchen until he found tape and a small roll of string. Five minutes later, Phyllis, the left side of her face and neck purple and swollen, sagged chin down on her chest, over the tape and string that secured her to the kitchen chair.

Satisfied, Edvard noted the time on the microwave and spoke to the children.

"It's seven fifteen. Mommy and Daddy should be home soon. Then we can have a little going away party."

Thirty-One

Still dazed and in shock, Anna didn't protest Krystyna's roughness as she pushed Anna into the passenger seat. Only when Krystyna let slip the clutch too quickly and bumped the car against a wall did Anna return to the present.

"What are you doing, Krystyna? What's happening?"

Gears ground as Krystyna reversed, changed to first, and stabbed the gas pedal.

"Where are we going? Krystyna, you're scaring me. What..?"

"It's Edvard, Anna. He, he's at my house and I . . ."

"No, no, the children . . ."

"I know, I . . ."

"But how, why do you think he is . . ."

"Edvard came to the café. He spoke with Jill, and she told him where I live. I called home, but when I spoke with Phyllis, someone came to the front door, and the call ended. I called again, but no answer."

"Oh God, no, no, no. We must call the police; we must save George and Robert."

"No, Anna, no police."

"But what can we do against Edvard? He is an animal. He doesn't care about anything. He will kill us all."

"Anna, what we did at the wharf, we can't call the police. Not yet. We must face Edvard."

Traffic forced Krystyna to slow. Two blocks from Braddons Hill, Krystyna stopped the car.

"What are you doing? We must hurry."

Krystyna unclenched her hands from the steering wheel, pushed her palms into her eyes, and sobbed as years of stress finally breached her resolve. She hunched her shoulders, and her chest heaved with rapid gulps of air until a scream, filled with anguish and fear, ripped from Krystyna's mouth. Tears ran and mixed with saliva as Krystyna's head shook left and right.

"Krystyna, stop. Stop it, Krystyna," pleaded Anna, her hands reaching to comfort her sister.

Krystyna's breathing slowed, her head stilled, and her hands fell to her lap. Nervous, Anna brushed Krystyna's cheek and whispered, "Krystyna?"

"I'm all right, Anna," replied Krystyna, as she checked her shoulder for cars as she pulled into the road. A left and right put them on Braddons Hill. Krystyna stopped the car ten houses short of her own and turned to Anna. "Anna, you get out here."

"What? Why? No, I want to help. Edvard has my son too. You can't go alone."

"Listen, Anna, Edvard is only expecting me. You walk from here, and go to the back of the house and to the workshop off the kitchen. It's probably unlocked, but you know where the key is, right?"

"Yes, under the third plant pot, but what am I to do?"

"I don't know, Anna. Just watch and wait. If something bad happens, if Edvard does anything to, to harm me or the children, then you call the police. You have your phone?"

"But, it will be too late then, Krystyna. Call the police now. They will know what to do. They can save . . ."

"Anna, Anna, this is between Edvard and me. He wants me. I must face him. Now go, Anna."

Reluctant, Anna got out and stood silently as Krystyna started the car and pulled away.

~

The tires crunched on the gravel driveway and skidded when Krystyna applied the brakes. Out of the car, Krystyna stood still and silent. Cautious, despite a desire to run, Krystyna approached the front door, hesitated, then grasped the door handle. With one turn to the left and a gentle push, the door edged open.

Light and sound bled through the narrow gap between door and frame. Krystyna stepped into the hallway and closed the door behind her. On the floor, her foot nudged one of several portable house phones. A pair of silver-rimmed glasses, one arm bent, lay close to the phone. To the right, the living room was dark and silent. Ahead, to the left, the flicker of the TV and the unmistakable sound of a cartoon pulled Krystyna forward.

At the doorway to the kitchen, a gasp sucked the breath from Krystyna. Phyllis, a savage gash between temple and ear, sat bound and gagged on a kitchen chair. Blood, fresh and crimson, dripped and pooled on the tile floor beside the chair. To the right, unaware of the pain and suffering of their grandmother, George and Robert faced the TV giggling and snorting as animated figures chased each other across the screen. Torn between the instinct to protect her child, and the desire to aid her bloodied mother-in-law, Krystyna froze.

Edvard, gun first, stepped into the kitchen from the workshop. Triumph and malice rippled his distorted face as he motioned for Krystyna to sit on the chair he had positioned next to Phyllis. Defiant, despite Edvard's gun, Krystyna did not move. Confident, Edvard stepped toward Krystyna. He stopped three feet in front of Krystyna, transferred the gun from his right hand to his left, and holding the gun on Krystyna, delivered a full-bodied right fist into Krystyna's face. The impact knocked Krystyna off her feet, and she sprawled on the floor.

"Get on the chair," said Edvard casually.

Up on her knees, Krystyna wiped a sleeve across her mouth and nose and stared at the wide stain of blood.

"Get up," commanded Edvard.

Gripping the chair, Krystyna pulled herself to a seated position and glared at Edvard.

"You still have your spirit," mocked Edvard as he lifted his arm for another blow. Krystyna flinched, but the blow did not come. Instead, Edvard leaned back against the counter and sighed.

"Did you really believe you could leave me, Krystyna? That I wouldn't come for you?"

Her lips swollen and bloodied, Krystyna didn't answer.

"Did you forget what I told you when you accepted my protection in Prague? Did you forget that you belong to me? That you are my property until I am done with you? Did you, did you?"

Licking blood from her lip, Krystyna jutted her chin forward. "No. I didn't forget. I remembered every day. Every day you used me, sold me, hurt me. I remembered every day, Edvard. That is why I left."

Edvard toyed with his gun, spinning it on a finger and passing it from hand to hand as he spoke. "Where is Anna?"

"She is gone with her husband to get groceries."

"Yet her brat is here. Why has she not come to collect him?"

"Anna and her husband also go for dinner, and I look after Robert until later."

"Where is your husband?"

"He plays darts tonight. He won't be home till late."

Rueful, Edvard changed tack. "What happened to Ennis at the Wharf?"

Krystyna, unsure of Edvard's connection with Tyrion, or if he would care or not, weighed the options of evasion.

"Ennis," barked Edvard, "what happened?"

"A man came. I don't know who he was. Ennis attacked him. They fought and fell over the wall onto the rocks."

"Where is Anna?"

"I told you. She's with her husband."

Edvard pushed off the counter, moved behind the two boys, and aimed his gun at the back of George's head.

"Where is Anna?"

"I told . . ."

Edvard cocked the hammer of the gun back.

"All right, all right, she's at home. Both our husbands are playing darts together. Anna will come later to collect Robert."

The hammer on the gun clicked as Edvard eased it closed.

"Call Anna. Tell her to come now."

"No," said Krystyna. "I will take you to her. We leave the children and their grandmother here."

A rage surged through Edvard as he rushed at Krystyna and stood over her with his gun pressed at her neck.

"You do not tell me what we will do. You are a whore, my whore. You and your bitch sister are responsible for my face, and you and your children will watch as I do the same to Anna. Then we will go. Now call Anna, or I will split open one child's head and pull its brain out in front of you. Do you understand?"

Edvard's voice overwhelmed the sound of the television, and George and Robert wriggled in their high chairs and turned their heads. The children's eyes widened, their breathing stopped, and for a moment, silence dominated the room until in unison George and Robert cried and screamed for their mothers.

Behind Edvard, just within Krystyna's peripheral sight, the door to the workshop eased slowly open. Pushing herself to focus on Edvard and keep his attention away from the workshop door, Krystyna goaded Edvard. "You are a coward, Edvard. You only hurt women and children. The man in the square, the one who broke your face, he was a real man and he beat you, you . . ."

Edvard's right hand, balled tight, plowed into Krystyna's head and knocked her off the chair. Edvard's right foot followed into Krystyna's stomach, then another to her hip, and a third to her back. Edvard, teeth bared, loomed over Krystyna, hacked up a glob of phlegm, and spat in Krystyna's face.

"You fucking filthy Roma whore," shouted Edvard as he stomped on Krystyna's chest. "I'll fucking kill you now, and then I'll kill your kids. Do you understand that?"

Agitated and frightened, the children, restrained by the straps in the chairs, flailed and screamed.

Edvard stepped back to gain momentum to deliver the killer kick to Krystyna's head. As he placed his weight on his left leg and drew his right leg backward, Anna screamed from the doorway to the workshop.

"No, no!"

Startled, Edvard turned.

"Ah, the bitch sister finally appears. Come in, Anna. I was just about to have some fun with Krystyna, but I think you deserve to be first."

Anna turned and fled back into the workshop.

"Come back, you bitch, or I'll kill the kids."

Below Edvard, Krystyna, semi-conscious, flailed and moaned with ragged shallow breaths. Adrenalin pumping, Edvard left Krystyna and strode with a predator's confidence to the workshop. Enjoying the fear he instilled, Edvard taunted Anna.

"I'm coming for you, Anna."

Edvard paused at the doorway and peered into the darkness.

"Come out now, Anna," commanded Edvard. "I will count to five. If you do not come, I will kill the children by the time it takes you to count to ten."

A whimper of defeat and helplessness pushed out from the workshop.

"One, two," said Edvard.

Feet, reluctant, scraped the workshop floor.

"Three, four," said Edvard, triumph and amusement in his voice.

From the gloom, Anna's voice screamed "five!" as she hurled herself toward Edvard. Too late, Edvard registered the glint of the sharp points of a three-pronged garden fork with a spade handle used to turn soil and rotate compost.

Fuelled by years of fear and insecurity, and overcome with the rage of a protective mother, Anna plunged the three prongs into Edvard's chest. Anna's momentum carried Edvard across the kitchen until his back collided with the counter top beside Krystyna. With the centre prong embedded in Edvard's sternum and the other two punching holes in his lungs, Edvard collapsed.

Anna let go the handle and fell beside Krystyna.

Bleeding from her face and clutching her chest, Krystyna grabbed Anna and gasped, "Is he dead?"

"I, I don't think so," said Anna. "His chest is moving a little. What should we do?"

"Momma, Mummy," called George and Robert.

"Anna," gasped Krystyna, "try to calm the children."

Krystyna, her breath laboured, leaned against the counter and regarded Edvard. His coat had fallen open in the struggle, and the tip of a photograph stuck out of the top of the inside breast pocket. Curious, Krystyna took the photograph and held it to the light.

With Anna's presence, a TV channel change, and a handful of Fishy Crackers on each of the highchair tables, the children quieted a little.

"What is that?" said Anna as she watched Krystyna hold the photograph to the light.

"Oh God, no, no, Anna. It can't be, it can't be."

Anna took the photograph. Her hand trembled.

"Is it, Krystyna, is it?"

"Yes. We took that photograph a few days after you arrived in Prague. I remember the day. I was so happy and so sad at the same time."

"But," said Anna as she held the photograph to Krystyna, "we sent the photo to Mom and Dad. How can Edvard have it?"

Edvard groaned and twitched.

"He must have gone to them. He must have found them and taken the photograph."

"Yes, Anna, that is the only way he could have gotten it."

"But, Mom and Dad would never have given it to Edvard."

"You're right, Anna. There is only one way Edvard would have gotten this photograph from Dad."

"You mean, you mean Edvard killed our parents?"

Edvard, groggy and hardly conscious, rolled and lunged for the gun that had fallen from his hand when Anna struck him. Anna, closest to Edvard, grabbed a short kitchen knife from the knife block on the counter and plunged it into Edvard's leg. Edvard's scream set the children in a frenzy, and they sobbed and cried.

Dragging his leg, Edvard inched closer to the gun. As his fingertips pawed at the barrel, Anna leaped on Edvard's back and stabbed and hacked at the nape of Edvard's neck. Blood, skin, and cartilage sprayed and flew under Anna's frenzied assault. Edvard ceased to breathe long before Anna, exhausted and spent, released the knife and slid off Edvard's back to the floor.

Through the blood and gore, the sisters crawled to each other. Anna, unable to stop shaking, burrowed into Krystyna and cried. Krystyna, her face battered, stroked Anna's hair and soothed her with quiet words.

"It's all over now, Anna. It's all over."

Anna pulled away a little from Krystyna and searched her sister's eyes.

"Is it really, Krystyna?"

"Yes, Anna, it's over. We have escaped Prague forever."

Epilogue

Unable to withstand the investigation, Krystyna and Anna confessed to their real identities, the blackmail of Ennis, and the fight they witnessed between Ennis and Stringer on the wharf. Fortunately, for Krystyna and Anna, the woman on the hatch who had, through binoculars, seen Edvard at the wharf, also maintained that she had witnessed Ennis and Stringer fighting and they had fallen over the wall together.

With no evidence of their involvement in Ennis' death, the undoubted evidence indicating self-defence in the death of Edvard, and without any willingness on the part of Taffy or Phil to testify about the blackmail, no charges were laid against Krystyna and Anna.

However, Krystyna and Anna's marriages, and their new lives in Torquay, did not survive. David and Mike, unable to reconcile the past lives of their wives, and the deception they had endured, obtained uncontested divorces and gave up all rights to their children. The café business was dissolved, and the proceeds divided equally.

More thrillers from Colin Knight

Some People Deserve To Die

Alan Davies, a naive and vulnerable teenager, is tricked into committing an immoral and abhorrent crime. Riven by guilt and remorse he runs, but he can't outrun his conscience.

For twenty years, Alan tries to silence his conscience with alcohol and drugs as fate and chance propel him in to the dangerous world of smugglers, nationalists, guerrillas, and mercenaries.

Battling alcohol and drug abuse, Alan dodges death and betrayal as life erodes his humanity and transforms him into a merciless killer until, used up and spent, he returns home.

Destitute and dysfunctional, a street scuffle brings him eye-to-eye with the men responsible for his heinous crime. Harnessing skills and cruelty learned through a crime and violence-laden life Alan seeks justice for himself and his victim.

But when justice has been served, Alan discovers the devastating truth about his crime, his family and himself.

Public Service

Not many jobs are for life.

Jeff Parsons was angry, angry enough to kill. A reliable, dependable, and mostly honest public servant, Jeff expected to ride the government gravy train undisturbed until his retirement in 2025.

On Friday March 2, 2012, Jeff's train derailed; a confidential email revealed that Jeff's boss, under the guise of government-wide cut backs, planned to 'let Jeff go' so they could use the savings to reward and promote their sycophant lackeys and painted whore.

Unemployment at fifty would destroy Jeff's life and threaten the security and health of his children. That was not acceptable.

Desperate and determined, Jeff analysed the problem; six deaths in seven days ought to be enough.

All he needed was a killer.

Bad Analysis

In London, a delusional racist aristocrat, invisible, privileged, and well-protected by his station, ruthlessly coordinates a diabolical attack, a slaughter disguised as a domestic terror assault.

Deep in the core of MI5, a traitor, misuses, redirects and controls official resources.

Manipulating a group of cowards, rapists, murderers, and virulent racists culled from the ranks of the English Defense League, the aristocrat and the traitor aim to throw England into a state of xenophobic frenzy.

Only two men stand a chance of stopping their fanatical plot.

One is a victim of state-sponsored madness twice over, a humble Egyptian cab driver who brought his family to England in search of a better life. Aalim is meant to be a scapegoat for the actions of his captors, a "rag-head" who can be made to take the blame for their actions lest his innocent wife and son, taken hostage, suffer a terrible fate. The other, Wilson, is a crotchety intelligence analyst. An iconoclastic workaholic, rapidly losing patience with his superiors' political gamesmanship, Wilson relies on his own brand of intelligence analysis when one of the plotters makes the attack personal and when one of his closest friends at MI5 pays the ultimate price for discovering too much.

Can Aalim's faith and humanity overcome his fear of the monsters keeping his family captive? And can Wilson overcome the Bad Analysis that infests a system that, from the very beginning, was set against him?